WARREN FITZGERALD

The Go-Away Bird

blue door

FT
Pbk

Blue Door
An imprint of HarperCollins*Publishers*
77–85 Fulham Palace Road,
Hammersmith, London W6 8JB

www.harpercollins.co.uk

Published by Blue Door 2010
1

A catalogue record for this book
is available from the British Library

ISBN: 978-0-00-731737-0

Typeset in Minion by Palimpsest Book Production Limited,
Grangemouth, Stirlingshire

Printed and bound in Great Britain by
Clays Ltd, St Ives plc

Mixed Sources
Product group from well-managed
forests and other controlled sources
www.fsc.org Cert no. SW-COC-001806
© 1996 Forest Stewardship Council

FSC is a non-profit international organisation established to promote the responsible
management of the world's forests. Products carrying the FSC label are independently
certified to assure consumers that they come from forests that are managed to meet the
social, economic and ecological needs of present and future generations.

Find out more about HarperCollins and the environment at
www.harpercollins.co.uk/green

For 'I'
and the kids of LRC and Kazo,
who saved me . . . in so many ways.

ACKNOWLEDGEMENTS

Huge thanks to Ian Golding and Leigh Singer for your object-ive and thorough reading, comments and criticisms long before a deal was ever on the horizon. Big love.

I'm indebted to you Frank Ntale and Jeanine Ngarambe for your comments, trust and friendship.

Much gratitude to David Grossman, my agent, for noticing and for persistence.

Thank you, Patrick Janson-Smith for meticulous editing, advice and support and for caring about my characters almost as much as I do. Much respect.

Thanks to Claudia Leisinger for your awesome photography.

Nan, thanks for telling a great yarn and inspiring me to start writing. R.I.P.

Roger Harcourt, much love and thanks for your unwavering encouragement and enthusiasm for so many years, for your infect-ious passion for literature and love of the *camping lark*!

Lama Mugabo, bless you for all the great connections in Rwanda and for being a wonderful host. I have so much respect for all the bridges you are building. **www.bbrwanda.org**

Alphonse and Prosper, I am honoured that you shared your stories with me. Thanks and warmest wishes to Peter, Gilbert and all my friends in Kazo and Kibungo.

To the DWC team (Kazo, September 2009), my love and respect. **www.developingworldconnections.org**

Thanks to Matt and Wavey (my very own Roddy and Dave!) for your love and support. And to Saire, my 'twin', for always being there and helping me hatch the plans.

1994

1

I live here because I can't afford to live anywhere else. Well, you wouldn't live here for any other reason, would you? It's a hole, but where else can you live in central London for forty quid a week, eh? Nowhere, I tell you. And I'm only here because I was lucky enough to know 'Chelle from my time at the charity, and she moved up north and sublet the place to me. So, yeah, I always have to think twice before answering the buzzer, or turn down the telly and creep to the peephole for a squiz if someone hammers on the door, but . . . central . . . forty quid.

Nearly there. Hold on, a couple more minutes.

Surprising I get any students at all when you think about it. I can just imagine their faces as they look up from their A–Zs, reckon they've found it . . . Well, this is Couper Street. They see the tall glass-fronted foyer with the concierge's (don't have a go if I've spelt that wrong! Not many of you would get it right first time. And as for my pronunciation . . . there's only one person who's allowed to correct my French – you'll know why when you meet her) . . . Anyway, where was I . . . the concierge's desk with alien green light all round the bottom of it, so the bloke looks like he's hovering above the metallic turquoise floor in a little spaceship, ready to welcome the residents, or to exterminate the uninvited filth. They see the massive potted plants with polished green leaves that match the spaceship lights; they see the rows of locked pigeonholes, one for each flat . . . sorry, *apartment* . . . lined up behind the concierge and his floating desk, as if he's standing guard over loads of little safes in a bank vault or something. And they see nothing else in this huge foyer that stretches the length of the block, except for the big cardboard sign in the corner window advertising the fact in blue and yellow that for a mere £475,000 the 'penthouse' apartment is still available – I wonder why?! They look impressed, even a bit excited. Then I can imagine their faces as they read the tiny letters on the glass door that say: CATHEDRAL APARTMENTS. So they turn round, looking for Frapper Court. Right street, wrong side. And their faces drop as they see the defaced council sign welcoming them to /rap/e/Court.

Nice.

Why do I find it so difficult to remember that I would've found that bloody hilarious when I was their age? Because I seem to take everything so personally these days, I suppose. Because, although I'm no little shrimp to look at – well, not particularly – if I'm honest with you then I'd have to say that I'm a bit scared of the little bastards, dressed in their baseball caps, enormous jeans and huge plastic clocks hanging round their necks, trying to be Flavor Flav or Chuck D. I'm scared of the feeling of humiliation if I get another football smacked into the back of my head, and the laughter that ricochets off the beige hard face of my block, so it's like even my own windows are dissing me:

No sanctuary for ya, even here, mate!

You can shut up. Call yourself windows! You're so thin and weak I could push you out with one finger from your grotty metal frames – laugh at me then as you plummet down eight storeys and shatter on the pavement with nothing but a puny hiss. You can't even keep the rain out half the time, let alone the cold and the noise. Christ, if this was my own place I would've been in touch with that nice old bloke from Everest, had him come and 'fit the best', had you out on your ear and replaced with some lovely double glazing ages ago.

I tore my screwed-up eyes from the windows of my flat as I ducked into the stairwell of the block. The stench of piss and wet dog slapped me round the chops and made me realize that I'd just been having a barney with a piece of glass!

Don't worry, Ash, you're seconds away now.

I took the stairs, of course. I needed the exercise, and I just couldn't risk the lift. It's not the getting stuck in there that bothers me. I sometimes wish for that. Then everything would have to stop. *I* would have to stop for as long as it took. It's the closest you could get to having the world stop turning for a bit so you could jump off, if you know what I mean. But I wouldn't, not in that lift, 'cause when my legs got tired I couldn't sit on that floor knowing what's been puked, pissed and gobbed on it.

By the time I got to Floor 4, I was already flagging. Man, you're thirty-nine, not fifty-nine! A door slammed some-where up at the top of the block and gave me my second wind so I could get to my place before I'd have to pass whoever it was on the stairs coming down. Floor 6, and right on cue the theme music to *Casualty* blasted from Number 57 so loud that their front door buzzed at me as I flew past. I had absolutely no idea who lived there, never seen them, but I knew exactly what they liked to watch on TV – we all did. Even though there was another floor between me and them, I knew they couldn't get enough of *Casualty*, *EastEnders*, *Coronation Street*, and now this new version of *Casualty* called *Cardiac Arrest* – it can't last, not two dramas about hospitals and blood and grief: surely people don't have the stomach for it?

Floor 7 and Roddy and Dave in Number 58 were pumping out the House hits as per.

'La da dee la dee da, la da dee la dee da,' went Crystal Waters with her voice like the phlegmy mutterings of the old girl who sits outside Costcutter dozing in her wing-backed chair.

Here's me trying to teach people what makes a good voice and a classic performance and these two dopes below will slam on another Acid track like they're trying to undermine me. And now this stuff's crossing over into the top 40 I can see that look in my students' eyes sometimes that says: I just wanna be a star, be top of the charts, where 2 Unlimited and Snap! are, so why you getting me to sing all this old Stevie Wonder and Aretha Franklin crap?

Nearly there, Ash, nearly . . .

I finally reached my floor and the door opposite mine, Number 61, gently clicked shut like it always did when I reached the landing. It's enough to make you paranoid, don't you reckon? But I knew that her eye wouldn't be at the peephole for long once she'd seen it was me. It wasn't me she was waiting for. It was that bloody ape Daryl. I knew his name 'cause I'd heard her squeak it a thousand times through bruised lips as he crashed down the stairs telling her she's dumped (again), and that she's a whore and a fat one at that. Her name's Rachel – I knew that 'cause he'd be roaring it into her door later, and she'd open it, like she did every time, and she'd let him in. Why did she let him in? Is it that she actually liked it, the way he treated her? It's beyond me, I tell you.

My hand shook as I turned the key – it's nothing though, just the fact that it's bloody freezing tonight. It's March, what do you expect? The heavy door slammed behind me and the windows all shook as if to try and get the argument going again, but I weren't rising. I was going to be sorted in a minute.

I whacked on the TV. I already knew what was on BBC1 thanks to my neighbours down below, so I started flicking almost before the tube was warmed up. I landed on *Channel 4 News* first. There was talk of Nirvana's lead singer again, put himself in a coma this time, it seems, after a cocktail of champagne and Rohypnol. Jesus, look at Courtney Love, what a state! Although I blamed the likes of Kurt Cobain for the lack of interest the music industry has in really fine singers today, I couldn't tear myself away from the news, any news about celebs in the music biz. If it was good news I'd search between the newscaster's words like someone reading their horoscope, vainly trying to find a comparison that signalled imminent success for me. If it was bad news, and it usually was, I'd just use it to feel better about the state of my life. So I dived in the kitchen and grabbed a pot of houmous and a bag of Doritos, the black-handled knife and the Red Leicester from the fridge, holding the crisp packet between finger and thumb, out in front of me like a dead rat so it didn't make a racket and block out any of the sound from the TV. I was back on the sofa in a flash. I had a bit too much momentum in the rush, forgot to sit down gently and so a cloud of dust puffed up around me from the frayed green armrests. I could taste it. I'm such a scumbag! But where would you start? The sofa's beyond saving. I'll chuck it out and get a new one . . . when I get the time . . . and the money.

They've finished with Kurt and Courtney already, back to Iran . . . The time! As if you haven't got the time, Ashley Bolt! You teach about six hours a week, drop off and pick up a few things here and there, do the odd gig – once in a blue moon – and you reckon you haven't got the time. Ah, houmous and Doritos! Better than sex, eh? Haven't got the money then . . . you can't argue with that. I don't earn enough to waste on sofas, furniture. It's just things; things don't matter. That's what Kurt, even Kurt Cobain, would say. But then he can say that, can't he? – he can afford to. Better than sex! Finish the cheese, quick! Like, when was the last time you got your end away to know about that? Iran, Iraq – how could you live like that? That would be the time with the bondage girl, who pulled a cat-o'-nine tails from her bag and told you to whip her from behind. Harder, she said. You can't do it hard enough, she said. Bloody right, I couldn't! Me and Jim had a laugh about that one. But then I bet she did too – probably thought I was a right letdown. I wonder whether it would make any difference if I lived in Cathedral Apartments . . . 'Course it would. People would come back. More students. I wanted to make a proper dinner, something hot. Now I've had all this cheese and crisps. You knew you would. Don't kid yourself, you dick! Now the knife's here. Must phone Dad. Why should I? Why does she do that, that Rachel? They know I teach singers. Do you reckon they do it on purpose, those two, play it loud to undermine me? I'd probably get complaints myself in Cathedral Apartments. Got crumbs down the side of the sofa. Like it matters! But it should. Perhaps I should change the way I teach, add some of this House stuff. Stick to your guns, boy, that's your trouble. Kurt Courtney Rohypnol Good for a comedown after a night on the pills Date rape Cheese Clean off the knife It's clean Ah

Ah

Ah.

Peace.

The more it hurt the more I cut. The knife with the black handle had a short, sharp blade. I slid it backwards and forwards on the inside of my forearm, pressing harder each time. And the chaos all went. Everything just stopped. Except the to-ing and fro-ing of the shiny blade. All was peace and quiet in my head. Nothing existed outside either. I couldn't hear the TV. I drew in the smoothest, longest breath. I rushed. An endorphin rush, if you know what I mean. Sex, orgasm – you're on the right lines. The buzz off a pukka E – maybe. Scratch an itch, an itch that you couldn't get to for ages because the time wasn't right, or the place. Yeah, any itch, on your inside leg, your back, your bum, anywhere. It wasn't appropriate in public, that paralysing relief you know is coming when you scratch the itch; it's going to make you look weird in front of others. But the longer you leave it, the more frustrating it gets, and the greater the relief when you finally get on your own . . .

So what if that itch is deeper? Deeper than your skin, I mean. What if that itch isn't an itch at all? What if it's a place, a person, something they said, something they didn't say, a thought, a dream, a nightmare, all of these things and more, crashing into the little space inside you?

The relief. The stillness. And then the blood popped out of the space between the blade and a flap of my skin and slid so fast, like a red and silent bolt of lightning looking for earth, down my forearm to my elbow. The first sound was the tapping, fast tapping of the blood dripping onto my khaki combats, making a dark purple stain. The sight of the blood on my arm had already made me stop pressing with the knife. But it was still held in place, the edges of the wound were hanging on to the blade, they were lips kissing it, thanking it for the feeling. The only feeling that made sense sometimes. The little alarm of dripping blood brought me back to reality.

Fuck, my combats'll be ruined!

And so the next part of the ritual began. I jumped into the empty bath and dropped my trousers, turned on the taps and tried to soak them before the blood stained, at the same time running my arm under the cold one. I reached over and opened the cabinet above the sink, pulled out my brown bottle of hydrogen peroxide – magic stuff this; every home should have one. Did you know hydrogen peroxide breaks down really quickly when exposed to light? That's why it's in a little brown bottle: the brown filters out the sun's rays. It's a great antibacterial thing – you can use it as mouthwash, clean kitchen surfaces . . . even highlight your hair! I held my arm over the sink, whilst my feet kneaded my trousers in the bath, and poured a little over the cut. It fizzed and bubbled, all pink. Stung a bit too, but that's a small rush after the main event. I poured again and again until the fizzing was white – it stops the bleeding and cleans the wound simultaneously, you see? Grabbed a bit of gauze from the cabinet and stuck it over the cut with tape, nearly slipped in the bath, my feet tangled in my combats – Christ, I had no intention of killing myself!

I wandered in my boxers back into the living room, switched off the TV – it was threatening to invade the little bit of peace I'd just created for myself, pull me back into chaos again too quickly. I sat back in the sofa, saw the bloody knife on the table and had to get up again, take it to the kitchen and give it a quick wash before I could sit and enjoy my peace properly. I tell you, I love this flat . . . no, there is something about it, honestly. Sat there, slouched on the sofa, I stroked the rough armrest as if it was a balding cat, and all I could see out the window was sky. Sky and the tips of the big tree across the road, the only one round here; its naked branches looked swollen in silhouette with budding leaves. The thin red clouds against pale blue could've been the sky outside a plane window or something, as I'm on my way somewhere warm, with fresh air and a beautiful land-scape, shitting myself about this new life I'm going to, but knowing I'm alive – for the first time in ages having some-thing worth shitting myself about. Then, as if to remind me that that wasn't the case, a black dot of a plane weaved through a couple of clouds, flashing its lights smugly, and those thin red clouds were suddenly scar-shaped and sore-looking.

More flashing lights, coming from the street below, made the black tree top turn blue every few seconds. Curiosity dragged me from the sofa. The crowd was in the way, kids, women, blokes, so I couldn't see what they were so inter-ested in. But judging by the ambulance and the only car in the middle of the road, the driver still in his seat, but with his feet on the road and his head in his hands, it was pretty clear he'd just knocked someone over.

So if the ambulance is there, what are you lot doing, eh? Helping? No chance. Enjoying the show, more like. Getting your next fix of grief and drama since *Casualty*'s finished and *EastEnders* ain't on till tomorrow. But what if I went down there in the street now, with my cheese knife, and started cutting my arm outside the Costcutter? They'd all run a mile; lock themselves in their scummy flats until the nutter had gone. Why? It's OK to stand there and watch the little girl's brains leaking onto the tarmac, but not me making a little cut in my arm. Because she didn't do it to herself. If I hurt myself then it's not just blood and guts and broken bones, it's mental and emotional pain too. And no one wants to deal with the kind of emotional pain that makes you do that to yourself. That's not entertainment, is it? It's not good drama. And it's certainly not art, right?

2

'Go go go! Go go way!' Jeanette is copying the sound of the big green birds in the fig trees. The ones with the tall white hats. She is running in and out of the trees trying to make them fly off. One does. It spreads its pretty purple wings and looks down at me as it goes. Its eyes are red apart from the black in the middle – red like Uncle Leonard's after he has been at the cabaret all night with Dad. The bird looks unhappily at me, just like Uncle Leonard does if I wake him too early. I try and tell the bird, with my eyes, that I was not the one who scared it. But I laughed when Jeanette did it, so he is bound to blame me too.

Mum clucks like a chicken because she is unhappy at the noise we make. 'Go and take your swim now if you want it, Clementine,' she says. 'Be quick! I need you to help carry the water back – that is if you want any breakfast today.'

Jeanette and I run on ahead. We know we must hurry. We are so lucky. My family are so lucky to live this close to the Nyabarongo. I try not to show it, but I feel bigger, more clever than Jeanette – even though we are both ten years old – because she always prefers to come and stay at our house. We are close to the river, you see. As we run past the last stretch of the marshes I puff the air out of my nose, so that

I do not have to smell it. The smell of the marshes makes me feel sick. Jeanette has to smell that every day when she goes to collect the water with her mum and sisters. The water in their cans is always brown, the colour of the marshland. Mum walks to the edge of the river to get ours – so it is always clearer, and it tastes sweeter. And it is great to—

'EEEE!' Jeanette screams and falls into the mud up ahead of me. And I stand as still as a statue because my heart jumps and tells me to stop. But just for a moment.

Then I laugh at her. I laugh high and loud, louder than usual because I am relieved that it was just a big grumpy pig that came running out from the papyrus and knocked her over. The pig squeals as if it is copying Jeanette and disappears into the papyrus again just as quickly as it appeared. I jump over Jeanette and run ahead, sliding down the muddy bank. I leave my sweater and my dress on the rocks and run again – I like to try to keep running until the water slows me down and lifts up my feet and—

SPLASH!

Jeanette jumps in close to me.

'EEK EEK, little pig!' I say.

'WHOOP WHOOP, little monkey!' I suppose it was the only thing she could think of quickly.

We don't have the breath to say much more, as we use all our energy to splash and swim. The water is nice and warm. I look up to the hills where we live. The mist is sliding away so I can try and spot my house. But all I can see from here is the banana groves. The bunches of bananas poking out from the trees look like the hands of giant green creatures holding back the branches so that they can spy on us swimming far below. I search for a moment for their eyes in the darkness and start to scare myself, so I turn the other way

14

and watch the sky turning from pink to orange to blue. It is so pretty. Jeanette looks pretty too as the new sun sparkles in the water drops on her face. I smile at her. She kicks water in my eyes.

As I blink the water away, I feel a little moment of panic – just a tiny moment, because I cannot see – and I start imagining a big wave of water coming at me and covering my mouth and nose because I cannot see it coming to get out of the way. So, as my sight returns, I feel like I should look to the river bank to find my mum. She is there, where the water curves around the marshes, with the big papyrus plants looking over her shoulder as she crouches down and fills up our water cans. Mum is tall and thin – I think she is one of the most beautiful women in our village. If she stood up now she would just about be able to see over the top of the papyrus and over the marshes. Jeanette has disappeared under the water, swimming like a fish in case I try to splash her back. I make sure I can feel the river bed under my feet, in case she tries to pull me under, and I keep my eyes on Mum. I think she is filling the third can already, but because she is quite far away it is not easy to tell. She usually brings only two or three, but she has brought one more today because we have Jeanette's hands to help too.

An antelope bounces through the marshes and catches my eye. They are my favourite animal – so soft and gentle, but so scared of everything. I dream about stroking their red fur and the white spots on their cheeks, but you can never get that close to one in real life. The river bursts behind me and Jeanette gasps for air, but I do not move. I'm trying to keep the antelope in my sight for as long as possible.

'Who is that?'

'Where?' I say, still looking at the marsh, but I am only

15

imagining the antelope now, following the swaying tops of papyrus and telling myself that it is the antelope that is making them move.

'Behind your mum. Look! Over there!' Jeanette grabs my chin and moves my head in the right direction. She does that a lot, probably because I daydream a lot, but I like the feeling of her hands on my face – it is a nice way to come back to real life.

I look back to the bank and my heart jumps, just like when the pig ran over Jeanette. A dark figure is coming round the edge of the papyrus and creeping towards Mum as she starts filling the last can. It spreads its arms wide as it gets close to her and just as it is ready to pounce I see a flash of white teeth and eyes as it smiles towards us. Then the man jabs his fingers into my mum's sides and she screeches and drops the can into the water as she jumps up to see who is attacking her.

My dad lets out a huge, deep laugh as he hugs Mum close to stop her from slapping him. My heart is light again and excited at the new task we girls have – to catch the empty can floating off down the river. I swim as hard as I am able because I know Mum and Dad will be watching me and proud if I save the can for them. But I was never as strong as Jeanette in the water and she reaches it first and holds it up as she runs along the bank towards my parents, as if she has won the soccer championship.

I run from the river, but I stop by the edge for just a second to catch my breath – and to look at the picture of my dad greeting Jeanette and my mum cheering her for saving the can. All at once I am jealous of her and happy that she is treated as part of our family – she is like my sister. I do not have any real sisters, only a brother. These feelings are quite confusing so I run on again and concentrate on the mud oozing between my toes – that is a feeling that makes sense.

I throw my clothes on over my wet body and shout: 'Daddy! Daddy!' as I jump into the air towards him, and he catches me like I knew he would – he always does. 'I saw a sitatunga over there just now, before you came. It was beautiful, all red, and it came so close I could see its white cheeks.'

'That close, eh?'

'So close. I think it knew that it did not have to be scared of me.'

'I am sure it knew. I am sure.'

Mum is back, crouching by the water, filling the last can. When she finishes she gives one to Jeanette, places one at Dad's feet – for me, picks up the other two herself and marches off up the hill towards home. I stand on Dad's arms as if they are the branches of a tree – they are as thick and as strong – and clamber up from his chest to his shoulders, as far from the heavy water can as I can go! He does not complain, he just bends his knees, scoops up the can and follows the others, with his free hand wrapped warmly all the way around my little, cold ankle – his one hand goes easily round it, but my two arms just about reach around his neck. I have to hold on tight as I bounce around high above the sloping path on the side of the hill. So my voice wobbles when I say,

'Tell me a story! Tell me a story, Daddy!'

'Mmm . . .'

His voice vibrates against my hands wrapped round his throat. It is such a big voice that it vibrates all around his head and so my tummy buzzes with it. Because I am so high up on his shoulders, all I can see ahead of me are the sky and the many hills in the distance that still look blue at this time of day. It is like a fresh blue piece of paper that I can paint onto, paint the picture of the things that the voice tells me about. Dad's voice. But I can't see Dad from here, I just hear his voice, like a magic voice bringing characters to life in my mind and on the paper in front of me. That is why I always ask for a story when we are walking like this. I think Dad expects me to ask too, because he only hums for a second before he starts.

'Many years ago, a man called Sebwgugu married a young and very beautiful woman. The day after they were married there was a severe, terrible drought. Food and water became very scarce.'

I paint the hills a hot, dry red – the colour of the main road to Kigali.

'One day,' Dad's voice warms my belly, 'Sebwgugu's wife set out to collect firewood. And, while walking the forest floor, she came to a clearing and happened upon a thriving pumpkin patch . . .'

Trees cover the red hills and there is Sebwgugu's wife clapping her hands,

'. . . pleased with such a rare and lucky find, under the dry conditions. Carrying as many pumpkins as she could possibly manage, she returned home. That evening she and Sebwgugu had a delicious pumpkin meal. The newlyweds were very happy.'

I dare to lift my hands up from Dad's neck and hold onto the top of his round head instead – still looking ahead at the scene, I can feel a big round pumpkin beneath my hands.

'Miam, miam! Pumpkin!' I giggle, and bounce my teeth carefully off Dad's short hair – carefully because we are still wobbling on up the hill and I do not want to knock my teeth out on his hard head, or hurt his head, because then the fun would really be over. My giggle sounds funny and muffled when my mouth touches his hair so I want to do it again, but suddenly I feel Dad's hard hands on mine. He scrunches up my hands like they were just leaves – he does not hurt me, he just slaps my hands back around his throat and the voice comes back. He has not finished.

'One morning, Sebwgugu's wife noticed their supply of pumpkins was running low. She decided to walk back to the patch and collect more. Out of curiosity, Sebwgugu followed his wife. He simply wanted to see from where the pumpkins were coming. When Sebwgugu arrived he suggested to his wife that the pumpkin patch be weeded in hopes of growing bigger pumpkins. She disagreed and kindly asked that he leave the patch be and let it grow naturally. The next day, without his wife's knowledge, Sebwgugu returned to the patch and weeded the entire area.'

I hear a sharp click – as if it is the sound of my painting snapping in two because it falls away from my eyes now and I see real life again all around. The dusty path ahead, the banana plantation now very close by, Jeanette down below and the back of Mum's head, where the click came from. She is unhappy about something and I think that it is either Dad or Sebwgugu himself. As Dad continues the story quickly, I put my picture back together, but I have a good look at the banana trees first. Just hundreds of bunches of smooth green bananas under the shade of big shiny leaves. I can see each one clearly, just trying to grow. The giant scary creatures that I thought I saw from a distance are not here.

'Soon after,' booms the voice, 'the pumpkin supply at home was again low. Sebwgugu's wife returned to the patch and found it dry. There were no more pumpkins. Although very upset that he had weeded the patch after she had asked him not to, she said nothing to her husband. The pumpkins stored at home were quickly finished. The morning after the last pumpkin was consumed, Sebwgugu's wife told him that she was going to search for water. She lied. Still upset that he had weeded the pumpkin patch, their only source of food during the continued drought, she decided to run away.

'Later that evening, Sebwgugu's wife stumbled upon a splendid house. She knocked on the door but nobody answered. Surprised to find the door unlocked and needing a place to sleep for the night, she entered the house. Although there was nobody home the house was filled with food. She cooked herself a nice dinner and went to bed. The next morning, Sebwgugu went looking for his wife and found her at the splendid house. She told him that she had got lost and had to spend the night. He believed her and they sat down for dinner.

'While eating, Sebwgugu's wife shared that, the night before, a big and mean animal arrived to the house and asked for help unloading what it was carrying. Scared, she told the big animal to go away, locked all the doors to the house and went back to bed. She then asked Sebwgugu to please not help the mean animal if it returned.

'Sure enough, later that night under the moonlit sky, the big animal knocked on the door.'

I am glad that Dad says that the night was lit by the moon, because I am having trouble painting such a dark scene – the sun is quickly climbing in real life, beating us to the top of the hill and shining straight into my eyes. So the moon in our story is very, very bright, OK?

'Sebwgugu answered the door and the animal asked for

help. Ignoring his wife's warning, Sebwgugu obliged. When he stepped outside to help, the big animal ate Sebwgugu in one bite – RAHH!'

My heart jumps and I hold tighter to Dad at the beast's roar. Jeanette turns her gasp into a little giggle. She must have slowed down to let us close the gap so she could enjoy the story also. When I look down at her I see that Mum is now closer too. And because the sun rises in front of us, I can see Mum's thin shadow stretching out towards me, and her other shadow next to her – Jeanette.

'Proud of his tricking Sebwgugu, the animal yelled into the forest, "I have eaten a man and will now look for a woman to do the same." Startled by this, Sebwgugu's wife jumped out of bed and grabbed a machete to protect herself. When the mean animal tried to enter the house, Sebwgugu's wife smote it in the head, killing it at once.

'She then found a drum and beat it joyously as the sun rose, all throughout the day and all through the night. The entire forest echoed with her brilliant drumming. The next morning a handsome man appeared. He was the king of the forest and the owner of the splendid house, yet was frightened away by the big and mean animal. Hearing the familiar drum, he returned to investigate. Sebwgugu's wife told the king all that had happened to her. IMPRESSED BY HER BEAUTY AND BRAVERY . . .'

Dad's voice became much louder right then – my hands could no longer touch each other as his neck grew thicker to make the sound – and he raised his head as if he was shooting the words straight towards Mum. At this she slowed down even more and cocked her head to one side, as if my dad's great words weighed heavy on one of her ears.

'. . . IMPRESSED BY HER BEAUTY AND BRAVERY, the king asked for her hand in marriage. She agreed with a smile; they were married and lived happily ever after.'

Jeanette and I both cheer at the happy ending, but Jeanette's cheer is a little breathless – I think she has had enough of carrying the can up the hill.

'Why do we tell the story of Sebwgugu and his wife, Clementine?' Dad says seriously, like a teacher at school.

I think I know the answer, but I am scared to say it, just in case it is not right after all and I disappoint Dad and look silly in front of Jeanette.

'Clem?'

The pathway stops rising as we enter our village and Dad puts his one free hand behind his head so that I can hold on as he lowers me to the ground. As my feet feel warm hard earth again, Dad, crouching down, is looking straight into my eyes. He is looking for the answer to his question. And now I do not mind trying to tell him, because I can start my answer slowly and I can see from his face – the way his nose moves and the way his eyes change shape – whether or not I am getting things right.

'It tells us . . . to not waste . . . the chances,' I can see that I am right and I just want to kiss his cheeks as they rise with his eyebrows, 'the chances given to you in life.'

'And . . . ?'

The words come rushing fast, now I am sure, 'And be satisfied with what you have.'

'Very good!'

I take my kiss and he returns one on my forehead, holding my shoulders as he does so, otherwise I am sure I would fall over with the force of it.

'And . . . ?' Mum has stopped outside our house. *She* sounds stern like a teacher now. 'What else does the story of Sebwgugu and his wife tell us?'

I look to Jeanette – she is too busy shaking her aching arm about. I look to Dad – his lips are squeezed tight. Either he wants another kiss or he is trying to stop a smile.

'Respect what your wife has to say!' I did not hear Pio come to the door. Mum does not seem surprised, though. She does not even look at him. She keeps her big eyes on me – and Dad – and says,

'Well done, Pio. Respect what your wife has to say. Remember it well.' And she turns and steps past Pio's smug face, with both her shadows following closely.

'Remember it well,' whispers Dad like an echo as he rises – I cannot tell if he means me to hear it or if he is only telling himself.

'It is no great thing that you know the answer,' I say to Pio's face which is frozen in its know-it-all grin at the door. 'You are older than me. Four years older than me – you have probably been told it hundreds more times than me.'

'Or perhaps I am just smarter than you, *my little sister*,' and he says these last words in English as if to prove how smart he is.

But I understand it. I am doing very well at English in school, so I say – in English – as I step inside,

'*Excuse me, brother, I will take my breakfast now*,' and I prod him in the stomach and run before he can return it.

We stop running almost as soon as we start because of the look Mum gives to us through the doorway to the back yard where she prepares the porridge.

'What shall I do, Mummy?' If I help then it will feel like that look was more for Pio than me.

'Bring the sorghum.'

I prefer the porridge when it is only made from corn, but we grow the sorghum ourselves so we have it nearly all the time. Dad is good at growing things. Everyone says so. People come to him for advice about their fields sometimes. They say he is a natural. They say it is his 'Hutu blood', whatever that means.

The porridge is OK today – I put extra milk on to make it sweeter. The milk comes from our cows. Granddad gave them to Mummy when she married Daddy.

'Miam miam! The porridge is lovely!' Jeanette says to Mum. I am not sure whether she really means it. She says it every time. Her family does not have any cows though. I know I am luckier than her.

And that makes me think of this morning down by the river and the birds with the red eyes – and the one that seemed to blame me for the things that Jeanette did. And the eyes make me think of Uncle Leonard so I say,

'Where is Uncle Leonard today?' because he has been sleeping at our house so often for the last few weeks.

Mum gives Dad the look that she gave him when she asked me the meaning of Sebwgugu's story.

Dad adds more sugar to his tea and as he stirs it says, 'Uncle Leonard has gone away. He has gone far away, so we may not see him for a very long time.'

'Where has he gone to, Dad?' Pio seems as surprised as I am to hear the news.

'He has gone to England.'

Lord, that is far away. I have sometimes dreamed about going to England – by aeroplane.

'Why?'

'Pio, it is complicated, but he was not very happy here any more. He needed to make a fresh start.'

It feels like Dad does not want to say any more, and so I say something to stop Pio asking more questions,

'One day perhaps we can all visit Uncle Leonard and Auntie Rose in England!'

Dad finishes his tea, gets up, kisses my head and grabs his machete from its place by the door.

'It is time for me to go to work and you to go to school. Nice to see you again, Jeanette. Say hello to your mother and father for me tonight.'

'I will!'

But as Dad walks out into the brightness, Mum hurries after him.

'Finish your breakfast and prepare for school,' she says over her shoulder. Then in her stern voice we hear, 'Jean-Baptiste!'

Pio and I look at each other for a moment to see if the other is going to do as they were told or do what is more tempting. We quickly jump up and go to the doorway, being careful to stay just inside where it is dark, and we listen.

'Jean-Baptiste, do you leave me to explain the truth to them when they see Rose is still in Nyamata?'

'She rarely comes this way and it is not likely they will go that far if they think she has left too.'

'Do not fool yourself; they will see her eventually and they will ask *her* where Leonard is if we have not told them the situation.'

'I will explain later, darling.' Dad sounds tired suddenly. 'I will!'

'You tell that story to Clem this morning to mock me then.'

'No! Chantal, perhaps I tell that story to tell myself what an idiot Leonard has been. But he needs help too. He is my brother and I pray he will find the help he needs in England.'

'You pray he will not bring shame on your family, so you help him to go as far away as possible.'

'It is for the best. Especially now.'

Nobody is speaking. There is just the sound of the earth in our courtyard being scraped by a foot.

'I must get to the field. I love you.'

I think I hear the sound of a kiss but Pio has run to our room so I follow before Mum returns. As she enters the house I hear her say,

'Thank you, Jeanette, but you must leave for school now. I will clean things away.'

Lord, I bet Jeanette does not bother to help out so much at her house!

'Clementine! Pio! Are you ready?'

We both shout out that we are as we gather our books, staring at each other – I think we are both trying to work out if we understood more than the other about what we just heard. But I think we are both still unsure of it all, except for the fact that Auntie Rose has not gone to England with Uncle Leonard.

We do not talk about it on the way to school much – I am not sure what there is to talk about. I do not feel so sad that Uncle Leonard has gone. For the last few months he always made it feel awkward or a bit frightening at home when he was there.

'What is your Auntie Rose like?' says Jeanette.

'Haven't you ever met her?' says Pio.

'Never.'

'I am surprised, with the amount of time you spend at our house!'

'Shut up!'

'You shut up!'

'Auntie Rose is lovely,' I say before they start fighting in the road, 'isn't she, Pio?' but he is marching off ahead.

'Good!' Jeanette says to his back. 'I do not want to walk the next five miles with him. Is she as pretty as your mum though?'

'Rose? No way. Mum is the most beautiful in our family. She is the tallest, the thinnest. It is because she is Tutsi.'

'What is that?'

I was hoping she would not ask that.

'I don't know – beautiful, I suppose.'

Although Jeanette and I both speak Kinyarwanda and French, we do not know what the word 'Tutsi' means. Perhaps it is an English word. Or just a word in French or our own language that we have not learnt yet.

'I'm nervous.'

I am surprised to hear Jeanette say this as we take our places in our new classroom. But I have not really thought about it, even on the long walk, a much longer walk to this school – the school for older children. All I have been thinking about is this new word. And Mum's sternness this morning. And her conversation with Dad about Auntie Rose. I had almost forgotten my own nerves about starting at the big school today.

'Hutus, stand up!'

The teacher's voice makes me jump as he marches into the classroom. He looks as if he has no neck, as though his wide face is just stuck on the top of his enormous shoulders and, as three quarters of the class stand up, I can see that he is not really that tall either.

Jeanette is standing. I suppose I should too then. So I do.

She gives me a quick, frightened look as my eyes rise to find hers – I am trying to find out why we are standing, searching for the answer in her face. 'Hutu,' he said, I think. He is taking each child's name now and checking it against his list, and then he tells each of us to sit down afterwards. They say Dad's Hutu blood makes him a great farmer. If he is Hutu, whatever that means, then I must be too.

'Jeanette Mizinge.'

'Sit!'

'Clementine Habimana.'

The teacher takes a pause – he said 'sit' so quickly after everyone else said their names, but he does not do so after I speak. He looks hard at me, narrowing his eyes – I think he might need glasses.

'Sit!'

I do quickly and search for Jeanette's hand under the table. Her hand is damp, but I squeeze it anyway and she squeezes mine in return. This makes me feel better.

'Twas, stand up!'

Only two boys stand – they look the same, perhaps they are brothers, but they look different from the rest of us. They are very short. I have never seen anyone else that looks like them before. Their names are unusual too – they sound almost as if they are speaking a different language when they answer the teacher. I feel nervous and strong all at once. Strong because I am glad it is not me standing up with just one other in front of everyone like that. Stronger because nearly everyone else is like me, a Hutu. But I feel nervous for the Twa boys – I have the feeling that they are in trouble with the teacher, in trouble for being . . . only two. Then my heart almost leaps into my mouth when the teacher shouts his next word as if it tastes horrible on his tongue.

'Tutsis, stand up!'

There is that word again. Tutsi. I cannot believe it – we were only talking about it this morning on our way here. Tutsi – that is what they say my mum is. So I must be too. Nine or ten children in front of me start to rise from their seats, and some behind me too (I could feel them, hear them, I am not sure which because it all happened quickly in real life, only slowly when I remember it). I am not sure whether I even turn to look. But I feel myself untangle my hand from Jeanette's, because she is not getting up with me, although I thought she would. She is my mum's shadow. She thinks Mum is the most beautiful too. And if to be Tutsi is to be like Mum, then I must be Tutsi as well as Hutu. I look down at Jeanette as I stand as straight and as tall as I can. She looks confused and scared.

The teacher starts to take the names of all the Tutsis standing up – there are a lot less of us than the Hutus – but he stops suddenly. The sudden silence makes me look up from Jeanette and into the angry eyes of the teacher again.

'Clementine – ' he is checking his list – 'Habimana, what do you think you are doing?'

The children in front all turn to stare at me too and I know how the Twa boys felt now. What do I think I am doing? What . . .

'Well?' His wide head looks like it is swelling up, getting wider, perhaps going to explode. 'You are either a Hutu or a Tutsi! Now, which is it?'

Which is it? You mean I can only be one or the other – not both? I am not sure what to do. It feels like an age before I decide. Most of the class are Hutu – it felt powerful to be the same as everyone else. Jeanette is Hutu. And we must be the same. But perhaps she does not realize if she is

Tutsi too. So she cannot know how nice it is to feel special, not the same as everyone else, one of the beautiful ones. But it does not feel that good right now. I feel Jeanette's hand on the back of my knee – she only touches me lightly, but I tell myself that she has almost beaten her fist there so I have no choice but to sit down, otherwise I might have been standing there all day! I want to tell the teacher that I think my mother is Tutsi and my father a Hutu, but he does not seem in the mood for any more words from me. He just stares through the standing Tutsis at me – I feel like an antelope hiding in the forest and he is the hunter peering through the tall trees trying to find me. He keeps looking, even as he starts checking the next name on his list. Then his eyes finally leave me and I start to breathe again – it is only when I start that I realize I had stopped!

3

'Tell me a story. And remember to breathe!'

'What do you mean?'

I pressed 'stop' on the tape deck before the song kicked in again. Sometimes when I'm teaching I feel a right fraud, I tell you. I mean, when there's someone in front of me with a great voice already, I just want to say, 'Go away, save your twenty quid: there's nothing I can teach you!' But then I think about my own bank balance and I ask myself, why are they here? If they're such good singers, if they *think* they're such good singers, what are they doing coming to a teacher? So I start to look for faults, scribbling frantically in my important-teacher-looking file (99p WH Smith) as they sing Mariah better than Mariah again. That 'all' was a bit shorter than Mariah's = she has a problem with her breathing. Hits every bloody high note without fail = needs lower range developing. Looks a bit nervous standing in a scummy room in the middle of the scariest council estate in London singing to a stranger with a receding hairline = has a confidence problem.

Bingo!

That's why the singers who can sing come looking for a teacher – they lack confidence. It's like paying twenty quid to go and see a therapist, I suppose, and I'm happy to play Dr Bolt for an hour – everyone's a winner! Except . . . then I feel even more of a fraud. Me, teaching confidence. Hey, student, this is how I deal with my stresses: grab a knife, any knife, but it must be sharp, really sharp, then pull up a sleeve and find a bit of skin that isn't already cut or scarred (obviously this gets more difficult the more you do it, but for a novice like you the world is your oyster), sink in that knife as if you were slicing bread, not too fast and not too deep (we don't want to damage tendons if possible), just deep enough so that the pain blots out the stresses and the nerves. Some rock stars take copious amounts of cocaine to boost their confidence – OK if you can afford it, I suppose – but all you need is an everyday kitchen knife and you can manufacture your own drugs, your own anaesthetic, free of charge whenever you want.

That's not what I tell the eighteen-year-old Mariah-wannabe fiddling with the edge of her lyric sheet, by the way! Because when it comes to teaching confidence in singing, really I'm selling myself short if I say I'm a fraud. If there's one time in my life when I'm truly confident, when I don't think for a second about cutting myself, or even so much as a little burn, then it's when I'm on stage singing. One minute before I go on, maybe, as I pace the dressing room. Two seconds after I get off, probably, as I remember the tiny mistake I made that no one else noticed. But while I'm on stage . . . I'm in heaven, I tell you . . . If only the gig could go on for ever . . . And if only I could get a bloody gig these days.

So yeah, *sometimes* when I'm teaching I feel a right fraud. But when it came to Lola, I earned every penny.

'What do you mean?' She sat down again behind my flimsy

metal music stand, which had seen better days since I bought it when I was learning the violin at school, and she rubbed her enormous calves, tired from the heels, I suppose, pursing her lips so hard that I thought the collagen would start oozing out any second from between the glossy too-brown-to-be-red-and-too-red-to-be-brown lipstick and the dark brown lip liner.

I called her 'she' because . . . well, she would kill me if I called her 'he', and because, although she was clearly a bloke dressed up like a woman, she did it with such conviction that you started to believe it yourself, I tell you. Lola needed no lessons in confidence. But she really needed them in singing.

'I mean you'll never make it to the ends of these lines with power unless you take a breath before each one, as I showed you.'

'I was.'

'Lola, if I can see your shoulders going up and down like they're on strings then you're not breathing from the diaphragm, you're just taking shallow breaths.'

She started looking at her nails, looking out the window – you could just see her twenty years ago in the back row of a French class refusing to join in. Perhaps she would've paid more attention if she'd known she was going to be singing Edith Piaf songs and '*Voulez-vous coucher avec moi, ce soir*' for a living by the age of thirty. She didn't take well to criticism; I was going to have to tread carefully here.

'The lamé dress you told me about for this number sounds . . .'

Grotesque.

'. . . grrrreat; but it's hardly going to show off your figure if it keeps riding up with your shoulders as you gulp for air, don't you reckon?'

She looked back at me, down her long nose, fiddling with the crucifix around her neck. I was getting through.

'It's just a matter of practice, until it becomes second nature. And it will, I promise you.'

She uncrossed her legs and stood up, smoothing down her pink skirt.

Result!

I rewound the tape a little and pressed play. The music of Barry Manilow jumped with jazz-hands from my speakers and I felt my face get a bit hot. Lola pushed her fingers into her diaphragm, just as I had taught her, and breathed in so that the muscle pushed her fingers back out again.

'Good!' I felt a buzz, a flash of pride even, and in my moment of optimism I stupidly added, 'And remember to tell me a story.'

'What do you mean?' Lola let her hands flop to her sides and her bum flop back into the chair.

You idiot, Ash!

'Nothing,' I shouted over Barry, 'I mean, don't worry about that yet. Just concentrate on the breathing this time round.'

'But I don't understand. Why do you keep asking me to tell you a story? If I'd wanted a job on fuckin' *Jackanory* I would've gone to the BBC not COME TO YOU.'

I stopped the tape again just before she finished and her last few words boomed around the suddenly quiet room, sounding more aggressive than even she intended them to be. I think she even rattled herself a bit, so she patted her black bobbed hair in case her rant had knocked something out of place.

'OK,' I said, as if I was talking to someone suicidal on the roof of a high-rise, 'it's just that with Barry Manilow, probably more than any other singer, his lyrics are telling a story, taking you on a journey. And this song is probably the most . . . story-like of all. So let's hear in your voice and see in your face the story of the showgirl, every man's dream, top of her game at first; then, by the last verse, she's a tragic figure, lost her love, lost her mind . . .'

Actually, underneath all the cha-cha-cha and brass fanfares this is a bloody depressing song, don't you reckon?

'Go for it and you'll knock 'em dead, trust me. And who knows, if there's anyone from the BBC in the audience you could be the first drag-queen presenter on *Jackanory*.'

She almost smiled, but she sucked it away like she was eating a sherbet lemon. She stood up, though, and smoothed down her skirt. Tapped each stiletto, the same colour as her lips, into threadbare bits of the carpet and pressed her finger into her diaphragm.

Result!

I rewound the tape to the beginning of the song – must get a new deck, it sounds like one of those crappy scooters the kids burn up and down the estate on thinking they're the mutt's nuts. I pressed play. It's going to start chewing the students' tapes up soon, by the sound of it, and I don't need to drive any more away.

Lola started singing about Lola, a showgirl with her hair full of yellow feathers and a dress cut down to . . . somewhere. It sounded like a cross between Mr T and Cilla Black, but at least she was starting to breathe in the right places and in the right way.

Perhaps I should invest in one of these new minidisc things. It's bound to take over the world and I'll get left behind as usual. Ten years ago when *Brothers in Arms* came out on the first CD I dismissed them as a fad . . . derr! And now I wouldn't go anywhere without my CD Discman.

Lola followed Manilow like an echo in a haunted house as he crooned about Tony and the showgirl, working late nights in this cheesy club, where at least they had each other . . . Whoopee.

'Good, keep it up, this is great!'

Oh my God, I'm looking at Lola's tits! Or bra full of socks, or whatever it is she's got stuffed down there. Ash, you've really got to get out more. Yeah? And we all know what happens if I 'get out more' – I keep a journal of my social life on my arm, written with a cheese knife.

But Barry and Lola loudly suggested that I should get myself down to the Copa, Copacabana. Music and passion are apparently always in fashion there. As long as I don't go and fall in love, they warned in suddenly sombre tones.

'*Don't fall in love* . . . Well?'

'I agree,' I said, then quickly realized I was not having a conversation with Barry about relationships. 'I . . . think we've nearly cracked it. Seriously, there was much more power in that, right to the end of even the long lines.'

Lola stood there, arms folded across her . . . chest; she raised her eyebrows and the stud through her right one shot up in the air like an antenna searching for bullshit waves. I thought for a second she had sussed that I could've been paying a little more attention during that run-through. But then I saw her surprisingly-white-given-all-the-cigarettes teeth for the first time today as her inflated lips peeled back like a horse's into a smile, her eyelashes whipped her cheeks and she clicked her heels together like Dorothy wishing her way back to Kansas.

'You think so?' Her voice went from its usual foghorn bass to Mariah's fifth-octave squeak in just those three words. 'Do you think I'll be ready for the show next week?'

'We've got another lesson before then, haven't we?'

Idiot!

Lola flopped to the chair and searched in her bag for a cigarette. 'So you're saying I'm not ready.'

'I am saying that after our next lesson you will be completely ready.'

I started making a meal of putting away my folder of notes to signify it was time for Lola to go. She offered me a Marlboro so I couldn't resist one more lesson for today.

'No thanks, I don't smoke – and neither should you if you want to improve your singing, especially the breathing.'

'Oh fuck off, Mother Teresa!'

Nothing like respect for your teacher, eh!

'Sinatra smokes, Robert Plant smokes, Edith smoked,' Lola smoked. 'It didn't do their voices any harm, did it?'

I was dying to point out the *slight* difference in the quality of their voices and Lola's at her age, and the fact that Piaf died of cancer, but I thought she might beat me with the sharp end of her stiletto. Besides, Lola's attention was fixed on the ceiling now and other voices barking through it.

'Jesus Christ!' In her posh-camp bass you felt every consonant and vowel of a phrase like that. 'What the hell are they up to?'

'Oh, don't worry about them, they're at it all the time, sounds like they're tearing strips off each other, don't it? Usually it's at seven in the morning, although what there is to argue about at that time of day is beyond me, I tell you.'

Lola blew her smoke at the ceiling in disgust. 'Listen, Ashley, I'm not racist but . . .' Here we go, that magic phrase that always comes before a racist comment. 'With those kind, even when one of them says "hello" to another it sounds like he's saying: "Your mother's a whore."'

'Those kind' are Africans. I couldn't tell you what country exactly, but I've lived in London long enough to know a lot of people from a lot of countries and I know they are from Africa. And there was an element of truth in what Lola said, in her sledgehammer-subtle way, but I prefer to see it in terms of music. That's what it is – just a different song, a different style. Heavy metal may sound aggressive to your gran, but it's a beautiful thing to a metal-head. A different language, and the culture it has evolved in is just a different style of music – each to their own, I reckon.

But when they argue like that, the bloke with his booming tone to rival Lola's and the woman like a Rottweiler with broken glass in its throat, it's got nothing to do with the fact that I don't understand the language – you don't need a translator to know that there's venom in those words. It's like an alarm clock, most mornings at seven o'clock – as if I need to be awake at that hour! I don't even function before ten.

They only moved in a couple of weeks ago. Perhaps it will die down soon – they say moving's one of the most stressful things you can do. But in that weird world between sleep and awake, where what you hear in the real world forms the soundtrack of your dreams and where what you do in your dreams is acted out on your face in the real world, that vicious arguing sets off something in me. It triggers memories. I'm sitting at home, I'm six years old perhaps, stuffing my face with Space Invaders crisps and watching cartoons on TV. Upstairs, there's arguing: Mum and Dad are at it again. Something gets thrown, someone stumbles, and I flinch, half expecting the ceiling to collapse on top of me. I cough up the Space Invader that got caught in my throat when I jumped – it makes my eyes water. I blink away the tears and try and fill my eyes with Road Runner instead, but my eyes are still watering. And the strangest thing of all, my parents aren't arguing in English, but some African language.

So I give up trying to sleep, pull myself out of the crater in the middle of my bed where the springs once were, and put the kettle on. But the rude awakening has left my head in chaos again. I turn on the TV and turn it up to try and drown out the arguing. Breakfast news: 'The Rwandan capital of Kigali descended into chaos yesterday as troops, presidential guards and gendarmes swept through the suburbs, killing the prime minister, United Nations peacekeepers and scores of civilians. Gangs of soldiers and youths kidnapped opposition politicians, and killed members of the minority Tutsi tribe, clubbing them to death with batons, hacking them with machetes and knives, or shooting them.'

Nice.

I flick to *The Big Breakfast* for something lighter – at least I would flick if this bloody remote was working properly, it can't be the batteries already. So I turn the TV over to Channel 4 myself and stand in the middle of the lounge watching Chris and Gaby campaign for Barbara Windsor to join the cast of *EastEnders*, waiting for the kettle to boil.

Nearly there, Ash, not long now.

I'll have this cup of tea and then get back to bed. Got nothing on till I meet Jimmy later. 'Old Ford Lock, London, E3 2NN.' Gaby gives out the address if you want to write to them. Where is that? Must be over in Hackney somewhere. What a cushy job they've got. What have I got in for breakfast? Oh, that milk better still be good, I hate having to go out before I've had a bowl of porridge. Especially in this weather. April showers, feels colder than a snowy day in December when it's this grey, this wet. Madonna swore on the David Letterman show. New bassist in the Rolling Stones. *Big Breakfast* news. Tom Jones is now a Doctor of the Welsh College of Music and Drama. Thunder rumbling? No, it's the kettle boiled. '. . . umuntu . . . !' African, Nigerian? Road Runner, '. . . igicucu . . .' clubbed to death, gangs of youths, her name was Lola, she was a showgirl, girl or bloke? Bloke or bird? Broken glass barking dog bedspring Jimmy hugged me last time I left Ah

Ah

Ah.

Peace.

The more it hurts, the more I press the old metallic kettle to my thigh. If someone could see me now! In my boxer shorts, bent over, head resting on the kitchen work surface, the kettle between my legs as if I was having sex with it. Well, in a manner of speaking I suppose I am. I keep the kettle in place, press a little harder and I don't care what I look like, and I wouldn't even care, wouldn't even know if someone was watching. I'm nowhere. In a peaceful place, where all the adverts, the news, the arguing, the laughter that I'm not in on, the chaos, is silenced. I allow the rush that fills my body to escape through my mouth in a long breathy groan. That's the first thing I hear, just the end of it. And my breath misting up the tin with TEA engraved on it is the first thing I see. And the smell of burning flesh is the first thing I smell – it's like chicken being barbecued in a marinade of Radox shower gel.

'We're trying to have a lesson down here, keep it down!' Lola bellowed at the ceiling.

I put my hand on my thigh, my folder of notes over my hand, and pressed gently. Ouch! Still tender. Lola stuffed her fags back into her handbag and grabbed her fur coat.

'You shouldn't have to put up with this: you need to make a stand before they think they can get away with it,' and she marched out of my front door and trotted up the stairs, the sound of her heels ricocheting around the concrete stairwell like the slap of a teacher's ruler on a schoolboy's hand.

'Lola.' Trying to keep up with her was a sore mission as my thigh kept chafing on my combats. 'Leave it, it's just the way things are round . . .'

She banged so hard on the door of Number 62 that she nearly fell back off her stilettos and I swear I saw her fringe move an inch down her forehead. But the moment she did it, the arguing stopped. Lola put her hands on her hips and stared down the peephole like it was a makeup mirror. I knew what Lola looked like in fish-eye-lens view from the other side of those peepholes and I had to stifle a giggle.

'Thanks, Lola, it seems like they got the point.'

Lola pounded on the door again. 'Not so loud now, are you? Are you gonna answer the door or what? Some of us are trying to work round here, you know.'

I could feel eyes at peepholes and doors opening a fraction up and down the stairwell, but not the slightest sense that there was anyone inside Number 62 now.

'Lola,' I whispered.

She raised her antenna again, searching for signs of life. Nothing. So she slapped and clicked back down the stairs again. 'Probably not even living there legally anyway.'

Aren't we all!

'I'm no racist, you know, Ashley . . .'

But . . .

'. . . but those lot, they're all the bloody same. Don't let them get away with it. Keep an eye on them.'

I reached my doorway first and stood in it just in case

Lola had any intention of coming back in, but she pressed the button for the lift. Somewhere below us was a sound like a giant toilet being flushed with scrap metal instead of water and I knew the lift was on its way.

'Well, keep up the good work, make sure you practise . . .'

'Will you come to the show next week?' Lola was smiling again and fluttering her lashes.

The idea of going out on my own to a bar full of loud queens must've sent a dark cloud across my face – I saw it reflected in Lola's and realized that it actually meant a lot to her to have her teacher see her performance.

'Yeah,' my mouth said, 'I don't think I'm booked up.' Ha! 'I might not be able to stay long after though.' Lola clicked her heels again and the lift door screeched open as if it was petrified of what it was about to carry. 'Oh, and can you put me on the guest list?'

The lift door scraped shut behind her. 'No problem, sir!'

I closed my heavy front door and my mind was already in chaos imagining all the worst possible scenarios of an evening at a drag club in Soho. I looked round the kitchen door at the drawer where I keep the knives, but then the great metal throat of the lift shaft choked, pressing pause in my brain. I leant against the doorframe and laughed loudly as Lola's voice drummed up the lift shaft,

'Fucking lift! Help!'

4

As I arrive home after my first day at school I am tired. More tired than I have felt before in my whole life, I think. But I am not sure that it is just the seven-mile walk that has made me this tired. I think it is also the worry and the fear with which my day began. My head aches, but not with lessons – I found them interesting and not too difficult, as I have always done. But doing those lessons under the terrible gaze of Claudius Kagina, my teacher – the one without a neck and with a wide head – this I feel is what has exhausted me.

Mummy is much brighter than she was this morning as I drag my heavy feet into our yard. She throws down the machete she is using to chop the firewood and pats the rock next to her for me to sit. Her face is light, it has an orange warmth to it, as if her shiny skin is a mirror for the red earth glowing in the evening light. I take a bit longer to get to the rock than I really need to, just so Mum will understand how tired I am. But I cannot help a smile bursting through my sour face because I cannot wait to tell her all about my day and I know she cannot wait to hear about it too – it was all I could think about since Jeanette and I parted as we reached Kibungo.

'My baby, growing up and going to the big school! How was your first day?' she says, squeezing me hard.

'It was good, Mummy, really good.'

And while I tell her about all the new English words I learnt and my agriculture class I forget my aching head until she says,

'And how are your teachers? Are they nice?'

Then I look up at my mum, but I feel I have to shut my eyes the moment they rest on her face, as if I have just looked into the setting sun – the pain behind my eyes returns.

'Well . . . ?'

'Mum.'

'What is it?'

'Are you a Tutsi?'

The scrape of metal along the ground makes me look back to her. It is the sound of the sharp machete as she moves it out of the way so that she can gather up the pieces of wood safely.

'What happened at school? What have they said to you?' she says, looking serious, as she was this morning.

I feel disappointed with myself for sending Mum so quickly back into this mood, so I reach for some wood too and try and forget that I ever asked her the question. But she is not about to forget.

'Clementine. Did someone upset you today at school?'

'No, Mummy. Why should you being a Tutsi upset me?'

'That is not what I asked, darling. Who told you I was a Tutsi?'

'No one, but my teacher made all the Hutus in the class stand up, and then all the Twas and then all the Tutsis, and I did not know what I was. I did not know what to do, Mummy!'

I suddenly feel like crying, especially because Mum looks so concerned as I tell her what Claudius Kagina made us do.

'And when did you stand up, Clem. Did you stand . . . ?'

'Yes,' I say, 'when he asked all the Hutus to stand.'

Mum looks relieved now. She places the wood at my feet and rubs my arms slowly and firmly, as if she is kneading dough. It is a strange feeling. It is like she is trying to make sure I really am there in front of her and not a ghost, but at least I do not feel like crying any more. I want to tell her that I stood when all the Tutsis stood too, but I am so glad that she is smiling again that I do not want to do anything to change it.

'I stood because Jeanette stood and because I have heard people say that Dad has Hutu blood.'

'That is right, darling, that is good. Very good.'

'But I have heard people say that you are a Tutsi. And I am like you, aren't I?'

Mum stops the rubbing, but does not let me go. 'Your father is a Hutu and I am a Tutsi. But it means nothing really . . . just that I come from a family of cattle herders and your father from a family of field workers.'

And a cow – perhaps one of ours – from somewhere beyond our house makes a great 'Moo!' just then, as if to tell me that Mum is right. She bends her head to gather the wood again, but I do not move. My arms are still stuck to my sides where Mum has pressed them – there is something I still need to know. Mum senses this and looks up. Now her eyes are questioning and I feel her face is a mirror again.

I say, 'Sarah said in the schoolyard that Tutsis are more beautiful than Hutus. That they are taller and slimmer. That they have lighter skin. And Hutus are shorter and darker and have wide noses . . .'

Mum grabs my hand and leads me quickly round to the kitchen. She drops the wood into the fireplace and leads me inside to her bedroom. On top of the chest of drawers is a little mirror, which she takes, sitting me down on her big mattress.

'Too dark,' she clucks, looking into the glass, and grabs me again, leading me back out to the yard quickly, as if time is running out.

'Look, Clementine!' she says, holding the mirror in front of my face. 'Look at yourself. Are you light-skinned?'

'. . . No.' I am darker than Jeanette anyway.

'Are you tall?'

'. . . No.' I was always one of the shortest at school.

'And your nose. How is it? Is it wide, like mine?'

I am excited and sad all at once. My nose is thin, it is a Tutsi nose, a beautiful nose. But for the first time I realize that my mum has a wide nose. Not like mine. She is tall and slim, but her nose is like Claudius Kagina's – and he is the ugliest man I have ever met! But Mum is beautiful. Everyone says so. *I* think so. This is getting confusing.

'But you are a Tutsi, Mummy. Your nose should be thin.'

She holds the mirror like a plate in her hand and drums her fingers on it. 'If what Sarah says is true then my nose should be thin, but it is not. I do not think it is my imagin-ation. This *is* my nose. I can feel it.' She stops the drumming and uses her finger to squash her nose instead. She makes both her eyes look towards it – her cartoon face makes me laugh. She laughs too. 'Many, many years ago, perhaps it was easy to tell a Tutsi and a Hutu apart by their looks alone. But many Hutus have married Tutsis and given birth to beauti-ful children, with wide or thin noses. We are not so different anyway. We speak the same language, sing the same songs, go to church and worship the same God. Your father is Hutu, so you stand with the Hutus at roll call. But you, my baby, you are lucky; for you have the best of both worlds – you are both Hutu and Tutsi, outside and inside.' She presses her hand to my heart and I think she is a doctor listening with that metal disc, listening for my double heartbeat – the Tutsi and the Hutu beat. And I do feel lucky. With my Hutu skin and Tutsi nose, I feel powerful and beautiful all at once. 'Now you must help me cook quickly before your brother and Daddy come.'

'What are you staring at, Clem?' says Pio.

I look down at my plate and fill my mouth with more of the isombe that Mum and I have cooked. I love isombe, because it has eggplant in it, my favourite vegetable. But my eyes keep wandering all through dinner. I cannot help it. I have to look at Pio and Dad, study their faces. Everything about Dad says Hutu – he is dark, not very tall, and every-thing about him is wide. His nose, his neck, his arms, his legs. But Pio is tall for his age, tall and slender. And his skin is lighter than Dad's, lighter than mine. But his nose is thinner than Dad's, thin like mine. Yet he must stand with the other Hutus at roll call. Sarah really does not know what she is talking about!

Dad is chuckling. At first I think he has noticed what I am doing and I feel my face get hot, but then he says, 'Bikindi! That man is so naughty. How does he get away with it?'

'Habimana is as bad,' says Mum, squeezing her lips together, trying to stop the smile growing on her face. 'Listen!'

And I realize that they are laughing at the radio, at the song that has just finished and the announcer who is now talking so fast I can barely understand him. Habimana, Mum called him.

'Habimana is *my* name,' I say.

'No,' my dad is still chuckling, 'Kantano Habimana. That is the name of the announcer.'

'And never was a man so wrongly named.' Mum rises to collect our plates. 'He is a little devil.'

I do not know why the announcer is so naughty, but I know what my mum is talking about. My name Habimana means 'God exists'.

'And if ever a girl was so perfectly named, it is you, angel.' Dad rises too and kisses my head. Pio pretends he is choking on his isombe. 'Ah, do not fear, my soldier.' Now Dad is squeezing Pio's shoulders tightly – if Pio's smile was not so wide, his scrunched-up eyes would make me think Dad was hurting him. 'Your mother and I never forget that we were blessed twice, and that before Clem came we had our first-born, Pio *Sentwali*.'

Sentwali? Courageous? Ha!

Pio's chest swells over the table, but I do not wait to see it grow further. The naughty announcer with the same name as me is still firing words from the radio faster than fruit bats fly from the caves at twilight. I think he says something about *Inyenzi*, but perhaps I misheard because that means 'cockroach'. Then the singer starts his song again and *n'umututsi* is the phrase that jumps out at me. But I think every time you learn a new word, as I have done today with *Tutsi*, you feel like you hear it everywhere. Perhaps it was always there, perhaps it was just a sound that meant nothing before. But I am not concentrating on noisy songs from the radio, I am trying to catch up with Dad as he leaves for the cabaret.

Of course I am not going to the cabaret with Dad – at least, no one knows when I am there. The cabaret is for the men, where they go to meet their friends after a hard day in the fields. Where they drink that disgusting beer made from banana and sorghum flour, urwagwa. I know because I had a sip once, when no one was looking – just one sip and I was nearly sick. It was like drinking the smell of cigarettes. I wanted to cough and shout the taste from my mouth, but that would have given away my hiding place.

I love to walk with Dad, to ride on his shoulders and to hear his stories. His journey to the cabaret is usually our time for this. This morning, coming up from the river, was an extra treat – Dad does not usually come to the river to collect the water. The cabaret he goes to is only on the other side of the village, so the walk is less than two miles. It is the same place we go to buy rice when we need to, and potatoes. Joseph also sells underwear and some other clothes, and beans, oil, batteries, shampoo . . . Some people say that Joseph can get you anything you need.

'Tell me a story, Daddy!' He has just helped me down from his shoulders so I know we must be close to the time when he tells me to run home. He has been quiet for most of our walk, but if I get him to tell me a story then perhaps we can stay together just a bit longer. But he says,

'A story . . . Mmm . . . Once upon a time there was a little angel called . . .'

I look up at his face. It is getting hard to see now the sun has gone, but I know his eyes are bright, I know what he is going to call her.

'. . . Clementine.'

Yes!

'She fell from her home up among the stars one night.' Dad looks up to the sky and the millions of twinkling stars light his face so I can see it much better. 'And if she does not get back home soon, the devil will take her out on this lonely road.'

He reaches down to tickle me and shoo me off home. I laugh – I cannot help it, I love it when Dad tickles me – but I scrunch up my nose, my thin nose, to make sure Dad knows that I am not really happy with his story or the idea of going home now.

'Hurry home, Clem! And do not find too many distractions on your way. Mummy will be angry if you are late.'

We both start walking in opposite directions. Dad is striding fast into the dark, eager to see his friends and taste his urwagwa. I stop after only three steps and watch him until he is almost out of sight. Then I follow. 'Women do not go to the cabaret,' Mum said to me once. 'And it is certainly not a place for a young girl.' What is so special about the cabaret? What is so secret there? I thought. I could not resist trying to find out, so I have been there three or four times now. It is funny to hear the men gossip about their wives and about other men who are not there. It is funny how their eyes begin to change, as if they are about to cry even though they are very happy, and how they become unsteady on their feet when they get up to piss in the road the more urwagwa they drink. Many of the men have been drinking at the cabaret for a long time before Dad arrives – you can tell by the way they sway on their stools. But I am never sure if Dad becomes like the others, because I cannot stay too long, otherwise Mum will be angry.

Joseph lives in a house like ours behind the cabaret. The cabaret is really just an extra room on the front of his house. The back wall of the cabaret, where all the cases of beer are stacked, is really the front wall of his house. But he has built extra walls – adobe, like the rest of his house – that come out only a bit further than the counter, where all the bottles are lined up. From there, the corrugated metal roof turns into a thatched one and the walls become fences of woven papyrus and grass. There is no wall at all at the front, just a big old sofa and stools around a low table, where most of the men like to be, if it is not raining. Once Dad has finally stopped shaking everyone's hands at the table and they have finished shouting out his name and saying things like, 'Hey, Jean-Baptiste, you are late tonight, working too hard again, eh?' and he has gone to the counter to buy his drink, then I can run to the fence and hide in the grass there. The weaving on the fence is so loose that I can easily see through it and hear everything the men say, even if it does not always make sense to me.

'So Leonard has escaped, Jean-Baptiste! Paul tells me he has flown to England, is this true?'

'Mmm.' Dad pays Joseph for a bottle of urwagwa and nods his head as he takes a sip through the reed straw.

'Lucky bastard! I wish I could get that far away from my wife sometimes!'

Everyone laughs at once and it sounds like the roar of the beast that killed Sebwgugu – it makes my heart leap and I sink my nails into the grass and the old newspaper that is lying there.

'So, Jean-Baptiste, did he take that sexy little whore with him to England?' That is Paul speaking. He is sitting in the middle of the sofa with his arms spread out along the back of it and his legs spread wide so that there is hardly any room for the others to sit. I think he thinks that the old sofa is his very own throne. I do not understand who he is talking about – I have never thought that Auntie Rose could be sexy and I know that Dad would not allow anyone to call her a whore. I do not like the way Paul speaks. I do not think Dad does either.

'Now, Paul, I think that is enough on that subject, don't you?' Dad takes another sip and passes his bottle to Augustine sitting next to him.

But Paul goes on. 'I just wanted to know if she was still around here, so I could go and take my turn.'

Most of the men are smiling, some of them are also making sounds like they have been punched in the stomach, but they are clearly enjoying themselves. Dad is saying nothing, but staring straight at Paul.

'Hey, hey!' says Augustine. 'Leonard is a—'

'An alcoholic fool? A coward?'

'A brother of Jean-Baptiste. He is his family, so respect that. You know that family is everything – even you, Paul. Or should we start talking about your family?'

Augustine passes Dad's bottle to the man next to Paul, but keeps his eyes on Paul. Paul looks as if he is searching for a piece of food stuck between his teeth, then eventually he jumps up and shouts, 'Another beer! My round, I think,' and he marches to the counter. 'Please, Joseph . . .' and Joseph prepares another bottle.

'Not joining us tonight, Adalbert?' Paul is talking to the only other man at the counter, who is sitting at the end of it on a high stool, but he is making sure everyone can hear what he is saying.

'No thank you, Paul.' Adalbert is looking embarrassed. 'I am still temporarily strapped. I must watch my money carefully for now.'

'What happened, my friend?' says Paul, but I do not think he sounds like a friend to Adalbert.

'You know, my field just seems to be failing again this year.'

'Bloody Tutsi cattle trampled your crops, I suppose.' Paul

says this more to everyone else than to Adalbert – half of them laugh. Dad smiles to the ground and shakes his head.

'No, no. Just one of those things. But I'll have to ease up on the urwagwa for a while, that's all.'

'Then how do you manage to still look so bloody drunk, my friend?' Paul slaps Adalbert's back as he says this to his audience and everyone laughs, even Augustine and Dad.

I know what Paul is talking about, because from where I hide I can see behind the counter and there, by Adalbert's feet, Joseph has placed a huge water can full of homebrew. Homebrew is another kind of beer I think, but it is very, very cheap. Many of the men say that it tastes awful. I do not know why they have to keep it hidden behind the counter. Every time Adalbert wants to take a mouthful he has to ask Joseph's permission, then suck through the very long reed that stretches from the can, up behind the counter. And after all that, he makes a face that says it was horrible, as if he has just taken medicine from Ruzi, the healer. Poor Adalbert! Even without the funny face, he always seems to look ill – he is very thin – too thin – and his short hair has patches missing at the back.

At least the atmosphere in the cabaret is happy again. I look down at my hand, stroking the rough newspaper beneath it. There's a cartoon. Perhaps a good story too. I fold it up slowly and quietly – I can read it in bed tonight. Paul sits back in his throne and passes his bottle to the man next to him, who has to shuffle to the end of the sofa as Paul spreads his legs again. The squashed man says,

'Did you hear Kantano Habimana tonight – he was funny, no?'

There is a mess of sound as all the men answer at once and all seem to have different answers. Paul's answer is,

'Yes, put the radio on, Joseph! Let us see if there are any more good things on.'

Some of the men groan, but Joseph disappears into the house. I suppose he is going to get the radio. The men start to talk in smaller groups. Augustine is asking Dad how Mum is. Paul is trying to get the other men on the sofa to sing a song. It is no good when they start doing this – it is so difficult to hear what is going on when there are too many conversations. I think about slipping away home when a great *Hiss!* is spat out of the darkness behind me. I become still as stone. And although I fear for my life, I'm not sure what would be worse – to be killed alone here in the dark by a snake, or to cry to my dad for help so that he would know I was here and know I had disobeyed him.

But as the hiss turns into a long crackle and the smell of cooking goat meat fills my nose, I realize that Joseph has just thrown the meat *en brochette* onto the grill at the back of his house, ready for the men when they are hungry later. It is a wonderful smell. I stay still in the grass a moment longer – to make sure that Joseph has gone and to enjoy the smell a little more. Even though it is not long since we had our isombe, my stomach starts to grumble. We do not eat meat very often at home, so before my stomach gets too excited, I start to slither away through the grass back to the road – now *I* am the snake!

Joseph must have found the radio because I recognize the voice of Kantano Habimana, as if he has joined the men in the cabaret for a drink.

'We began by saying that a cockroach cannot give birth to a butterfly. It is true. A cockroach gives birth to another cockroach . . . The history of Rwanda shows us clearly that a Tutsi stays always exactly the same; that he has never changed.

The malice, the evil are just as we knew them in the history of our country. We are not wrong in saying that a cockroach gives birth to another cockroach. Who could tell the difference between the Inyenzi who attacked in October 1990 and those of the 1960s? They are all linked,' his voice does not sound as if he is looking for laughs any more, 'their evilness is the same. The unspeakable crimes of the Inyenzi of today recall those of their elders: killing, pillaging, raping girls and women . . .'

I do not understand what he means. What attacks? What cockroaches? Why is he talking about Tutsis too? I feel scared and, as if it is reading my mind, the radio starts spitting out some scary, noisy music. The singer is Simon Bikindi again.

'I hate Hutus, I hate Hutus . . .'

Lord, now it seems like there is something wrong with the Hutu also!

'. . . I hate Hutus that do not think that Tutsis are snakes.'

I stop sliding through the grass. It is as if Bikindi is singing straight to me. I was being a snake! I am Hutu! I am Tutsi! What have I done? What should I do? I run to the road and I keep running towards home. The lovely smell of cooking meat that filled my nose and lungs before soon changes – it is replaced by the feeling that Joseph has thrown my lungs onto his grill instead of the meat. I am not halfway home yet, but I have to walk the rest. I walk fast. Taking big gulps of air, squeezing the newspaper in my hand with each gulp because I need to hold on to something, my chest swells in front of me and I remember Pio at the table as I left the house. I wish I had stayed with him and Mum tonight.

5

The sun was out and it even felt like I might be a bit over-dressed with this coat on. I could just hear Dad, ordering everyone about in the garden and congratulating himself, 'See? I knew i' would turn ou' nice for a family bar-bee. May bank holiday weekend – gotta be done! Listen to yer Uncle Tel, he knows best!' It seemed a shame to ferret my way down the Tube with the rest of the rodents, but it was quicker, so I could drop the stuff off at Jimmy's and still have plenty of time to get to Dad's before I started getting slagged off for being the 'prodigal son'.

No police with dogs at the barriers – handy. As the Northern Line train rattled into the station, I stuffed my headphones into my ears and pressed the tiny 'Play' button, followed by the 'Random' one on my beloved Discman, before shoving it safely back in my coat pocket. The clanging and scraping and groaning of the train quickly faded out as bluesy Fifties electric guitars faded in, then an electric bass like something out of Grandmaster Flash reminded me that we were in the Nineties and the drums kicked in and we were off.

I used to find travelling round the city such a stress, I tell you, but now with my own personal soundtrack pumping through my head it's just like being in my own music video. People don't seem so threatening any more – they're just actors in my video. A funky song from Prince and I'm strutting through the crowd like a Sexy MF, a ballad from Boyz II Men (hey, don't knock 'em, they're great vocalists; cheesy, I know, but they can sing) and I'm sauntering through the street annoying everyone trying to get past me who thinks that I must be a tourist otherwise I'd be scurrying along as frantically as them. And as I stared at the wooden slats that made up the floor of the train, I imagined I was on a pier – not Brighton or Southend, Christ, no! Somewhere a bit more . . . classy, romantic even . . . I don't know, on a quayside in Miami or Venice Beach perhaps – this music was transporting me. And now this voice, sighing goodbyes, stabbed in the guts by the inevitability of dying love. Looks like *Melody Maker* actually got something right for a change when they said that this debut by Jeff Buckley was important, a future classic album. There's not much coming out these days with powerful songwriting *and* great singing, I tell you. It's either great singing and crap songs – Boyz II Men. Or crap singing and great songs – Oasis. Buckley's voice was . . . beautiful . . . got to try this out with some of my students. The song was sad, but I was enjoying the technique and feeling a bit superior that I had not made the same mistake as the character in the song – getting involved.

As the song just continued to build, without looking back, one crescendoing chord sequence after another, I became self-conscious for a moment that my exhilaration might be showing a bit too much on my face – I wasn't sure if that was a smirk from the girl sitting opposite me from inside her cave of black hair, as black as the little mice in these tunnels, their fur dyed by years of grime and fumes. Funny . . . I couldn't've cared less if she was a minger or twice my age. But she wasn't, so I grabbed the discarded newspaper on the seat next to me (luckily it was the *Guardian* and not *The Sun*) and I held it up to my face.

UN troops stand by and watch carnage

said the headline. I read it probably ten or fifteen times without taking it in, as my mind was still on the passionate end of the 'Last Goodbye'. But then another track started, all harp-like guitar and choirboy falsetto. I checked the track number on the Discman: 8. I laid the newspaper on my lap and pulled the CD's booklet from the inside pocket of my coat – I never leave home without the booklets, I tell you, I'm the kind of music anorak that has to know the track titles, who wrote them, who played drums, who produced, blah, blah, blah . . . This one was 'Corpus Christi Carol' by Benjamin Britten, apparently. I stuffed the booklet away again, flicking my eyes ahead to try and see without really looking if the girl thought I was sad . . . Is that a stud above her lip or a mole? Either way it's . . . I hid behind the newspaper again . . . saucy.

The classical vibe of the track swelling in my ears and its almost unintelligible words meant I found myself focusing on the words on the page in front of me instead.

French and Belgian forces are evacuating expatriates but leaving members of the Tutsi minority, including local employees of international organizations, to their fate, reports Mark Huband in Kigali.

A few yards from the French troops, a Rwandan woman

was being hauled along the road by a young man with a machete. He pulled at her clothes as she looked at the foreign soldiers in the desperate, terrified hope that they could save her from her death. But none of the troops moved. 'It's not our mandate,' said one, leaning against his Jeep as he watched the condemned woman, the driving rain splashing at his blue United Nations badge.

'Not our mandate' – what's that supposed to mean?

The 3,000 foreign troops now in Rwanda are no more than spectators to the savagery which aid workers say has seen the massacre of 15,000 people – mainly from the traditionally dominant Tutsi minority. The killing started after President Juvenal Habyarimana and his Burundian counterpart – both from the majority Hutu tribe – died in a rocket attack on their plane while returning from peace talks. His presidential guard and the Hutu-dominated army unleashed a campaign of terror. Opposing them is the rebel Rwandan Patriotic Front, dominated by Tutsis.

The Belgian and French troops are here to get foreigners out. So far they have ferried about 1,000 from an assembly point at the French school to military aircraft. Rwandans, including staff of international organizations, are left to their fate.

About 275 Rwandans staying in one hotel have been barred from leaving on European military aircraft, a Belgian Red Cross employee said yesterday. 'All of them are Tutsi. They are going to be assassinated. It's disgusting that they don't take them. We have all their names and we are going to publish them when we get to Belgium,' he said, before being evacuated with his Rwandan wife.

Sick!

Less than a mile from the airport yesterday, army trucks filled with foreign evacuees were blocked when they drove into a massacre where machete- and knife-wielding Rwandans lined the roads smiling as their victims lay dying.

On the way to pick up the evacuees, the convoy had passed the bodies of two newly killed men sprawled in the muddy courtyard of a house. As the convoy returned past the same house less than an hour later, the body of a woman and two more men lay with the two already dead, their eyes wide open. The woman had had one of her legs cut off.

On the other side of the road the bodies of three men lay with fresh wounds. Watching the convoy were the killers – young men, two women with clubs, old men and children. Close to one body stood a man with a clipboard in office clothes. Beside him stood a well-armed government soldier in smart uniform. Halfway up the hill lay a pile of corpses. From nearby houses women, old and young, were casually led to the pile and forced to sit down on it. Men with clubs then beat the dead and dying bodies which surrounded the women as they sat, screaming, pleading for their lives . . .

The music in my headphones was too mournful, too perfectly suited to reading about such awful things. It was as if a gushing tap had been turned on in my chest and it was quickly filling up. Once my chest was full, the warm water had to flow up my neck and into my head, and if I didn't do something about it quick, it would overflow from my eyes. I chucked the newspaper back into the seat that it came from and popped the headphones from my ears like a couple of corks that let the vintage 1994 Northern Line plonk fill up my world again.

Phew! That was close. I flicked a look at the girl opposite to see if she'd noticed anything. She stretched her green and white striped sleeves, gripped them and buried her hands between her thighs as if she was trying to keep warm. It wasn't cold in the train. I was probably giving her the creeps. Camden Town couldn't come soon enough. I jumped up before the train stopped – a split second before, so did she.

Oh, great, now she thinks the creepy bloke is following her!

I tried to get ahead of her, so she couldn't possibly think I was after her, but just succeeded in colliding with the people in the flood coming the other way. So I tried walking slowly, so she would quickly lose me in the crowd, but that just got me a barrage of 'tuts' and huffs aimed at the back of my head. So now I was walking side by side with the girl and I had made myself just about as conspicuous as possible – as conspicuous as an average-looking bloke can down Camden Tube on a Saturday with its time-warp tunnels of skinheads and punks from the Seventies and cyber-Goths from somewhere in the future in their black PVC macs, fluorescent green dreadlocks, and platform biker boots.

When we got to the escalator I tried to let someone get on between me and her, but as I tried to stand to one side I became the head of a chain of zombies bumping into the person in front like some Marx Brothers moment. After about two seconds, the chain was nearing twenty zombies long, so I gave up and found myself face to back with the girl and her low-cut top. I held my breath in case she felt it on her skin and found my headphones dangling round my neck. I stuffed the cork back in this dodgy sparkling wine and, since I hadn't bothered to press 'Stop' when it was all getting a bit emotional back there, Jeff Buckley was still going – and this time he was rockin'! Led Zeppelin would have been proud of this hard, dirty groove and it injected some conviction back into my step as I slid off the escalator – so much so that I almost forgot to get ready to slip back down again if the barriers were crawling with police and sniffer dogs.

But they weren't. And stripy girl went left as I went right – I tell you, all you need is a good tune keeping the world at bay and everything seems to go your way.

I marched down the high street, blinking at the sunshine and dodging the crowds in time to 'Eternal Life'. As I got nearer to the Lock I wanted to take my coat off, but I thought I'd better wait till it no longer had two thousand ecstasy pills in it.

Jimmy Riddle's tattoo shop is just after the Lock, on the way up to Chalk Farm, between a second-hand furniture shop and a second-hand clothing shop – or *vintage* clothing shop, as it calls itself. Jimmy Riddle's not his real name, of course. And *he* doesn't call himself Riddle. He calls himself Jim, but I doubt that's his real name, that's just what he calls himself to everyone but those he trusts with his life . . . and I guess that's just Elaine. And that's why everyone else calls him Riddle – 'cause that's the way he likes to be. Elusive is safe, protected if the shit hits the fan, you know?

They do piercing at Jimmy's too. Elaine does the piercing out back and Jimmy does the tattooing in the front – he likes people to see 'the artist at work', although there's a curtain, heavy and red like in an old theatre, which he pulls across if the client insists – but I'm not sure if anyone has the balls to insist on anything from Jimmy. He's your classic British Bulldog, at least he looks like one anyway – what's left of his hair shaved bald; thick, shiny neck that you just want to slap to see how it sounds (never done that, of course!); shorter than most but wider than most – and on a day like today he'll be in his England top and shorts, and won't probably take them off till after the World Cup (even though England didn't even qualify . . . or perhaps *because* England didn't even qualify).

That's not to say he's dirty, quite the opposite. Him and Elaine always have the best gear on, the most expensive perfumes and aftershaves; they look like they have four showers a day and Jimmy has a permanent tan as if he lives in Tenerife – it's from a sun bed, of course, but no one knocks him for it. Like I say, no one insists on anything from Jimmy . . . but he'll pull the curtain without you asking if he's doing your bum or your—

'Cock?!'

'Yep.' Jimmy kept his eyes on the TV screen, as if he was just telling me the football scores, 'and he wan'ed me to wri' 'is girlfriend's name up it, in calligraphy, like.'

'How does that work then?' I was genuinely curious. 'Do you do it when it's hard or floppy?'

'I don't bleedin' care, Ash! I told 'im, as long as 'e wants i' done in my shop 'e's havin' i' done on a floppy.' He looked at me for the first time since I came in. 'And 'e should think 'imself lucky that I'll stretch to that.' He noticed the potential in this line, 'If you'll pardon the phrase, matey!' and he stuck his tongue out as he laughed just in case I needed another reason to think of him as a bulldog.

I laughed too, but I could never fully relax with Jimmy until the business was out the way. But that's not the way things were done. Whenever I arrived at the shop Jim would say hello and chat as if it was a nice surprise that I had just dropped in. If he was working on someone he'd finish the job, chatting to me all the while, no matter how long it took. If he wasn't busy, like now, he'd stare at the little portable TV on a bracket high on one of the clinical white walls and comment on the news or the sport for a while.

'See those poor bleeders in Rwanda, Ash?'

'Just read something about it on the train.'

'Some BBC journalist managed to get the bastards on film hackin' at some poor women with their fuckin' machetes . . . Animals.'

'And they showed it on the news?'

'Yeh . . . it was 'orrible . . . Sad, innit?'

'Yeah,' I said, feeling strangely chuffed at how my pal Jimmy always surprised me with his compassion.

And he was my pal . . . I suppose . . . At my shaky times I realized that I probably didn't even know his real name and that I was just the mug who was stupid enough to look after his gear for him (for a fee, of course), so that if the fuzz came knocking he would have nothing harder than some paracetamol in his house . . . but the rest of the time I liked to think that he'd really taken to me. He'd even taken to hugging me when I left. It nearly blew me away the first time he did it – not just because I hadn't felt a hug from anyone in God knows how long . . . but because I didn't know where to put my hands. Jimmy being that much shorter than me, his face was in my chest and there was that shiny head and I just wanted to pat it, see if it made the same sound as the old bloke's on *The Benny Hill Show*. Needless to say, I didn't.

Elaine loves me; she says I'm 'nicer than all the other

arseholes he hangs around with', so I guess that makes Jim see me in a better light too. I love Elaine too. She's gorgeous. Trust Jim to not only have the flashiest car and jewellery, he has to have the tastiest bird too. Elaine's parents are Indian so I'm not sure how she ended up with a name like Elaine, but she's definitely got all the best bits from their genes – she has long thick black hair, perfect skin . . . quite a big nose if you think about it, but her smile, as white as the walls of the shop, just makes you want to melt. And as for the body – athletic, I tell you. She had a kid with Jim a couple of years ago and she still has the body of an eighteen-year-old gymnast.

'I thought I heard your lovely voice, Ashley.' She bounced through from the back room after a pale white girl with burning cheeks and a glowing red ear from where Elaine had just skewered it.

The girl ducked out of the shop without a word and covered her ear with her hand the moment she got outside.

'Hiya!' I said like a little boy.

Twat.

Elaine sat on the back of a plastic chair; her white trainers on the seat, elbows on her knees, she leaned forward, 'Got any more gigs coming up? We're dying to hear you sing again. You've got a beautiful voice, you know.'

She was only wearing a black vest with thin straps, no bra – she's not exactly overloaded in the chest area anyway, but nevertheless it was difficult not to stare.

'Not had a lot of offers, to be honest, just concentrating on the teaching mostly at the moment.'

'That's a shame, innit, Jim?'

'Yeh.' Elaine seemed to have brightened up everything since she walked in the room except Jim. ''Aven't you got stuff to do in there? Me and Ash are tryin' to talk business 'ere.'

Are we? At last!

'I can spend time with my husband and his friend if I want, can't I?' and she hopped off the chair and sat on his lap.

Jimmy pulled a face like she'd just dropped one or something. 'You see, matey, this is the reason why you're be'er off on your own, take my word for i'.' Elaine slapped his chest then buried her head in it. 'They carn be on their own for five minutes,' he said with a mouthful of Elaine's hair. 'I've gotta go to Spain next week, you know, drop something off . . .'

That'll be a suitcase full of money more than likely, and he'll just waltz through Customs with it – got connections everywhere, has Jimmy Riddle – half the Customs officials buy their coke from him – seriously.

'. . . I'll only be gone for a few days but she carn stay here withou' me . . . just for a few days, innit, but she carn do i', wants to come with me, as if I'm going on some bloody beano or somink.'

'What about the little one?' I said.

'Exactly wha' I said, bruv, and so now we gotta ask 'er mum and dad to look after 'im and then they star' askin' all sorts of questions about where we're goin' and wha' for.'

'Oh, shut up, Jimmy!' Elaine bounced off to the back room again. 'Look, I'm going . . . to be on my own. Get on with your "business".'

Jim put his feet up on the white counter next to the till and leaned back grinning again. 'You see, Ash,' he said loudly so Elaine could still hear, 'yer women, well, they're the same as drugs, same as booze. They piss you off, cause arguments – that's the hangover or the comedown. And that's when you say, never again, I'm jackin' it in, kickin' er ou'. And a few days later, where are you? Down the pub getting pissed up, a' the club grinding yer teef, sayin' this is great, I'm 'avin' the best time ever! That's the bi' where you've made up and you fink she's the best fing since sliced bread, see? Memories like goldfish, us humans, that's our problem. Fick as shi'!'

Elaine's voice shot through from the back room. 'Wanker!' I didn't think she could sound so . . . ugly.

I stood in the middle of the shop, flicking through a book of tattoo designs, feeling awkward and at the same time smug that I didn't have to go through that kind of relationship stress on a daily basis – I'm not sure I've got enough room on my arms!

'So,' I was riding a rare wave of superiority when it came to me and Jim and enjoying the idea that all that glitters perhaps isn't gold after all, 'family life's not all it's cracked up to be, eh?'

Jimmy took his feet down and pulled a sports bag out from under the counter. 'Matey,' he looked at me so straight that for a second I thought I knew his real name, 'I wouldn't be without them for all the coke in Colombia.'

I handed over the pills and he put them into his bag. For someone so guarded, he didn't seem to mind doing stuff like that in the front of his shop with a mini version of Pearl Jam hanging around outside, looking at the designs in the window and daring each other to go first. Jimmy chucked the bag through the doorway to the back room.

''Ere, make yerself useful and put that away!'

He walked in his waddling way – which wasn't the least bit funny, more physically impressive (how can you walk with your feet at right angles to the direction you're walking in and not fall over?) – to the shop door and yanked it open.

'You.' He pinned mini Eddie Vedder to the window with his stare. 'You're first. Stop pissin' abou' and get on wiv i'!'

The other boys squealed with laughter, relieved that it wasn't them, and bundled Eddie into the shop. It suddenly felt busy in there – time to get going. Jim was getting the inks and needles together; he looked like he could tell what the kid was going to choose, probably because of the book the boys were now crowded around, or possibly because he'd done the same tattoo on the same kind of kid a thousand times.

I took off my coat now it was potentially twenty grand lighter, and stuffed my Discman into the huge pocket in my combats instead. I looked at the boys in their black T-shirts, Jimmy in his England one, and me in my long-sleeved shirt. No matter how hot this summer got, I'd be in long sleeves, the same as every summer. No matter how sweaty I got, I couldn't handle people staring at my scars . . . let alone the questions. There's twenty years of cuts on my arms: you can just imagine the reaction!

I needed to feel . . . normal, so I moved nearer to Jimmy and quietly said, 'I'm off now then.'

'OK, matey.' He was putting a CD in the stereo to get everyone in the mood – Soundgarden's latest: *Superunknown*. Their singer, Chris Cornell, had an unusually fine technique for the grunge scene.

'It's funny . . .' I chuckled.

Lame.

'What, Ash?'

'You know, why people would want to . . . mutilate their skin like this with tattoos and piercings.'

'All right, bruv, piss on my picnic, why don't ya!'

'No, I'm not knocking what you do.' Of course! 'It's just strange when you think about it.'

Jimmy looked impatient and tested the gun thing with the needles in. It hissed its high-pitched note, like a dentist's drill, and the boys all went quiet.

'Fing is, Ash, it's no' mutilation, is i'? It's no' like you're cutting yourself like some of the loonies you hear about these days . . .'

This wasn't going the way I'd hoped.

'There's rumours,' he said, nodding up at the TV, 'that Princess Di is into all tha', you know, cutting her skin to block out the pain of being married to that ball bag, Charles.'

'Yeah?' I had the feeling my cheeks were the same colour as that girl's who'd just had her ear pierced.

'Difference is, havin' a tat is all about social inclusion – there's no psychosis involved . . . well, there may be in the parents when they find out!' He giggled and did his bulldog tongue in the direction of the boys. 'It's like those girls who get all anorexic. If Elaine goes on a diet she gets pissed off, she feels deprived. But when yer anorexic is starving herself, she feels satisfaction even though she's in pain, riskin' 'er life.'

I was staring at Jim, but all I could see was Oprah.

'Same way, when someone decides to get a ta'oo or a piercing you 'ave to go through the pain. You don' like it, but that's the deal. If you wan' the tat you have to endure the pain. When yer self-mutilator cuts 'erself, on the uvver 'and, she don' care about the result, the cut, the scar – the pain is the only bi' they're after. There's nuffink socially acceptable about it, poor bastards. They're jus' tryin' to block out the worse pain in their 'eads.' I didn't know whether to be impressed by Dr Riddle or embarrassed 'cause it felt like he was talking about me. 'Like I say,' he concluded, 'loons!'

The shop door twanged on the heel of a trainer and we both looked round. Pearl Jam had left the building.

6

I tell Mum I am very tired when I get home. I tell her I cannot wait to sleep because then I do not have to face her too much.

'You do not even want a story tonight, darling?'

Mum tells us a story nearly every night. Beautiful stories. I love them – it is the best way to end each day. But if we have a story there will be more time for her to see in my face that there is something wrong, and I won't know what to say if she asks me what has happened.

'No thank you, Mummy, goodnight.'

I jump into bed and cover my head with the blanket. I am not comfortable yet, but I stay very still, waiting for all the noise to leave my head – the noise of the men laughing about Uncle Leonard, the noise of the music from the radio and the angry voice of Simon Bikindi. And I wait for the silence of the night to replace it. I listen out for the gentle huff of Pio's breathing from the bed next to me, for the distant hoot of monkeys from the valley below.

These peaceful sounds are air blown into a balloon. My body is the balloon and it becomes lighter and lighter as it fills up, and my stiff limbs relax and float just below the blanket, which slides from my face as my hands slide down to my sides. I feel safe again now so I let my eyes pop open. The room is so dark, but I do not need my eyes to find the rolled-up newspaper, sticking up like a spear in the little mound my dress has made where I left it on the floor by my bed. I pull it up onto my chest and stroke the rough pages – it is a comforting feeling. Perhaps this is what a bedtime story about princesses and magic feels like to a blind child in Braille.

I pull back the curtain a bit above my head – it is easy to reach without getting up. The light of millions of stars falls onto my bed, making it easy to see my newspaper. At least I can find a story in here to send me off to sleep, without facing anyone. I see the cartoon that I saw when I first found the paper by the fence of Joseph's cabaret. It has a title. TUTSI, RACE OF GOD. I feel a little burst of pride that makes me wriggle under the blanket. The paper clicks – it is old and stiff – I must be careful not to wake Pio. Below the title is the cartoon of a man holding up a machete, like the one Dad uses in the fields, and the words:

What weapons can we use to defeat the Inyenzi once and for all? What if someone brought back the Hutu Revolution of 1959 to finish off these Tutsi cockroaches?

Before the noise of this evening at the cabaret can rush back in and kick out my peace, I turn the page. THE HUTU TEN COMMANDMENTS is the title of the next story. Everything I see or hear today seems to have something to do with Tutsis or Hutus. I have got a strange feeling that, when they get older, people forget that they are all the same and become obsessed with making up differences between themselves. I wonder why? It only seems to make them unhappier as far as I have seen. The story of the ten commandments looks more like a list on the page and I do not think I am going to find the bedtime story I am looking for in this newspaper after all. But my eyes are drawn to the list anyway and, although I do not understand all the words on the page, I can feel the hatred in them.

1. *Tutsi are blood- and power-thirsty. They want to impose their hegemony on the Rwandan people by cannon and sword.*

2. *Ever since the social revolution of 1959, not one day has passed that the Tutsi have let go of the idea of reconquering power in Rwanda and exterminating the intellectuals and dominating the Hutu agriculturists.*

3. *Tutsi use two means against Hutu: money and Tutsi women.*

4. *Tutsi sold their wives and daughters to the Hutu authorities. Tutsis tried to marry their wives to Hutu elite in order to have spies in the inner circle.*

5. *Tutsis did everything they could to erase the Hutu consciousness to the point that any Hutu that noticed the diabolical actions of the Tutsi was fired from their job without warning and thrown into jail.*

6. *Hutus must know that the Tutsi wife, wherever she may be, is serving the Tutsi ethnic group. In consequence, any Hutu who does the following is a traitor:*
   a) Acquires a Tutsi wife
   b) Acquires a Tutsi concubine
   c) Acquires a Tutsi secretary protégée.

7. *All Hutus must know that all Tutsis are dishonest in business. Their only goal is ethnic superiority.*

8. *The Rwandan Armed Forces (FAR) must be exclusively Hutu. The war in 1990 teaches us this lesson.*

9. No military man (i.e. FAR soldier) may marry a Tutsi woman.

10. The Hutu must stop taking pity on the Tutsi.

Hassan Ngeze

I throw the newspaper underneath my bed and feel the need to wipe my hands, so I do, on the edge of my blanket. I do not care about the noise I am making. I just want to get up quickly and find my mum. She is sitting at the table making some trousers by candlelight.

'Mummy,' I say, and she has put down her sewing already, 'can I have a story after all?'

I think Sunday is my favourite day of the week. Because in the morning we go to church and in the afternoon we go to see Nyamata play soccer. I am not that keen on playing soccer or watching it, really, but the atmosphere is heart-pounding. And most importantly I get to sing in the choir at church in the morning and I get to sing all afternoon at the soccer – and here the choir is thousands of people strong!

Dad, Mum, Pio and I walk through the forest along with hundreds of people from Kibungo. Dad sees Augustine in the crowd. He is with his wife – I think her name is Marie, and their little boy, John. Dad shouts to Augustine, Mum just smiles at Marie – it is difficult to make yourself heard anyway over the noise of the crowd. The trees just ahead of us are constantly waving their branches as birds flee from us humans – it makes me smile, I feel strong, but I know the birds will be OK. They will always be OK for they can fly. Crowds from Kanzenze and Ntarama march on other tracks through the forest too, and when we all meet at the edge of Nyamata it is as if we have all just been reunited after a long and distant war. The roar that erupts rips out my insides and in a split second fills me up again, pouring fizzing blood into my head – I feel it hit the bottom of my stomach and race up the inside of my chest, my neck, my head until I am full and tingling all over.

And then we sing.

I am always amazed at how we all, thousands of people, end up singing the same thing together so quickly. The idea to sing, or perhaps it is the song itself, seems to exist outside us all like a spirit that darts through each head in a flash, so that each of us begins to sing just a moment after the person next to us. I look to my left as we emerge into the blazing sunshine from the forest and I think I see the spirit causing a wave to flow through the crowd as each person lifts their head to let their voice ring out. Almost as soon as I notice it, the wave is upon me and my family, and we are singing too, but I still manage to look to my right and follow the wave right to the other end of the crowd that is starting to spill into the main street. I wonder where the spirit is off to now? At its speed it is probably at the great Lake Kivu already, shooting across the surface of the water, making ripples and making the kingfishers sing, on its way to the Congo to bring the people there joy. Like the joy I am feeling now as we sing songs about Nyamata and soccer heroes and songs about victory. I do not care that we are singing about soccer – the way the music lifts and falls, the way my voice tickles deep inside my ears and vibrates around my head and the way thousands of people are making a giant roar like one enormous beast, we could be singing 'Mwami Shimirwa' (Thank you God for the love that is beyond our understanding) as we did this morning in church.

The crowd sweeps us down the main street towards the

marketplace. There are stalls selling everything you could imagine and all the cabarets are open around the edge. Joseph is there at the bar of Madame Bunani's cabaret. He does not work there, he is out enjoying himself too – there will be no one back in Kibungo to attend his cabaret today.

'Look, Daddy, look,' I shout up, tugging on his shirt in case he cannot hear me over the crowd, 'there is Joseph!'

'Oh yes, darling, let us say hello,' and he begins to shuffle through the people, looking back occasionally to see if we are all still there and smiling to Mum. 'Look at him, Chantal! Even on his day off he is making connections and talking business.'

As we get near to the cabaret, Joseph notices us. I know he has because his watery eyes glisten. It is very difficult to tell what Joseph is thinking because his beard of thick, tight curls covers so much of his face. But it seems to make his eyes stand out even more – his beautiful eyes like the surface of the river at twilight. He hands some money to Madame Bunani and brings two bottles out to the roadside to meet us. He shakes Dad's hand and kisses Mum on both cheeks. He is smiling, but it is only when he looks at Pio and then me that his beard breaks open into a bright white grin.

'Pio, my man! Clementine, beautiful Clementine, how are you both?' He crouches down and gives us both a hug as we tell him we are well. I suddenly feel guilty as he speaks as if he has not seen us for a long time – and he hasn't! But I have seen him often from my hiding place in the grass.

After he has presented us both with a bottle of Cola, he gets up and his grin disappears deep into his beard again as he talks to Mum and Dad. Pio shouts to some boys he knows from school and they sing a song at each other through the crowd. I want to hear what the adults are saying so I move away from Pio's noise and try to slip inside the circle they have formed. Mum hugs my head to her dress so that one of my ears is buried in the bright blue material and the other is covered by her hand – it feels like I am being held under water, the noise of the crowd sounds like the rushing river, so I slide my head around under her hand so that both my ears are free again and Mum's hand is resting on my cheek and over one eye. Mum is so engrossed in her conversation above my head that she lets her hand remain that way. And I do not mind – it is not my eyes that I need now, it is my ears so that I can listen to what is concerning them so.

'. . . and the burgomaster sacked the trainer of the Nyamata team only yesterday,' says Joseph.

'What on earth for? For being Tutsi?'

'Well, that is, of course, not the reason he gave for his actions, but . . .'

Mum's tummy rocks my head back and forth a little faster as her breathing quickens. Joseph goes on,

'Half the Hutu players on the team are missing practice regularly to attend political rallies, and when they return they can barely bring themselves to pass the ball to their Tutsi team-mates. I will not be surprised if we lose today, even to this second-rate team.'

Dad speaks at last. 'I think losing at soccer is the least of our worries,' and he tilts his chin in the direction of the soccer field.

Mum and Joseph follow his gaze, but I cannot see from down here. I slip out of the circle and search among the men drinking their urwagwa for an empty stool. It seems like hours until I find one and, as I climb onto it and stand on my toes, I guess I am too late. But the adults are still staring. In fact, many of the people in the marketplace are staring at the cabaret nearest the field, where all the men seem to be wearing the same clothes and making the most noise. They are nothing to do with our team, I am sure, because they are not wearing the purple and white colours of Nyamata. They are all wearing shirts with a jungle of patterns of gold, green and red. Some have headscarves of the same colours and some have red berets on. They all look as if they have been drinking for hours and I am sure that their singing is not created by the same spirit as the one that moves through me – their voices turn a tap on inside me which lets all that fizzing blood drain away to be replaced by . . . nothing.

'*Umwanzi wacu n'umwe,*

Turamuzi . . .'

Our enemy is one, they sing, *we know him.*

'*N'umututsi.*'

It is the Tutsi.

I feel like crying until two big, warm hands grab me and lift me from the stool. I am so concerned about whose hands these are that I forget about the men and their terrible song for a moment. When my feet touch the ground I can wriggle free of them and turn round to find out who they belong to.

'What are you doing alone in a place like this, Clementine?'

It is Pastor Bernard. He sits on the stool where I was just standing and looks into my face for an answer. I want to ask him the same question too, but I do not think it would be respectful, so I just nod in the direction of my parents and mutter, 'Mum . . . Dad.'

'Oh!' He almost seems disappointed, but then he smiles at me and says, 'Your singing today in church was as wonderful as ever. I do not know what we would do without you, girl.' I cannot help staring at his big, flat, shiny nose – it is the shape of a crucifix, a crucifix turned upside down. 'You are the best singer in the choir, you know.'

I do not know what to say – I am embarrassed, but very proud at the same time, so I just say something stupid like, 'I love singing.'

'I can see that,' he says. 'Shall we go and exercise our lungs some more on the soccer field now? The game will start soon.' He looks at his watch and I look at Mum and Dad.

Joseph looks around as he gives a fat brown envelope to Dad and notices me. He tells Mum where I am. She waves at Pastor Bernard and he picks me up again and pushes with his big belly through the crowd to them.

'Good afternoon, Pastor,' says Mum.

'Hello again,' says Dad, pushing the envelope deep into his trouser pocket and keeping his hand there.

'Good afternoon, Jean-Baptiste,' says Bernard, 'I was just saying to young Clem that I think it is time to move to the field if we want to get a good position and see everything. I am hoping today's match will be an entertaining one.'

'Let's go then! Thank you, Pastor,' and Dad holds out his arms to me.

I am glad. I prefer riding on Dad's shoulders to Pastor Bernard's hot belly. Now those enormous guts lead the way through the crowd to the edge of the field and, as we pass the cabaret where the scary men in bright colours are, I can see from up here that most of them are not men at all, but boys. I lean forward and weave my arms tighter around Dad's neck – his head is a boulder I can hide behind as I spy on their faces . . . One face I recognize from school. That's Fari! He is one of the older boys that Jeanette said she fancied on our first day. Wait until I tell her! He looks so different. Not just because of his clothes, but his face – his jaw juts forward and his eyelids are heavy as if he will fall asleep at any moment. Perhaps he does not want to be there. Perhaps it is the man who is speaking to him, jabbing his finger at him with each sentence, who is making him stay . . . The man turns away from Fari so I can see his face for the first time. I should have known! Should have known from the jabbing finger and the back of his wide head that I watch fearfully from my bench in the classroom as he attacks the blackboard with chalk. I turn my face away in case Claudius Kagina sees me staring and a flash of purple catches my eye on the field. The crowd erupts again like they did when we first came from the forest – the teams are on the pitch.

'Evergiste Habihirwe! Evergiste Habihirwe!'

Everyone is chanting Evergiste's name – he is the star of our team. He is graceful, plays soccer as if he is dancing to the songs we sing for him. He is muscular, but slim, tall . . . and fast.

Perhaps Joseph was worrying for nothing about losing to Kiyovu – after only a few minutes we have scored. But I do not feel like singing. Our song does not sound so sweet. Something is out of tune, someone is singing a different song. Not the Kiyovu supporters – of course they have their own songs and they sing them from the other side of the pitch where most of them stand. But here among us I hear discord – it is the boys in bright colours, spitting bitter words against Tutsis onto the pitch. I look down around me – Mum is next to me, Marie next to her. Augustine is behind Marie with John on his shoulders and Joseph is on my other side. Pastor Bernard stands in front of Dad and me, and I feel safe surrounded by all our friends like this. But I am scared for Evergiste – I know Mum said that you can never be sure what someone is by the way they look, but I know, I just know hc is a Tutsi. There are three other men in our team who I think are Tutsi too, mainly because of the way they are beginning to look at each other with concerned faces between play. Most of the crowd are trying to ignore the boys and easily overpower them with their excitement as one of our Tutsi players tries to score.

'OH!'

The crowd is confused as well as disappointed – our player was tackled hard and falls to the grass clutching his ankle, but he was tackled by one of our own players. No Kiyovu player was even close. Other team-mates are running over to help . . . no, they are not helping, they are kicking him as they pass. The stubble on Dad's neck scratches my arm as his head twists sharply to the left – he is looking at Joseph. Joseph stares back and his eyes are full of knowing – they are sad, but not surprised. I look back to the field, the horrible players run back to their positions with their heads bowed as if they are ashamed at what they have just done, flicking their eyes up every few strides at each other and towards the boys who are laughing and cheering and pulling at each other's bright shirts shouting,

'Hutu power! Hutuland!'

Fari is still there, cheering with the others. I cannot see Claudius Kagina anywhere now.

7

Dad's house is in the suburbs, north of London, a twenty-minute train ride from King's Cross. You can pick his house out easily from among all the other identical ex-council houses, with their grey lumpy exterior walls that always make me think each house has had an allergic reaction to something inside. You can pick his house out easily from all the others with their grey wooden picket fences that I guess were once brightly painted, with the same grey wooden gate that you have to lift up entirely to open it or else the bottom will fire off great chunks of wood and splinters like spears as it's dragged across the concrete garden path. I tell you, on a day like this, you can pick out Dad's house easily from all the others, even when you get off at the station, five minutes' walk away – just follow the music.

Just follow the sound of The Troggs feeling it in their fingers and feeling it in their toes.

Just follow the sound of Dad, 'Ta da da da da, ta da da da da da!'

The gate fired off a few shards and the cat hiding in the long grass did a runner before it got speared. Then I remembered to lift it, but not before Dad's ears, tuned to every little creak and tick that his castle made, heard the scraping sound, even over the sound of 'Love Is All Around' cranked up to compete with the main stage at Glastonbury.

'Lift *it!*' he bellowed with venom and the emphasis on *tit*. Then I think he followed it with a quieter, 'Twat,' but a 'you know I love you' from Reg Presley covered it.

Great start! It was hard enough dragging myself here in the first place, and now I felt like turning round and following the cat. Considering this, I fingered the mildew on top of the gas-meter box on the lumpy wall until the back gate was yanked open.

'Oh, it's you! 'bou' time too,' said Dad.

He was made up of a load of 'O's, my Dad. His head was an O with just a bit of short blond hair left round the ears and the back. His eyes were two Os, green and wide like he was expecting a punch. His mouth too seemed to be in a constant O and you could only tell from his eyebrows whether he was joking or annoyed. His O head sat on top of his enormous O body, out of which stuck his O beer gut (already red from the sun) on the end of which, sticking out and topping things off like a cherry, was his O bellybutton.

''Ere, look oo it is, everyone, the prodigal son has returned!'

Dad went back to his place behind the bar while everyone said hello and I went around shaking hands with all the boys and men and waving stupidly at all the women and girls. There were about fifteen people in this little garden. Some of them I recognized, some I didn't, and some I knew I was supposed to 'cause they were family, but I really couldn't remember their names for the life of me, I tell you. Once that was all done I found myself standing in the middle of the patio being stared at like a water feature by everyone sitting around the edges. I looked to Dad for . . . something.

'What you 'avin' to drink then, son?'

Dad stood proudly, half naked, behind his bar. Yeah, his bar. Yeah, we were in the garden, but Dad had built a bar by the garage wall, underneath a bit of corrugated plastic in case it rained. He had painted it a deep blue and put shelves of the same colour on the garage wall so he could stack glasses there and put bottles of spirits there, 'just like a real pub'. There were cardboard XXXX coasters and Guinness towels on top of the bar itself and even a little fridge underneath with an orange extension lead running to the kitchen through the back door that you had to be careful not to trip on when you went in to use the toilet.

'Joo wanna try some of me speshal punch?' He stood all red and white Os against the blue shelves and the grey garage wall.

There was a mix of groans and cheers from everyone.

'You wanna stay well clear of that, if I were you, Ashley, mate.' That was Auntie Grace, Dad's sister.

'G'wan, mate,' my cousin Rob piped up. ''Ave a bit, it's wicked, if you can handle i'.'

Dad closed his Os for a second and just for that moment looked . . . serene, like a Buddha. He collected his thoughts, his eyes opened and he let forth his wisdom,

'You, Gracey, can fuck off! Listen to your cousin, Ash, he knows what he's talkin' abou'.'

To avoid making another *faux pas* so soon I opted to try the punch.

More cheers and groans.

Dad ladled some into a pint glass from the enormous bowl on the end of the bar where a bloke sat on a high stool. He had black-rimmed glasses and a thick moustache under his swollen-looking nose so that at first I thought he was wearing one of those crap disguises you buy in a joke shop. The bloke nodded at me while I waited for my drink.

'All right?' I said.

'Vic ain' moved from tha' spot yet,' said Dad, pointing his ladle at the bloke.

'Yeah, an' he ain' likely to neivva as long as tha' punch is there,' wheezed a woman from a deck chair in the sunniest spot in the garden.

Dad's mouth O quivered proudly at Vic's devotion to his punch. My lips quivered with trepidation as I went for my first slurp. The garden was suddenly quiet – even The Troggs seemed to hold their breath in anticipation.

'Mmmm,' I swallowed, 'it's good!' It was basically loads of vodka and a dash of Five Alive, so I wasn't lying.

'See,' Dad rejoiced, ''e knows what side 'is bread's bu'ered!'

Reg and The Troggs rejoiced by launching into the chorus, filling the air with 'I love yous' and 'I always wills'.

'My mind's da dup da da dee die feel.' Dad was in his element. 'Ta da da da da, da dee no end . . .'

'Uncle Tel.' A teenager that looked so much like a miniature of Auntie Grace with her *EastEnders*-chic hairstyle and her Burberry clothes that, even if you didn't know her, you'd know she was Grace's daughter wandered over to the bar cradling a baby. 'Uncle Tel, ainchoo go' the proper version of this song?'

'Wha' ja mean?'

'The one by Wet Wet Wet. It wen' in at number one this week on the charts.'

'Fuck off, Chrissy! 'Ere, Gracey, sort your daugh'er ou', will ya?'

Rob stood up to unstick his balls from his thighs, sweaty in those Farah's. 'No, she's righ', Uncle Terry. Who is this geezer anyway, he carn sing for toffee?' He sat back in his picnic chair and found his Stella. 'I know! Let Ash decide who's the best, he's the singing teacher, in'e?'

Cheers.

But I did have an opinion, so I perched on the other high stool at the bar and addressed my audience,

'Marti Pellow . . . actually a fine singer, of course much more accomplished than Reg whatsisname . . .'

Cheers and groans.

'. . . But, as for this song . . . it's a cheesy choice, only number one now because of the *Four Weddings* film and I'm afraid it'll sink without trace by next week.'

The cheerers groaned and the groaners cheered, not quite realizing that Reg Presley lost either way. I turned to pick up my drink from the bar, feeling clever, and saw Dad's unimpressed eyes flick up at me a couple of times as he sliced oranges. That gulp of punch tasted all vodka and no Five Alive.

'Parklife' by Blur kicked in next and Chrissy jiggled about with the baby next to me.

'We like this one, don't we, Tricksy?'

The baby actually seemed to agree, but it was a shot in the dark 'cause it was just like Dad, but a smaller bunch of Os.

Curiosity got the better of me, so I asked Chrissy, 'Is that your . . . ?'

'Yeah, didn't you know? Six months old now, she is.'

'Yeah, I told you, son! Memory like a bleedin' sieve 'im, Chris.'

No, you didn't, Dad. 'Oh, did you?'

'Joo wanna go?' Chrissy held out her new toy and its tiny eyes grew wide with horror.

Mine did too and I kept hold of my glass as if to say, 'Sorry, just don't have enough hands.'

''Ere are, quick, before I drop him.' Chrissy had the baby

held out with straight arms like a contestant on *World's Strongest Man*.

'Nah,' I waved my glass at her. 'Besides it's not really my thing,' and just in case she found that offensive I tried to make up for it with, 'That's a nice name.'

'What?'

'Tricksy.'

Vic sniggered and I saw Chrissy's shard of a laugh pierce the baby's brain as it screwed up its face and began to cry.

'She ain' called Tricksy, oo would call their li'le girl tha', that's daft.'

'Oh, sorry,' I tried to laugh along. 'What's her name then?'

'Fifi.'

?

Chrissy went over to her mum and a bloke that I guess was her husband, or at least the father of her . . . Fifi to tell them what an arse I was. Dad's voice gave me an excuse to turn away from them.

'If you spent a bit more time up 'ere, paid a bit more attenchun to yer family, you migh' no' make such a dick of yerself.'

Here we go. 'Ah, you know,' I said this more in Vic's direction; I never found it easy to look Dad in the eyes when I spoke to him, especially if what I was saying was a load of bollocks, like now – perhaps Vic wouldn't notice as easily; perhaps he'd be more sympathetic, 'with all the teaching and students coming at odd hours, my free time is always different to yours.'

'You can make time if you want to,' Dad said to Vic.

'I'm here now.'

'You don' even recognize Vic, do ya?'

Luckily he didn't give me the chance to answer.

'And Sonn. Over there.' He pointed his tea towel to the wheezing women in the sunniest spot.

'Don' you remember ya Auntie Sonia?' she wheezed again, and tried to get out of the deck chair, but thought better of it.

Then I did recognize them. They weren't my real aunt and uncle, just really old friends of my dad's. 'But to be fair,' I said, 'you've both changed a lot, especially you, Sonia.'

The Sonia I remember didn't have short tight peroxide-blonde curls that seemed even brighter next to her dark orange skin. And this Sonia was dressed in a bright red sleeveless dress with frills on every edge and it was low cut, showing off a considerable cleavage – she was clearly pushing sixty, but there was something sexy about her . . . in a dirty way.

'Well, we've been away for years, ain' we,' she shouted across the garden. 'We was livin' in Zimbabwe until last Christmas.'

'Well, you're looking good on it,' I said, trying not to sound like a perv.

Then it also came flooding back that you didn't have to say much for Sonia to find the pervy angle.

''Ere, you see, Tel, your son knows a good pair a tits when he sees 'em.' She was more determined this time and struggled out of the deck chair and, leaving her flip-flops behind, she cat-walked across the patio. 'My Vic . . . 'Ello darlin', good to see ya again, darlin',' and she kissed me on the lips. 'Vic doesn't even notice, don' know why I bovver, but I bough' one of them new Wonderbras. Thought I'd give it a go, you know. Probably just anuvver gimmick I ge' sucked in for, but wha'd'ya know?' and she straightened her back to give the fullest effect and at least ten voices all chimed together, like it was rehearsed,

'Hello boys!'

I laughed with everyone else. I'd seen the huge billboard ads too, the ones that were causing male drivers to crash 'cause they couldn't take their eyes off it. Besides, Sonia really did make me laugh; she was funny, she was warm and, although she said it far too many times, I really believed that she was happy I was there . . . unconditionally.

'Tell Ash about yer uvver fing an' all, Sonn!'

''E doesn' wanna 'ear abou' tha',' she wheezed.

'What?' I said.

'Well,' that was as much persuading as she needed, 'I thought I'd spice things up in the bedroom a bit and I bough' this studded leather G-string at one of them Ann Summers parties last week.'

Rob nearly choked on his Stella, Auntie Grace screamed with joy.

I didn't know what to say. '. . . And did it work?'

'Did it fuck!' she pointed her empty glass at Vic who was sharing unimpressed looks with Dad. 'And I kept gettin' me pubes caught in i'.'

More choking and screaming.

'I've got it on now.'

'Show us then, Sonn!'

'You should be so lucky, Simon! No, I sorted that little problem out,' she said to me as if she was giving me cooking tips. 'I just shaved me pubes off.'

How do you follow that? When the choking and screaming died I said, 'So you were out in Zimbabwe . . . for how long?'

'Oh, darlin' . . .' She was shuffling about like she needed the toilet. 'Fill tha' up, Tel, please, I gotta sit down again, come over and sit wiv me, love and I'll tell you all about it.'

We went over to Sonia's spot and as I followed her I couldn't help visualizing what was under that dress. She slipped into the deck chair again and I sat on the floor, like a child waiting for a story – that feeling was as warm to me as the paving stones on my arse.

'We were out in Zimbabwe for ten years, give or take. Oh, it was beautiful, darlin', how do you think I got this colour? Nearly like one of them, ain' I?' she said proudly. 'The scenery, it's like nothin' you could ever imagine, mountains on the horizon and our gardens were kept ever so nice in the village.' I was trying to imagine Sonia and Vic in a little earth house surrounded by identical ones in a village of black farmers, until she filled me in: 'We 'ad everyfing we needed in this village. 'Ardly had to step outside, you did. A little shop and a bar, most of us were English or spoke English at least, all friendly . . . it was just like being 'ere, but wiv bloody great weavver all year.'

Great. 'So you never got to know many . . .' how shall I put this '. . . natives then?'

'Oh no . . . Well, we was 'appy in our village. We 'ad a huge wall all the way around it, quite high, and broken glass, you know, all stuck around the top.'

I drew a question mark with my face, my mouth full of punch.

'Oh yeah, you had to have some protection 'cause they can kick off sometimes, the blacks, and when they do . . .' Perhaps she saw that I needed a bit more convincing so she added, 'Look at 'em in Rwanda now, with their machetes and tha' . . . Savage. That's the reality of it, darlin', I'm afraid.'

I was starting to feel uncomfortable sitting on the hard stone. 'So is that what made you come home then?' I said, shifting to a crouching position.

'No, Gawd, no . . . missed the children, the kids and the

grandkids, especially a' Chris'mas time. That's why we came 'ome last Chris'mas, i' was one too many, they couldn' ge' over to us too often wha' wiv work and money and tha' and I was missin' the best years of their lives.' I thought she was going to start crying for a moment, her eyes started glistening in the sun. 'So I said to Vic, "that's i', sod the weather and the peace and quiet, we're goin' 'ome!"' She put a red fingernail to the corner of one eye and scraped at her mascara as if it was irritating her and, as she raised her voice again, I realized we'd just had the only conversation that afternoon that wasn't performed to the audience. ''Ere, ain' you 'ot in that shirt?' I stood up. 'Why don' you take i' off, like ya dad?'

'Watch out, Vic!' Uncle Pete, Grace's husband, joined in. 'The dir'y cow's after Ash now.'

Vic didn't seem to mind. I announced to everyone that was listening that I wasn't that warm, Dad announced that I'd been like that for years and that I needed a bit more meat on my bones, and I announced that I was bursting for the toilet before tripping over the orange lead and unplugging the little fridge.

Going into Dad's house, where we'd lived since I was eleven, was always a trip at the best of times. And now, with everything taking a minute to come into focus – the living room with its aristocratic blue and gold sofa with tassels on the bottom, the mahogany-look display cabinets with photos and naff souvenirs from Spain and Zimbabwe – gradually bubbling up from the darkness after the contrast with the bright outside, it felt more trippy than ever. I walked sharpish through the room, throwing a quick glance at the photos to see if the one of me playing the violin at school was still there – it was – and went upstairs to the bathroom.

After a much-needed piss I sat on the edge of the bath – to take a bit of time out and work out my excuse for leaving so soon. The party was reaching full swing outside below the bathroom window.

'Twat,' Dad mumbled as he put the fridge back in its place under the bar.

'Leave 'im alone!' wheezed Sonia.

Not sure if she was talking about me or someone else, but the words made me feel the need to go and check the bedrooms . . . for memories, I suppose. There's only two. My old room, which Dad now seemed to use as a shed, by the looks of all the DIY tools and bits of shelving lying on the bed. My awards were still on the wall though – for swimming 200 metres, violin grade five, even my two A-level certificates in Art and Philosophy. But there was nothing to do with my singing. He never seemed to approve of that. Took me swimming every week, encouraged me to practise the violin every day, even had a go at the teachers at school if I asked him to, but when I moved down to London to become a star, he didn't want to hear about it.

I stood on the tiny landing with my old room on one side and his room on the other.

I pushed the door open and crept in, as if he was downstairs watching TV and would go ballistic if he heard a floorboard creak above him, knowing I was where I shouldn't be. The room had hardly changed, same old blue and brown carpet, sky-blue bedspread with valance all the way to the floor, with a quilted diamond design, like the inside of a deluxe Barbour coat but as naff as that is posh, you know? The walls were still . . . turquoise, I suppose you'd call it, and one wall was still fitted with white wardrobes.

On one of the white doors, stopping it from closing

properly, a couple of belts were hanging. Dad had probably left them there when he realized he didn't have to choose which one to wear today, it was going to be hot enough just for his safari shorts and they didn't need a belt. One of them I didn't recognize; perhaps it was new. But the other was familiar, like an old friend, I tell you, that I rushed up to and touched. It was a fat belt. Everything about it said that the wearer was tasting the good life – or wanted us to think he was. It was a J. R. Ewing oil baron's kind of belt, thick black patent leather with an enormous rectangular gold-coloured buckle with sharp corners almost like horns. If I didn't know it came from Burton's, I might have thought it was from the state of Texas.

I gently lifted my old buddy down from the wardrobe door and went and sat on the sky-blue bed with it – just as I did twenty years ago when I came back from London for the first time to visit, about six months after leaving home.

Then I suppose it was the belt that I'd come back to see really, not Dad . . . and certainly not Mum. I cradled it in my hands, like I'd seen Auntie Grace do with her new baby Chrissy, and ran my finger along the smooth surface of the buckle and out to the sharp corners. Something clanged in the kitchen and I felt all the blood in me rush to my feet – but it was only Mum, washing up or something, Dad wasn't due home yet for half an hour. 'It'll be a nice surprise for him,' Mum said. That's why I came upstairs, I wasn't going to stay down there with her for half an hour – I told her I was looking for something in my room.

It must've been because of these corners that it hurt so much when Dad whipped me with it. That and the fact that he used to hit me so hard, I tell you, he used to beat the living shit out of my arse with this belt. He must have held the leather end and hit me with the buckle end. I could hardly sit down the next day at school; the other kids used to love it, saying I had piles or something. The skin burned like it did on my back that time in Wales on holiday when I spent hours boogie-boarding in the sea and got too much sun – I remember Dad looking really worried and telling Mum to put more calamine lotion on. But after the belt there was blood as well. When I took off my white pants in the evening they were streaked with red. The first time I saw that I was so scared. I ran to the bathroom and tried to see my bum in the mirror over the sink. It's hard to see your bum in a mirror at the best of times, but when it's high up over a sink . . . I was standing on tiptoes, standing on the scales, and eventually I managed to see a wobbly image of pink tracks across my white skin, as if I'd been run over by a steamroller, and parallel with the tracks were red cuts where the blood had come from.

It was these corners that did that then. I used to run upstairs when Dad came into the living room after I heard them talking in the kitchen, 'cause I knew what was coming. Where did I think I was going? The only place I could've locked myself in was the bathroom and Dad could've knocked that door down easily, or just waited until I got hungry and had to come out – then the whipping would've been ten times worse. But he always grabbed my leg before I got to the top stair and I'd drop to the floor. His big hands would work their way heavily up my legs and back as he climbed the rest of the stairs using me like a rope, then he'd drag me to his room and push my face into the quilted diamonds with one hand while the other pulled down my jeans (I always wore jeans 'cause they're thick and tough, but he never fell for it). He kept his hand on the back of my head as I felt him stretching for the wardrobe, heard the squeak of the door and the click as he lifted the belt from its hook.

'I do everyfing for you, son, everyfing, and this is the fanks I ge', eh?'

The worst thing was the split second swish and jingle of metal against metal, because in that tiny moment I could anticipate the pain and that seemed to make it so much worse when it actually came – it made the whole thing last longer.

My screams were muffled by the bedspread and I felt like I was going to suffocate. My instinct to breathe was even stronger than his heavy hand every now and then, so I'd twist my head free and gulp for air.

'I'm only doin' this because I wan' the best for you, *we* wan' the best for you.'

We? Where was Mum during all this? She never once came upstairs when I screamed; she never once said to Dad that perhaps that was enough; and she never asked me if I was all right after, if I might need some cream put on it or something.

I soon learnt that if I put my hands in the way they'd just get it from the belt too, so I'd sink my fingers into the scratchy bedspread instead as if I was holding on to the edge of a cliff . . . for dear life. I could never guess how long it was going to go on for. Sometimes it was over really quickly; other times it seemed to go on for ever. Once I swear sunlight was coming through the net curtains when we started, and the streetlight when we finished. But however long it took, it usually ended the same way. Dad would chuck the belt into the corner of the room and would stomp off saying:

'It's 'cause I love ya that I have to do i' . . . twat.'

'Leave 'im alone!'

That's it! That's what I was thinking of. The time when he stopped and her voice came up the stairs,

'Tel, come down 'ere now and leave 'im alone, for Gawd's sake!'

It wasn't Mum's voice, of course. It was Sonia's. There was a short muffled argument in the living room while I ran – as fast as you can run with your jeans around your knees – to my room and threw myself on my bed. A few seconds later, there was a knock at my door. It was Sonia, because no one else bothers to knock. I pretended I was asleep – as if! But that meant I couldn't pull up my trousers and pants. I was lying on my stomach pulling a moon in front of a grown-up, and a woman at that, but the embarrassment couldn't outweigh the pain of pulling clothes on over my blistering skin, so I stayed as I was.

'Oh, love,' she whispered and promptly left the room again.

In a moment she was back. She pulled my wooden chair close to the bed. 'You just lay there, babe, it's OK. This might sting a bit, but it'll help.'

It stung, but apart from the occasional gasp and clenching of my bum, I stayed still and let her help. The room smelt of blancmange and McDonald's root beer so I knew she was putting Germolene cream on me – I loved that smell; right then it was my incense. Then she just sat there rubbing my back slowly for a bit. It nearly sent me off to sleep, until she said,

'Let's see . . . what we got here.' I heard some of the books knocking on the shelf as she gently went through them. 'How about this? Poor Flop the Dog had forgotten how to bark,' she read.

It was a baby's book, one that I should've chucked out a

long time ago. I wanted to sit up and say, 'I'm thirteen, you know!' but I was too exhausted.

'As he bounced out of his basket one morning he opened his mouth and shouted, "Meoooow!" "That's not right!" said the cat, "only cats go meow." So he tried again. "Squeak, squeak!" "That's not right," said the mice, "only mice go squeak!"'

Sonia read in her best and gentlest voice and I found the repetitive words calming.

'"Tweet, tweet!" "That's not right!" said the birds. "Only birds go tweet." Flop the Dog was very unhappy, but that night he heard someone creeping around in the dark of the house. It was a burglar! "Meow, meow!" shouted the little dog. "Squeak, squeak! Tweet, tweet!" All the other animals woke up and came running, chasing the burglar away. The humans woke too and, realizing what had happened, cried, "We're saved! You're a hero, Flop!" Flop the Dog was so happy, "Woof, woof!" he barked, and he never forgot how to bark again.'

I slept.

He did it almost to the day I left home. I was eighteen and I was still letting him whip me. And then I left and he couldn't do it any more. I was free. Gone down to the Big Smoke to be the king.

And I was lonely, I tell you. But that's only to be expected at first, isn't it? But I missed home. I missed my dad who did *everyfing* for me, who took me everywhere, worried about me, wanted *the best* for me. He only whipped me because he *loved* me. So I went back to visit and Mum said he wouldn't be home for half an hour yet, and I went upstairs and saw the belt hanging on the wardrobe door, and I cradled it in my hands like a baby's head. And I got a rush of power – I was holding the belt for the first time, I was in control of it – just think what I could do! I could bring some of that love back, to blot out the loneliness – I had the tools right here.

I lifted one cheek of my bum from the bed and held the buckle there, trying to remember how Dad did it. But that felt awkward and very difficult to do. I sat down properly again and looked down at the black belt in my white hands on the end of my white arms coming out of my Led Zep T-shirt. They'd just released *Houses of the Holy* – I'll be as great a singer as Robert Plant soon if I keep working at it.

I pressed the sharp corner into my left forearm and dragged it along till it cut. It was still so sharp. I made sure the cut was deeper and longer than any one I'd ever managed to see on my bum from when Dad hit me with it. The rush blotted out all the bad feelings, all the loneliness, just as I'd guessed it would. And I did it all myself. I didn't need Dad to do it; I didn't need him any more. The sound of blood dripping onto my jeans brought me back – one day I might actually remember to put something down first! But you never quite believe you're really going to do it again, even with all the build-up, right until the moment you feel your skin heat up around the cool blade.

I rushed to the bathroom and ran my arm under the tap, found a bandage in the medicine cupboard and wrapped it round and round, not exactly St John's Ambulance-style. I felt relieved and confident. I took a bit of tissue and bounced into Dad's room, wiped the blood from the buckle of his belt and hung it back on the wardrobe door. I knew I wouldn't be able to explain the bandage round my arm, so I shouted to Mum as I reached the bottom of the stairs that I had to go and I'd come back again soon – besides, there was no real reason to stay now.

'What about your dad?' she squeaked from the kitchen. 'He'll be home in—'

I slammed the door and strode down the street of lumpy houses, occasionally chucking a glance at my arm with its bright white band like the coolest new trend.

I had no intention of using my dad's belt today, upstairs while the party went on below. I usually saved it all up till I got home anyway. As Jimmy would tell you, it's not the most socially acceptable thing to do, cutting. I stood up to hang the belt back on the door and the sky-blue bobbles from the old bedspread clung to the buttonholes on my combats so that it started to drag itself from the bed. I thought for a moment it was trying to come with me – or perhaps trying to keep me from leaving. I ripped it away from my trousers and straightened it back on the bed.

'Get a new cover, for God's sake, Dad!' I said to the room and went downstairs.

I went through the patio doors, stepping over the orange lead like it was a sleeping tiger, and into the warm breeze that carried the sound of a wailing kid.

'What's up?' I said to Chrissy.

'Rob's give 'is little Steven a clout 'cause 'e's getting overexcited, tha'sall.'

'Wha'?' Rob grunted.

'You just don' 'ave to be so 'ard on 'im,' said Sonia. 'Some would call that abuse these days.'

'Oh, fuck off, Sonn!' Dad polished a glass with a tea towel from Wales.

'Yeah, it's *my* kid,' said Rob while his girlfriend cuddled it. 'Abuse, my arse!'

'Yeah, wha' joo know, Tel?' Sonia wheezed again.

'I know tha' *you* migh' call i' abuse, but that's only 'cause some dick'ead, pen-pushin' social worker decided to call i' tha' yesterday while 'e was scratchin' 'is arse thinkin' wha' the fuck he was gettin' paid all tha' money for. In my day it was called discipline. Now half the kids are off the rails and they tell us it's 'cause they've got speshal bleedin' needs, tha' they need extra help.' He slammed the glass on the bar and chucked in some ice. 'Wha' they need, and wha' even parents are afraid to give 'em in their own bloody 'omes, is a bloody good whack, then we wouldn't 'ave 'alf the delinquents we've got and the government could save us a bob or two instead of wasting it on extra help and therapy this and therapy tha'.' He poured the last of the punch over the ice straight from the huge bowl. ''Ere are!'

The drink was for Sonia. She stayed in her deck chair, her face tilted to the sun, eyes closed. Dad stayed behind the bar. The drink stayed on it.

Sister Sledge drowned out any uncomfortable silence and any last whimpers from little Steven while I went over to Sonia to tell her I was going.

'Oh no, love, why?'

'I've got a lesson to teach tonight,' I lied. 'Quite an important one for this student, they've got a big show on tomorrow,' and, just for good measure, 'at the Palladium.'

'Oh, 'ark a' you!' She pulled me down to her in the chair and kissed my lips again. 'Don't you work too hard though ... All work an' no play ...'

'Makes Vic a dull boy, eh?'

'Shut up, Pete!'

I went round and shook all the male hands again and this time kissed most of the women – I had the Dutch courage now. Dad saw me to the back gate.

''Erc arc,' he said, and stuffed thirty quid into my hand, like he always does when I leave.

'No it's all right, Dad, I'm fine, doing well with all the teaching and that,' I lied, like I always do when I leave.

'Take it,' he said. 'Won' 'ave you thinkin' I don' care.'

I think he knew I needed it, couldn't refuse it. Perhaps money was the new belt whipping.

8

'This is Hutu Power Radio. Stay alert. Watch your neighbours.'

Mum and Dad are sitting opposite each other at the table. They have the radio in the middle, between them. The flickering light from the candle makes it look like the radio is pulling faces as it speaks. The big round dial is its nose sniffing around like a pig's. The shiny label at the bottom is its mouth flashing its teeth in a vicious grin. The voice coming from it has no trace of laughter in it any more and Mum and Dad do not smile – they look sick.

'Soldiers, gendarmes and all Rwandans have decided to fight their common enemy in unison and all have identified him. The enemy is still the same. He is the one who has always been trying to return the monarch who was overthrown.'

I used to love the smooth wooden sides of our radio. I would just sit and stroke them for ages as it seemed to purr at my touch, playing bright songs and telling stories about the world.

'The Ministry of Defence asks Rwandans, soldiers and gendarmes the following: citizens are asked to act together, carry out patrols and fight the enemy.'

Now the box looks as if it will burn me if I touch it.

The wobbly candlelight makes the very grain of the wood move so that the orange-black sides become lava flopping from a volcano.

'RTLM brings you this terrible news, citizens . . .'

I want to run from the shadows of our bedroom and turn off this angry voice, but I hold back – not just because Mum and Dad would be annoyed that I was not sleeping, but because I cannot resist hearing what this terrible news is.

'. . . the president's aircraft has just been shot down as it prepared to land at Kigali airport. President Juvenal Habyarimana and President Ntaryamira of Burundi were among the dignitaries on board, returning from peace talks in Tanzania. All on board the plane are dead. This assassination represents the decapitation of our Rwandan government and army. It was clearly the work of the Tutsi-led RPF rebel army. We warned of what would happen if anything ever happened to our president. Now the time has come. It is time to cut the tall trees. Cut the tall trees!'

Mum reaches out across the table – the radio looks as though it might bite at her hand as it passes – and she grabs Dad's hand. All this talk of armies and planes, presidents and shooting. I am afraid there is a war going on. And I am afraid it is between some Hutus and some Tutsis.

Cut the tall trees! the announcer repeats again and again. What do trees have to do with it? And then I remember that feeling, the feeling I had on my first day in Claudius Kagina's class. When I stood up with all the Tutsis, when he told me that I could not be both Tutsi and Hutu, when I sat down and he stared at me through the standing Tutsis like a hunter peering through the trees trying to find an antelope. Through the tall Tutsi trees.

The announcer is excited now as he reports that roadblocks

and military checkpoints have been set up all over our capital city Kigali. So quickly. And he says that some Tutsi families in Kigali have been killed to avenge the president's death. So quickly. At least Kigali is many, many miles from here. Perhaps we will be safe . . . but then I think again of the way Mr Kagina looked at me in class, of the Tutsi players at the soccer match, and the horrible boys in their bright-coloured shirts . . . and I step out of the shadows,

'Mummy!'

I think it is me that makes my parents jump up and my mum snatch her hand back, but it is not. It is the frantic knocking at the door.

'Jean-Baptiste! Please, Chantal! Open the door!'

Marie rushes in, holding on tightly to John, and Augustine follows with his eyes so big and white in the dark doorway, as if he has seen a ghost.

He says, 'You have heard the news?'

Dad points to the radio still dancing on the table. Mum sits me on her knee and tells me I should go back to bed, that everything is all right. But she is not letting go of me so I stay where I am.

'We are going to the church. Many are already going. We have been promised refuge there.'

Dad says, 'By who?'

'Government officials. The burgomaster has sent people around in trucks to take us there if we want. We should go now before it is full. You must come too.'

Dad sits down again, he does not look in a hurry to leave. He scratches his stubble and Augustine looks at Mum instead.

'Chantal, you must come, with the children. It is not safe for you.'

'The children will be fine. Chantal will be fine,' Dad snaps.

'I am sorry, Augustine. I know it is different for me, but are you sure this is the right thing to do?'

'What choice do I have, Jean-Baptiste?' Augustine's big eyes are full of tears now. 'What choice, eh? Sit at home and wait to be cut?'

Dad follows him as he goes to the door. 'Look, Augustine, please, I will stay here and try to help us all. Perhaps I can talk to some Hutus, some influential Hutus. Perhaps they will listen to me.'

'Jean-Baptiste, you are just a farmer. What can you offer them?'

'Please, I will try.'

'And *who* will you talk to? The Interahamwe? Drunken, drugged-up youths, trained to kill? You think they will listen to reason?'

'I will try . . .' Dad embraces Augustine and kisses Marie and John, who is still sleeping, and they disappear into the darkness outside.

Dad shuts the door and leans against it. 'You will be safer if you stay here with me. If we run they will assume we have done something wrong. Everyone knows what everyone else is around here. They know I am Hutu.'

'And they know I am Tutsi.' Mum lets go of me and I only realize then how tightly she has been holding me as I nearly fall from her lap.

'But you are my family,' he comes and takes me from Mum, 'and I will never let anyone harm you. I will do anything . . .' He kisses her and carries me back to my bedroom.

'What is happening?' Pio is talking but I can tell from his slurred words that he is barely awake.

'Everything is fine,' Dad answers Pio, but looks at me. 'Go

back to sleep now,' and he whispers to my hair. 'It will all have calmed down in the morning.'

Pio has a watch. Dad bought it from Joseph when Pio reached fourteen. It has a strap the colour of the tastiest chocolate, a round, gold-rimmed face with a tiny knob at the side to wind it up. The face was white once, I think, but now it is many shades of yellow with tiny cracks across it – as if it was the ceiling of a rich man who smokes a lot. I love the hands best of all. They are gold coloured, like the rim, and they have sharp points so that they seem to be the blades of two gold swords – or should I say one sword (the long hand) and a dagger (the short hand). And the thin gold second hand sweeps around like a rapier defending them all.

Pio was so proud when he got his watch. And I was jealous. Just for a while. Until I realized that I could enjoy the watch as if it were my own for a few moments each day, because Pio leaves the watch on the table between our two beds every night when he goes to sleep. Before he wakes and the sun is beginning to light up our room, I turn the watch on its side to face me and I find out what time it is – and what date, because it even has a little window where the number three should be that tells you. And I allow myself to be hypno-tized by the sweeping second hand for a while before lying the watch down again so that Pio does not know I have been touching it. Today it says that it is the 7th – the 7th of April. And when the rapier reaches the number twelve it will be . . . eight thirty! Eight thirty? I check to make sure that the watch is still working properly. We should be at school by now – we will surely get into trouble for this. Why didn't Mum wake us?

I am just about to jump out of bed and shake Pio when

there is a loud knocking on the front door. Our window is at the front of the house so it is easy for me to see that it is Adalbert and Paul from the cabaret at the door. There is another man too, but I cannot see his face clearly as Paul's enormous body is in the way. Dad must have answered the door.

'Jean-Baptiste, are you ready to go?'

Adalbert and Paul work in the fields too, but they do not seem dressed for it today. Well . . . I could not tell with Adalbert – he only ever seems to have one set of ragged clothes that he wears every day. But Paul and the other man are wearing flip-flops, Bermuda shorts and shirts – and yet they still carry their machetes as usual. My dad's voice comes from the house – he sounds tired.

'Go where, Paul?'

'How could you not know?' Paul's huge face breaks open into a giant's grin – he is clearly happy about something. And Adalbert is excited, too, shuffling from one foot to the other, scratching at his patchy head.

'Everyone was called to a meeting at the marketplace this morning.' When Adalbert speaks I realize he is more impatient than excited. 'The messengers from the municipal judge went house to house to make sure we all knew. Did they not come up here?'

'We noticed you were not there,' chuckles Paul, 'so we thought we would be good neighbours and come and tell you before you got into trouble.'

'What have you been doing with my watch, Clementine . . . ?'

I put my finger to my lips and beckon my brother to the window too. He must be able to tell from my face that this is no time for petty squabbles because he creeps over without another word.

'Tell me what?'

The other man speaks and it is another of Dad's friends from the cabaret, Samuel. 'The market was swarming with Interahamwe and the judge told us that our job, our only work from this day on, is the killing of all Tutsis.'

Pio must see my shoulders start to shiver because he squeezes them tightly.

Samuel carries on, 'They made it very clear, very simple. We must keep working every day to cut them all, until the job is done. They threatened us with punishments if we bungled a job . . .'

'Adalbert has already had his wrists slapped, eh, my friend?' Paul is enjoying this. 'He did not turn up with his machete . . .'

'I was misinformed – not the only one!'

'. . . the Interahamwe leaders said they would not let such stupidity happen twice.'

'So I ran home and got it – no big deal. Now we should get going before we get into more trouble. Maintain a good pace, they said, spare no one,' Adalbert's face brightens, 'and loot anything we find.'

'That was the news that Adalbert was waiting for, Jean-Baptiste.'

'Yes?'

'Why not . . . ?' Adalbert is whining now. 'I struggle, we all struggle with a meagre plot of land and barren soil for years, and now it is official – we have orders to go and take whatever we want from those we cut. We use a machete as naturally as we use our arms. We pick it up every morning and go to work, but from today our work will be far more rewarding than sewing and harvesting. Tonight I could be wealthy.'

'And, more importantly, free of cockroaches, don't you think, Jean-Baptiste?'

Paul knows that my dad does not want this. He knows that my mum is a Tutsi. I hold my breath, waiting for Dad to tell them to get lost. But he does not answer, or if he does I cannot hear it over the roar of the truck, honking its horn, that seems to throw itself over the hill like a bull trying to buck the brightly dressed Interahamwe boys from its back. Interahamwe in Kinyarwanda means 'those who attack together' – and they look like a pack of wolves baying for blood as they come to a stop outside our house. Pio pulls me back from the window and he rushes from the bedroom as one of the boys booms,

'What have we got here? Stragglers? Dawdlers? Cockroach lovers . . . ?'

I want to know what is going on outside, but I cannot stay in this room alone, without Pio, with just an earth wall and a curtain between me and them. I run after Pio and almost knock him over because he has frozen outside our bedroom door, watching Mum and Dad performing some kind of mime show. Dad has picked up his machete from its place by the door and Mum is pulling at his other hand, pulling him away from the door, almost on her knees. Her mouth is a big black hole and tears drip from her chin. But both of them make no sound at all, until Dad has to put down his machete again otherwise he might lose his balance, Mum is pulling on him so. He crouches down with her, putting his fingers gently over her open mouth and whispers,

'If I go, if they think I am helping, they will leave you all alone. Please, Chantal, I have to go.'

Mum grabs his wrist and pulls his hand away from her

mouth. She looks as if she is going to shout at him, but instead she whispers too,

'Do not go! You must not be a part of this.'

'I will only seem to be; I would never kill anyone.'

'I would rather you refuse. Grab a gun from those animals and shoot us all in an instant. It would be better than this. Do not go – it will change you for ever. It is you I am thinking about, not me or any Tutsi. Do not do this to yourself.'

Paul's voice is as big as him – it rumbles through the door, 'Hurry, Jean-Baptiste! We have work to do.'

Dad twists his wrist from Mum's grip. That is when he notices us. He kisses me quickly on the top of my head and says to Pio, 'Keep the door locked; do not leave this house until I return!'

Pio nods, but Dad has already turned to the door, grabbing his machete again. There is a flash of light as he lets himself out, shutting the door quickly behind him. The truck roars to life again and the men all start cheering and chatting – all except my dad. The noise quickly fades away and I am staring at Mum on the floor, not quite sure what has just happened. When she looks up at me I run to her and Pio runs to the door, bolting it firmly. The radio is talking to itself on the table.

'. . . seeing people gather all through the night in churches is not good, not good at all, especially when the RPF have put them there along with grenades and other arms . . .'

9

My soundtrack for the journey home was Prince's new release, *The Beautiful Experience* – funky, hard, confident, liberated – and it made me feel the same . . . for as long as the EP lasted, anyway. As I got off the train and walked through King's Cross station, heading for the underground, the last track burst into life, all chiming guitars and ethereal synthesizers, like a euphoric gospel service. It made me look up, instead of looking at the ground ahead, where city people seem to keep their eyes locked. I looked above everyone's heads, as if there were beautiful sights on the horizon – mountains or a red sun setting over the ocean. I looked above the black roofs of the trains spewing equally black exhaust fumes and followed them up to the high ceiling, a great arching ceiling that looked as if it was made of glass, blue glass that you couldn't see all the way through, just the light – like stained glass. I realized then that this might be the first time I'd ever looked up there, even though it must have looked down on my receding hairline scurrying below thousands of times. It was actually quite an awesome sight (the ceiling, not my hairline), even beautiful, like looking up at the inside of a cathedral dome. But what is it we worship in this church? Prince responded with,

. . . the reason that God made a girl.

Not exactly what I had in mind, oh purple one.

I found another article about Rwanda in a newspaper left on the Tube, alongside yet another analysis of what made Kurt Cobain great. I tell you, this newspaper wouldn't have been seen dead talking about grunge a couple of months ago, but since Kurt blew his own brains out, they're writing about him like he's Mozart or something. Perhaps I can still be a star after all then, I just need to cut a little deeper, hit a main artery next time.

I resisted reading about Nirvana then and concentrated on what Lyndsey Hilsum in Kigali had to say. But as I read I found myself battling to keep Sonia's words from ringing round my head,

'You had to have some protection 'cause they can kick off sometimes, the blacks, and when they do . . .'

. . . An international Red Cross official who saw the bodies littering the street also reported finding about 350 bodies in the central hospital, and the Vatican ambassador in Kigali said that at least 25 Rwandan priests and nuns have been murdered.

In one incident, soldiers entered a religious centre, locked six priests and nine novice nuns in a room and killed them. Two Belgian Jesuits were spared.

Belgium was talking to France, the US and the UN about a joint military operation to take and hold Kigali airport . . .

. . . Chief delegate to the International Committee of the Red Cross, Philippe Gaillard, said the soldiers roaming Kigali's streets and setting up roadblocks were respecting the emblem of the Red Cross and allowing teams to move around the city . . .

... It is not clear why religious communities are being targeted. Soldiers who belong to the late President Habyarimana's majority Hutu tribe have been going from house to house kidnapping and killing minority Tutsis, but the priests and nuns were said to be of both tribes.

Nor is it clear who is a Hutu and who is a Tutsi. A Rwandan journalist, Nestor Serushago, described how youths armed with knives attacked a young couple with a baby, because, although they were Hutus, they looked like Tutsis ...

I decided not to leave the copy of the *Guardian* where I'd found it, but instead I rolled it up and marched from the underground brandishing it like a truncheon, feeling the need for extra protection tonight on the ten-minute walk to my flat – although I'm not sure what I intended to do if I got mugged, I tell you: beat the attacker with paper or bore him to death by reading to him. I did the ten-minute walk in just over five, desperate to get home after my trippy day, desperate to surround myself with me-things, no matter how dusty and dirty they were – they'd remind me of who I am and, most importantly, I wouldn't have to have conversations with my inanimate possessions so I couldn't put my foot in it or make a fool of myself. My sofa doesn't call me a twat ... if I sit down carefully enough.

I flew up the stairs, pulling myself up the cold metal banister with one hand and paddling the air with my newspaper truncheon in the other, so fast that I nearly fell over the woman rocking herself with her arms wrapped around her stomach on the stair just before the first floor. All in the space of a second, I sidestepped her but stopped my foot from landing in the puddle of puke next to her, keeping her company – my foot repelled the puke like a magnet facing its polar pair and threw itself on the landing of the first floor instead. Bloody heroin screw-up! Don't get me wrong, we all have our problems and I kind of feel sorry for the woman, but that's just it, we all have our problems, so we don't need to have hers literally shoved under our noses as we're trying to get home, don't you think? She lives in one of the ground-floor flats, I think. If she's not hanging round in the foyer arguing with her mates about who owes who what and whose turn it is to go and buy the next fix – making no attempt to keep her voice down when it comes to the words 'H', 'brown' or 'cook-up' – then she's turning herself inside out on the stairs like this, her guts on the tiles next to her and wearing her skeleton on the outside.

I was still muttering my disgust to myself as I paddled my way past the fifth floor, so much so that I didn't notice the little girl sitting on the next flight till I almost stepped on her too – Christ, what is this, National Get In Ashley Bolt's Way On The Stairs Day? My foot instinctively hovered until it was sure she had no little puke pal next to her too, then, as I stomped on the stair next to her, I gave a half-hearted tut and looked at her as if to say, 'Sitting on the stairs is very dangerous, you know, little girl, someone might trip over you.' I was gone, huffing and puffing up the final few flights before the look she returned really registered. Her little black face was streaked grey with silent tears and her enormous eyes had an experience about them which made the blood rush to my face when I thought of the patronizing look I'd given her – or was that just my heart working overtime as I darted up all these stairs?

My lovely African neighbours above welcomed me back with screaming and bellowing of such volume that I wondered if they even needed to use a phone to call their relatives back home. Woh! Sounded like their TV or someone's head just got bounced off the living-room floor. I dumped my coat on the sofa and rushed to the kitchen where it was a bit quieter, where it would be utter peace in a minute. The sink was full of washing-up, but I knew my trusty cheese knife would be clean and dry, ready and waiting in the drawer where I always left it.

And then I found myself opening the front door, stepping out and peering over the banister, peering so far my stomach folded around the smooth metal. The pressure and way it stopped me breathing properly had a dull pain of its own that kept me going till I could get back to the knife I'd left spinning on the kitchen worktop 'cause I'd dropped it so suddenly. I was trying to see the little black girl, see if she was still there crying on the stairs below. As the banister tried to cut me in two, my eyes bulged, making me see stars and Burberry patterns. I thought of Chrissy playing with Fifi like she was a toy and Rob hitting his son like he was a dog. I thought of sitting on the warm patio today at Sonia's feet and the way she told me the story of Flop the Dog all those years ago when tears streaked my face like they streaked the little girl's down there now. I wondered if Sonia could bring herself to soothe a little black, a little 'savage', like the ones kept at bay by the high wall round her Zimbabwe village, the wall with the shards of glass stuck in the top. The way she soothed me.

I couldn't see the little girl and I straightened up before I fainted. I had this crazy desire to run down the stairs and find her. Try and make her feel better, the way Sonia made me feel. I wondered if Sonia knew how, in a garden full of blood relatives, she was the one I wanted to spend my time with, to touch and feel her warmth returned. Be it Dad's 'discipline' or Chrissy playing with Fifi, it's all OK because they're family. If I go and see if this girl's all right now, this dark black girl who is so obviously not related to me, some arse will think I'm a nonce or something.

So I went inside, telling myself she was probably a little shit anyway, like the rest of the girls that hang around in gangs on the estate; she probably deserved whatever it was that made her cry. Don't get sucked in, Ash! Don't get involved. That's the whole point, remember? That's what leaves you needing this knife.

It had stopped spinning and was pointing at me as I went into the kitchen – a bottle at a party, ordering me to kiss a girl I didn't want to.

The last thing I saw tumbling through the chaos in my head, before the peace came, was the door of Number 61, Rachel's door opposite – it didn't do its usual click shut tonight as I arrived on the landing . . . and that was when I realized that the skeleton on the stairs, right down near the first floor, wasn't the cook-up girl at all. I'd just assumed it was, that was her 'patch'. I tell you, I couldn't believe how much Rachel had changed, but it was something about the way she wrapped her arms around her stomach tonight – that was what triggered it in my brain, the way she always hugged herself when she called to Daryl down the stairwell, hugged herself the way she wished someone else would hug her, I used to think from behind the protection of my peephole. What was she doing right down there? Too bad, I had my own hug to get . . . I wrapped my arm around the blade . . . Ah.

Levi had been coming to me for a few months. I was scared that in a few more he might suss me out, look at the progress

116

he'd made and beat the living shit out of me. Yes, Levi was only seventeen. Yes, he was the size of an average twelve-year-old girl. Yes, Levi looked like Bobby Brown did when he was still in New Edition – oversized dark blue denim coat, oversized denim jeans to match, his afro hair shaped like a black fez (without the tassel) on top of his head, and to make him look even more comical, an NYC baseball cap perched on top of his fez hairdo so it looked like he was wearing one hat on top of another. And yes, he had the highest, girliest speaking voice you have ever heard from a male, even Michael Jackson. Levi's voice was like . . . That's it! It was identical to Mickey Mouse's, I tell you. I knew it would come to me one of these days. So yes, Levi was not top of the list when it came to threatening appearances. But I'd seen Levi in action.

He had the reputation on the estate for being just about the meanest motherfucker around. I suppose he'd learnt to be, to avoid the bullying he'd surely get otherwise.

I was looking out my pathetic windows once, picking off scabs of white paint from the frames, just . . . surveying the grounds of my estate (!) . . . and there was Levi – or little Bobby Brown as I knew him then – standing by the phone box on the corner talking to two men, both twice his height. The estate was its usual hive of activity – kids and women in headscarves constantly in and out of the shop with all the fruit and veg outside, a gang of white boys trying out their latest skateboard tricks on the kerb by the bench, and two Tricky lookalikes perched on the wall watching what little Bobby Brown was up to, their white vests and gold teeth reflecting the sun as if they were flashing him a Morse code message. They pumped Public Enemy from the stereo on the wall between them loud enough so you could hear it wherever you were on the estate, from Frapper Court to

Westbrook House – even the double-glazed people in Cathedral Apartments must have had it in the background like badly chosen muzak in a department store.

The two men were starting to pace around a bit, pointing at little Bobby Brown, who was starting to shift his weight from one foot to the other and flap his arms with each shift as if he was showing them a new street dance. But this only lasted ten seconds at the most . . . Little Bobby Brown reached inside his denim coat and pulled an iron bar from his trousers. I blinked, just blinked, but when my eyes opened again one of the men was on the floor holding his head and the other was running across the street. Little Bobby Brown was fast, like a greyhound out of the traps at Walthamstow Stadium. Caught up with him before he reached the other kerb and swiped at his legs with the bar. The bloke went down and was beaten with the bar until he didn't move any more – it didn't take long. I could hear nothing, no shouts, no screams, just the hip-hop from the wall. Master Brown went back to the other bloke and did the same. The boys in their vests looked on like they were just in the cinema watching *Reservoir Dogs*. No one else seemed to notice.

So when he knocked at my door the following week and said, in his Mickey Mouse tone,

'You're a voice coach, innit?'

I was dying to say, 'Pluto!' but I didn't. I said, 'Yeah.'

'I want you to make my voice lower, aigh?'

Pluto! Shh! 'Er . . . well, I work on people's singing voices usually, not their speaking voices . . .'

'You're a voice coach, innit?'

Déjà vu.

'Yeah . . .'

'I want you to make my voice lower, aigh? What time's my first lesson?'

'Tomorrow . . . no sorry, booked up tomorrow . . . Wednesday?'

'What time?'

'FFFF . . . Five?'

'Aigh,' and he limped off down the stairs.

Of course I wasn't booked up at all tomorrow, and five on Wednesday was better than ffffour 'cause it would give me an extra hour – I realized that I'd need all the time I could get to go down the library and dig out everything I could on voice coaching and the physi-whateveryoucallit of the human voice. My life depended on it.

'Let's take it from the top one more time.'

African words were barked and spat above our heads. Levi looked up at the ceiling, I thought we could drown them out if we got on with the song quick enough, so I pressed 'Play' on the tape deck and Prince's 'Purple Rain' soaked the room.

Well, the way I figured it, if a girl singer came to me and wanted to extend their range higher we'd work on Mariah Carey songs, and if a bloke came to me and wanted to extend his range deeper we'd work on some of the grunge bands until he felt ready to take on Barry White . . . you get the idea, anyway. So, since no iron bar was pulled out of pants when I suggested the idea of singing to lower his speaking voice, Levi had begun with some of the soft falsetto soul classics from the likes of Al Green and we were working our way down. 'Purple Rain' was not particularly high, for Prince, and had verses that sounded more like speech than singing, so it seemed ideal for Levi.

Levi sang along with Prince, who was regretful about causing another's pain and sorrow.

If only the men with their heads all over the pavement could hear him now!

I held my breath as we approached the first note of the chorus, probably one of the lowest notes of the entire song. Levi kept his eyes screwed up when he was singing, but opened them quickly when there was a long break for a guitar solo or something, or at the end of the track – he'd look around the room then as if to make sure no one else had sneaked in to laugh at him. He'd even take a sidestep to the window occasionally, usually during the introductions to songs, and peer down to the street – this always made me particularly nervous – as if he was expecting someone. But right then his eyes were closed so he couldn't see me nearly falling forward out of my chair, my eyes as wide as his were small, dreading that first 'Purple rain'.

'GOOD!' I overreacted perhaps, but it was. Levi's eyes flew open to see what all the fuss was about, until I said, 'It's OK, carry on, this is good!'

'Purple rain . . .' I guessed that's how Stevie Wonder might look behind the glasses when he sings.

And now the lowest line of the lot. Levi pulled his chin down, as I'd showed him, but he was trying so hard to keep it back that he looked as if he was choking on something.

'Purple rain, purple REEEE.'

I pressed 'Stop'. Levi's eyes popped open and his face and neck stopped contorting, the skin settling back into its smooth blank way.

'Aigh?'

'Er . . . that was great. Did you hear how you were getting all those lower notes no problem in the chorus?'

'Yeah, you nearly put me off, mun.'

'Oh . . . sorry.'

'But that last note was shit, right?'

I love it when he says it first! 'It could've been better, but I'm going to give you a new exercise to practise at home till next time – that should help.'

Levi kissed his teeth and started flapping his arms like he'd done seconds before he'd twatted those blokes in the street.

Shit. 'Hey, man, what's the matter?' Now my voice was creeping up to Mickey's range. 'You know if you don't practise in your own time it's going to take a lot longer.'

'I know that, I trust you, mun, but it's . . . time's getting on, mun, and there's girls out there who ain't gonna take me seriously, innit, you know what I'm saying . . . ?'

As he let slip his reason for being here, the answer to Levi's problem was staring me in the face, but I just couldn't see it. I was too gobsmacked and wrapping myself up in the duvet of what he'd just said to me . . . to *me* . . . 'I trust you.' Levi trusts me.

Then, of course, I just couldn't accept that . . . No, Ash, if it's a sunny day you just spend it all wondering when the next rain cloud's going to appear. So I thought that 'trust' must be a new street word for . . . 'hear' or something . . . I don't know . . .

'What, mun?' Levi was getting bored of waiting for the exercise as I stared into space trying to work out what 'trust' meant.

'Sorry . . . I was . . . just working out the best way to do this.'

He kissed his teeth again and sat down behind the music stand. 'Well, while you're thinking I'm going to sort myself out, innit,' and he dragged the little glass coffee table closer where I put the jug of water and glasses for students (room temperature, of course, lesson number one: no point in warming up the voice if you're just going to chuck cold water over it. Warm is relaxed). But instead of taking a drink he pulled out a small triangle of folded paper and started chopping lines of coke on my table. 'Fancy a toot?'

'No, thanks, Levi,' I had to smile. And my ego couldn't resist just getting it confirmed, 'You trust me, don't you?'

'Yeah, mun, I said so, innit.'

Wow. 'So do me . . . do yourself a favour and save that stuff at least until we've gone through this exercise. Then we're done.'

Levi's Blockbuster video card hung in the air for a moment over the snowy rail track he'd made on my table. Then he put it back in his pocket and stood up behind the music stand, cleared his throat with a gentle cough and closed his eyes.

He'd only been gone a minute when there was a knock at the door again. The buzzer hadn't gone so I guessed he'd forgotten something and remembered before he'd got all the way downstairs. I chucked a quick look through the peephole anyway – instinctive nowadays. Saw a black face on a short body, but when I opened up it wasn't Levi. It was a girl. I was already regretting opening the door and waiting for some kind of prank or load of abuse, but I peered around the corner and up and down the stairs to see where the rest of her little gang was. But there was no one else and, as I looked at her waiting for her to speak, I got the impression that she wasn't up for a prank.

She was barefoot and wearing a cream-coloured summer dress with a print of branches with cherry blossom on it.

Her skin was so dark, so black next to this dress. Her eyes stood out, big and white, and, though her skin was so smooth, her eyes made me think of age. That's when I recognized her as the girl I'd stepped over on the stairs the other day. I'd felt a bit guilty then because I was so desperate to get in my own space I didn't ask her what was wrong, but I didn't have time for someone else's shit, I had enough of my own, right? She looked up at me and carefully smiled with her lips together. I figured it was safe to say something now.

'All right?'

She nodded and wiped her hand under her nose. It was a thin nose . . . I mean, it wasn't as flat and wide as I might've expected from someone so . . . black, I mean, she was clearly African . . . but different somehow . . . perhaps she came from one of those islands off the coast of Africa, in the Indian Ocean or something.

'You are a teacher?' she said.

'Er . . . yeah, yes.'

'You teach singing?'

'Yes, I do.'

'I would like lessons, please.' Her accent sounded possibly French and she pronounced every word immaculately, better than I did, so I found myself raising my game, getting a bit Queen's English.

'OK,' I said, 'but . . .'

And she smiled, this time all teeth, and stood on tiptoe for a second, as if a puppeteer had pulled a string above her head, bringing her to life. That's when I first appreciated how beautiful she was.

'But,' I said, 'usually I have to see your parents first to make sure it's OK with them.' I was all too conscious of the society we were living in, one united only in its disgust of paedophiles

– and for once I was in tune with society when it came to this. 'Perhaps one of them would want to come to the lesson too.' She lost her spark again, her smile faded and I thought I might be losing her, that English wasn't her first language, so I spoke more slowly, 'And I guess they would be paying. It's twenty pound per lesson . . . Your parents? What do they say?'

'Nothing.' My gaze went back from her mouth to her old eyes. 'I do not have parents.'

A bolt above us was yanked across a door and the couple upstairs in Number 62 brought their abuse of each other out into the stairwell for a moment. I saw the little girl duck as if she was expecting something to be thrown at her head from above and she looked at me with pleading, terrified eyes. It didn't take a genius now to work out that she was related to them. And it didn't take a genius to work out that she didn't want to be related to them. I had no problem empathizing with that, but it was more than that. From the moment she first smiled, I mean really smiled at me, I had stopped thinking about everything else. Like I nearly did on the landing when I'd stepped over her the other day. But now I'd *really* stopped, so much so that I didn't realize it till much later that day. I wasn't thinking about the weather, the fact that it was too hot for long sleeves, the food I did or didn't have in the fridge for dinner tonight, the way I could've taught that exercise better to Levi, the girl on the Tube, the news, the shit going on in Rwanda, Iran, the Middle East, what it is that makes people listen to Nirvana, why Prince can sing so effortlessly that high and that low, why the batteries in my remote control kept dying so quick . . . you know, all the things that go through my head whatever else I'm doing all day every day . . . except for the ten minutes or so after I cut myself or burn myself.

The row above threatened to spill down the stairs. The little girl's mouth was open as if the words, 'Let me inside quick, you stupid man!' were lodged at the back of her throat. I looked up towards the noise to let her know I understood, stepped aside and said,

'Why don't I give you a trial lesson for free to see if you like it?'

She was like an Olympic sprinter, poised on the blocks.

'Come in!'

That was the starting gun. She was over the threshold in a flash of cherry blossom and I closed the door behind us quickly but gently so it made no sound. We stood looking at each other in my dark hallway, her shoulders going up and down as if she'd really just done the hundred metres, my heart pounding as if I'd just popped an E, scared and excited by the trouble I was swallowing. We listened to the man's voice 'woof' the way a car does when kids set light to it, done with joy-riding. Once . . . twice . . . three times he made the sound, each time pounding on his front door, or trying to shut it, it was difficult to tell. There was a hysterical wail from the woman that continued long after the man had slapped his feet down the stairs, passed my door and stomped out into the street. She seemed to be moaning to someone, but I had the feeling there was no one else left in the flat.

I carefully slipped past the girl in the narrow hallway. I felt so big for a change, big and clumsy, I felt like I might knock her over if I wasn't extra careful – she was so small and delicate. I went to the window in the spare room (my teaching room) and peered out, just like Levi would at the beginning of a song. A balding black head over a dirty red Adidas tracksuit top wobbled its way across the street, past the shop and out of sight. I turned back to the little girl now standing in the doorway.

'Who is he?' I tried to sound as gentle, as unthreatening as I could.

'My Uncle . . . Leonard.'

'And her?' I chucked a look at the ceiling.

'His . . .'

'Wife?'

She shook her head and frowned at the floor.

'Girlfriend?'

She shrugged her shoulders, 'Yes.'

'They fight . . . argue a lot.'

'Yes.'

'Are they horrible to you too?'

'Can we sing?'

I laughed at the idea and she smiled her toothy smile again, each tooth separated from the next by a little gap. She was waiting for another starting gun. She was serious. She really did want to sing.

'You want to sing now?'

'Yes, please.'

'What about . . . upstairs? She might hear. She might hear you.'

'She will not know it is me.'

I thought about this for a second, thought about how it was probably true that this woman upstairs had never heard the little girl sing, or even talk for that matter. She only ever seemed to listen to her own gnashing voice or the bark of her sparring partner.

I sat down and pointed to the other chair behind my skinny music stand.

'So what do you like to sing?' I smiled, leafing through my file of lyric sheets.

She hoisted herself up in the wooden chair I'd bought

from a dining-room set on sale outside the charity shop, and her bare feet didn't touch the floor. As I looked at her little legs swinging slightly I felt two things all at once – I felt a fear of my own ageing and a desire to look after this fragile thing in front of me. Both made my heart try to leap from my chest like the monster-baby thing bursting from John Hurt's body in *Alien*.

'At church. Music at church.'

Oh.

I stopped flicking through lyrics and glanced up at the girl. Her feet had stopped swinging and she was looking worried again. She was looking worried because I was looking worried. I looked more worried because she looked worried and so she became even more worried. As soon as I worked out how this was going I smiled.

'We need *this* file then,' I announced, as if I was in pantomime at the Hackney Empire.

The little feet started swinging again and her face relaxed.

Oh, I'm good!

After my initial panic I realized that I had just what we needed. There's a direct line back to the church from the great soul singers like Sam Cooke and Aretha Franklin. In fact it was as gospel singers that they started. And it was the church that frowned on them when they decided they wanted to sing songs about boys and girls, cars and makeup, Cupid and sweethearts, instead of God. But it was those songs that made them stars, not the gospel music. I thought I'd save that bit of the lesson for another day, though, so I pulled out two copies of the lyrics for 'What a Friend We Have in Jesus' and slid my Aretha Franklin gospel tape into the player. I handed one sheet to the girl as the sound of a lively congregation and piano wafted round the room; she gripped the paper hard as the sound reached her and her eyes widened as if she'd just seen the burning bush or something.

'Just listen to begin with, just listen, OK?'

She nodded, her face bright, and she looked deep into the speakers as if they were a TV screen showing her favourite film.

By the time Aretha had finished the first verse, I could see the girl was bursting to speak and she began to raise her hand. I turned down the volume a bit.

'I know this. We sing different words, but I know the music.'

'Great,' I smiled, 'but you don't have to put up your hand here, OK?' She looked unsure. 'You can speak whenever you want to.'

She looked into the speakers again, so I turned up the volume – she threw a glance at me as I did, which told me I was doing the right thing. After the second verse I pressed 'Stop'.

'Now you,' I smiled with extra high eyebrows when I said this 'cause I know how daunting the first time can be for any singer in front of a teacher.

She jumped down from the chair and put her lyric sheet on the stand – I rushed over to lower it for her 'cause, although Levi had used it before her, even he was taller than her. She took a frowning look at the lyric again, as if the print was too small for her, then looked at me with anything but a daunted expression on her face. I lowered the volume a bit and started the track again. As the congregation got excited at the opening chords, the girl stood on tiptoe again for a second, as if the sound sent electricity through her. I knew that feeling – that's what music could do for me.

And then she sang.

'What a friend we have in Jesus,
'All our sins and grief to bear,
'What a privilege to carry
'Everything to God in prayer.'

I wasn't sure that she understood everything she was singing, and some of the pronunciation was weird – in the most endearing way – but for the first time in my life I felt a hymn like this made sense to me. She was filled with a spirit, a passion for the music, and my page for scribbling notes on range, breath control, performance and pitch remained empty. Her voice was naturally high and warmly nasal, but it was beyond analysis, it was pure . . . conviction. She didn't need a teacher; she just needed the opportunity to sing. I could give her that. In fact, I would pay *her* to let me listen to her sing again and again. In the little gap between verses I saw her old eyes appear for a split second as she glanced up at the ceiling. I turned the volume up a bit, keeping my eyes on hers as I did it. She looked at me and went on tiptoes again, as if I was in control of the voltage flowing through her.

'Beautiful!' I shouted. 'Can you sing louder?'

She nodded.

'Oh what peace we often forfeit,
'Oh what needless pain we bear . . .'

I turned it up a bit more.

Tiptoes.

'All because we do not carry
'Everything to God in prayer.'

I turned it up a bit more. I thought she might get cramp in her feet in a minute. But I couldn't resist. I felt like I had power over this girl, the power to make her happy. And I was buzzing on that power. I stood up too and grabbed my lyric sheet. I turned the music up so loud that it sounded like the Seventh Day Adventist Church next to Westbrook House had crammed itself into 60 Frapper Court for this week's service, and I joined in. Like my Discman, keeping the stressed-out London streets at bay, we blew Number 62 above out of existence.

'Everything, everything, everything, woh!

'Everything, everything, everyth—'

She couldn't finish the line; she burst out laughing and doubled over, slapping her knees that sprung her back upright again.

We sang some more from Aretha's gospel tape. I even tried her out with a bit of Gladys Knight – it was a relief for a girl not to ask for Whitney or Mariah. Every time I sat back in my chair, happily exhausted, she'd throw a worried look at the ceiling and get closer to the music stand, asking for the next song with her eyes, her fingers locked in front of her. I knew if I said that we were done with singing today but she could stay anyway, she would relax again. But I couldn't keep her here, downstairs from the flat where she was supposed to live. I'd be accused of child abduction or something . . . and besides, this was no place for a child . . . look at the state of it.

I cleaned the kitchen after she'd gone. No, I mean, really cleaned it. I actually picked up the microwave and wiped underneath it. There was only a dribble of Safeway cleaner in a bottle under the sink, but plenty of hydrogen peroxide in the bathroom, so I used a bit of that. I nearly cleaned the inside of the oven too . . . but one step at a time, eh! Besides, I didn't have the blowtorch and chisel necessary to get through the solidified lava that must've once flowed through these parts. I cleaned the toilet and the bathroom though, and hoovered everywhere, although more dust seemed to be blowing out the vent at the back of the Hoover than was getting sucked up by it . . . I was an archaeologist lifting the last layer to reveal the delicate and rare fossil below when I opened up the Hoover – just as I suspected, my find was a bulging brown bag from the *Crust*aceous period: one false move and it could burst its precious contents all over the floor, lost for ever to history.

I wished she'd started sulking or shouting at me when I finally said that she'd have to go. I wish she'd turned on the waterworks, as Dad would say. Then I would've been glad to get rid of her; it would've confirmed my suspicion that this wonderful time I'd just had was a fluke, a glitch in the normal way of things between people, between adults and kids. But she didn't. She smiled her lips-together smile, walked with her eyes on the filthy lime-green carpet to the door and turned to say,

'Are you a soldier *and* a teacher?'

'Pardon?' She nodded at my combats.

'Oh!' I giggled, suddenly embarrassed by my attempts to be fashionable at thirty-nine. 'No . . . er, lots of people wear these now . . . in this countr— How long have you been here, in England?'

'*Deux, trois* . . . three weeks.'

I thought so. 'From France?'

She shook her head. I decided to risk a bit of French, it'd been a long time.

'*Quel pays?*' That was as much as I could do for now – masterful!

She smiled her teeth smile again at my crap attempt, 'Rwanda.'

'Rwanda . . . in Africa?' No, the other Rwanda, off the Isle of Wight, dick!

She nodded. 'Thank you . . . *Merci, monsieur.*'

I tell you, to hear her speak French was almost as good as listening to her sing. Must dig out my French dictionary.

'*Je m'appelle Ashley.* No "*monsieur*".'

'*Pas monsieur?*' she asked and corrected.

'*Oui . . . Non . . . Pas monsieur,*' I was blushing, 'Ashley.'

She stuck her skinny arm out to shake hands. '*Je suis Clementine.*' She sounded so much more confident, stronger and in control, 'Clementine Habimana', as much as I felt out of my depth and stupid trying to speak her language. I shook her hand, although I wanted to give her a hug.

'*Enchanté, mademoiselle.*'

She skipped up the stairs. I saw her dusty feet stop at the big window between flights. She had obviously just remembered where she was going. I shut the door, its heavy click firing a shot into the stairwell.

10

Mum and I sit huddled around the radio, as if it is a fire that could keep us warm on a cold night – but there is nothing but ice-hard words coming from it. News about the number of Tutsi families killed so far . . . no, not news, but celebration. The announcer seems to be cheering the killers along . . . Stories about how the Tutsi do not belong in Rwanda, more calls to Hutus to continue the killing. The announcer says that thousands of Tutsis are already dead in Kigali. Thousands! I cannot imagine what that must be like. I think of all the people at the soccer match on Sundays and pretend I see all of them falling to the ground at once. Where are all these dead people? And how do the people in the radio know how many there are? I have never been to Kigali – it is very far from here – but I know it is an enormous, busy, dirty city, and things that happen there do not always happen here. Not even Hutus are safe there. The announcer tells people to 'slay Hutu traitors that try to protect any Tutsi or refuse to take part in the work'. And then, as if to show us what he means, there is an interview by phone with the Hutu prime minister, Agatha Uwilingiyimana. She says that she is hiding in her home with her husband and five children. I can hear gunshots in the background. She says the

United Nations are guarding her home, but that they are surrounded.

She says, 'There is shooting, people are being terrorized, people are inside their homes lying on the floor. We are suffering the consequences of the death of the head of state. We must ask for—'

The gunshots suddenly get louder, Mum twitches, but keeps her eyes on the table. There is a shout, a scream, or perhaps just the sound of electricity buzzing and then the phone line goes dead.

'Prime minister? Prime minister—?'

Then the interviewer is cut off too and the announcer's voice creeps across our table, slow and deep now, as if he was finishing a bedtime story,

'This is Hutu Power Radio. Watch your neighb—'

Mum switches him off.

'Pio, come away from the door . . . Pio!'

'I have to stand guard, Mum. Dad said.'

Mum seems too tired to argue.

'Listen!' Pio runs to our bedroom window.

I can hear whistles, many whistles being blown down in the valley. It is then that I realize that I have not heard the call of any animals all day, or the night before. The hoot of monkeys, the squeal of pigs. Even the big green birds with the white hats and purple wings – the ones with the red eyes that accuse, like Uncle Leonard's – even they are silent too. And now the only sound comes from the toys those stupid Interahamwe had round their necks this morning when they arrived in their truck.

'What does it mean?' I ask, but there is no answer. I guess no one else knows either.

I feel cold. It is not cold outside, but this is the first time

I can remember when the doors have not been open all day, letting the warm air run through the house like a third child in our family and the sun cut huge triangles and shapes with four sides that I do not even know the name of out of the dark corners of our little house.

'It's Dad! It's Dad!'

Mum looks up from the table as Pio sprints to the door and unlocks it. The road outside is noisy again, just like the end of any working day, but the men are so much more excited as they shout to each other, whistle and cheer. I see people pass our open door with sheets of corrugated metal – the type our roof is made from – on their backs. Some men are bent over like old women under the weight of it. Some carry comfortable-looking chairs, radios, clothes. Some push bicycles along, others pull cows. Some just wave their machetes in the air. It is a carnival, a festival, I feel my face begin to relax for the first time today as it reflects the joy in the faces that pass by our house . . . Until Dad's body fills the doorframe.

'Drinks are on me tonight, Jean-Baptiste!' Adalbert's voice comes from somewhere behind him. 'See you at the cabaret later to celebrate?'

Dad waves his hand to Adalbert without looking back and closes the door. His machete dangles by his side and I cannot help staring at it – if I am honest, I am looking for blood on the blade. But before I get a good look, he throws it into the corner, and it reminds me of the way I threw the newspaper with THE HUTU TEN COMMANDMENTS in it underneath my bed, except that the machete makes a loud clang which makes us all jump.

Now Dad looks smaller than usual, smaller than he was when he left the house this morning – I mean he looks thinner somehow. And paler. His jaw juts out and he is trying to turn his lips into a smile, but he just looks as if he has the most terrible smell in his nose. His eyes look huge, like Augustine's last night, and I have an urge to ask about him and Marie and baby John. Dad's big eyes are fixed on Mum's. She does not move from her chair by the table. He does not move from his place by the door. It looks like they are having a conversation by telepathy, because first Dad nods his head so slightly and slowly you could almost miss it, and then Mum shakes her head ever so slightly and slowly too. I cannot help myself a moment longer,

'Daddy,' I say it in a whisper though, it feels like the right thing to do, 'did you see Augustine and Marie . . . and baby John?'

Dad opens his mouth to speak and I can hear it unstick like it does first thing in the morning after he has had too much to drink at the cabaret the night before. 'Pio, Clementine, please, you must go to your room for a while. Please . . .'

'No,' Mum's words quiver, but the meaning is firm, 'they should know what is going on out there. They need to know. They need to know how hard they will have to run, how well they will have to hide.'

'Chantal . . .'

'Jean-Baptiste, answer your daughter! Tell us all, what has happened to our friends?'

'They . . .' He looks as if he will fall over at any moment. I am relieved when he finally comes to the table and sits down. 'They went to the church like they said they would. The authorities were saying all Tutsis would be safe there. So the church was full by sunrise, full of Tutsi families.

And that is where the Interahamwe led us first thing this morning. They had no chance, it was too easy for the Interahamwe – it was like sweeping dry banana leaves into a pile to make them burn more easily. We were told to go in and cut every person inside. There was no refuge there. As soon as a few rushed through the doors willingly, the rest followed . . . I followed too. Inside was chaos. It was dimly lit, there was uproar; men all around me striking out with their machetes without really looking, their elbows knocking into mine as they flailed their arms around. How silly! There are people being chopped, women and children in front of me and all I can remember is my elbows being bumped! I felt something spray across my face and I knew it was blood. And I knew it was not my blood. And I knew it was not from my machete, because I held it firmly by my leg. I did not raise it, Chantal, not once,' my dad is crying and so I do too – I think it is the first time I have ever seen him cry.

Mum's hand slides across the table to find his and after a moment he grabs it. 'I slipped back through the crowd of killers, and followed a few others outside again. I thought I would be in trouble for leaving so soon and my heart nearly stopped when I came face to face with a great bulldozer in front of the church. But the Interahamwe were cheering us and calling the rest out. But they hardly waited for them, their own killers, to leave . . . They sent the bulldozer towards the church. It flattened it, and anyone who might have still been alive inside . . . Perhaps, I pray, it released some from a slow, agonizing death from machete wounds.'

'But did you actually see Augustine, Dad? In the church . . . ?' Pio takes the words from my mouth.

'No, son, I did not see him. And I pray to God that he did not see me either.'

'Then perhaps he is still safe.'

'Perhaps, Pio.'

This idea comforts Pio and me, but it does not seem to have the same effect on Dad. He hisses through his teeth at Mum,

'Chantal, they even took the time in the church to hack at the statue of Jesus on the cross, because he looked more Tutsi than Hutu.'

'That is why you cannot go out there again tomorrow, darling.'

'I have to . . .'

'You will just be punishing yourself . . . and for how long? Soon they will have killed all the Tutsis out there and then they will turn on those Tutsis related to Hutus . . . and then they will turn on the Hutu themselves – on their own people! We have heard it on the radio all day.'

It is as if Dad has become deaf, or in a trance. He carries on talking like he is telling us a story. But this is the most terrible story he has ever told.

'There must have been one thousand of us this morning. So many faces I recognized, friends, neighbours. Just like a busy day in the market – except there was not one Tutsi in sight. And then there were the Interahamwe and a couple of soldiers with guns, who led us all through the forest down to the marshes. There was a group of Tutsi men hiding in the forest. They tried to run when they saw us coming. Celestin was among them.'

'Celestin Karikuwundi?'

'Yes, the old man. He is hardly able to run these days. He fell as he tried. Two of our group were on him like leopards, chopping across his back. I recognized one of them – Faustin, he lived in the next house to Celestin. Celestin had helped him out with milk from his cows when times were hard. Faustin had shared urwagwa with him, with us all, at the cabaret. As he finished him off, I heard Faustin say to the other killer, 'He is better off dead, at last I am rid of him.' Did I say I recognized Faustin? Perhaps, as he ran after the old man, but when he rose up and wiped the blood from his face I could no longer recognize him. He was no longer what he had been. And I could see that to him his Tutsi neighbours were no longer what they had been either – now they were just things to dispose of.'

'Shh, now, Jean-Baptiste,' Mum rubs his hands awkwardly and gets up, 'none of us have eaten all day. Clem, come and help me prepare something and then we will make some decisions.'

I do not think that any of us are really hungry.

'Jean-Baptiste, find the things that Joseph gave us in the meantime . . . Jean-Baptiste!' She has to shout to snap him out of his trance.

'Yes?'

'Gather the things that Joseph gave us. The envelopes.'

'Yes.'

I help Mum to peel and slice some mango and banana. The back door remains locked so it is the only thing we can make as we always cook in the outhouse. We have some avocados too. When we put the food on the table, Dad has lit some candles and the house smells sweet and warm. It is almost as if it is just another evening, until Mum says,

'When it is dark, later tonight, we will all leave here together.'

I am not sure whether it is these words that shock me back into our new life or the knock at the door that is so sharp I expect to see a hole in it when I look there.

'Jean-Baptiste Nduwayezu! Hey, cockroach lover! Outside now!'

Dad jumps from his seat, his old strong self again. 'Take the children, Chantal, go!'

Mum pulls Pio and me into her bedroom at the back of the house so fast that my heart is racing and my eyes are full of streaks of candlelight.

'Do not move! I will be back immediately.'

As Mum races from the room there is a crack as loud as a summer storm – the men outside could not wait for Dad to answer, they have smashed down our front door. I do not know what I expect then, but I do not expect it to be this quiet.

'They've taken them outside in the street,' Pio whispers. 'Stay here!' and he creeps round the bedroom doorway and out of my sight. But only for a moment – I am not going to stay here on my own.

'And how many cockroaches did you kill today, eh? None, traitor! Do not think that you were not noticed, hanging back, hiding in the crowd.'

When Pio and I reach our bedroom window we can see that the speaker is one of the Interahamwe resting a rifle on his shoulder. There is a gang of them, about six or seven. And even more people from the village watching the commotion – men, women and children. One of the Interahamwe has hold of my mum by the shoulders. She is almost as tall as him and he is young enough to be her son. In our old life she would be smacking him round the head until he begged for his mummy. Now she looks terrified.

'I came willingly,' says Dad, 'I will do better tomorrow.'

'Do not worry,' says the man with the gun, 'we have saved this one for you.' And he kicks out at the pile of rags on the floor between himself and Dad and I realize that it is a man. A puff of air comes from the man, but hardly a sound. The light is fading outside, but I can see that he has been beaten already.

'It is quite simple, Jean-Baptiste Nduwayezu. If you want to save the life of your wife, you have to cut this man right now. He is a filthy cockroach. Prove to us that you are not of his kind. Bring the man a blade!'

The Interahamwe begin to chatter and whoop like a group of monkeys as one of them drags a machete across the road so that the blade crunches and screeches through the gravel to Dad's feet. The boy with the machete then straightens himself and hands it to my dad and there is silence again, except for shuffling feet in the crowd.

'We do not have to do this now, like . . .'

'Then if you do not we will start on your wife.' He struts over to Mum and plays with her hand. 'Beautiful Tutsi women. This is the problem, you see? Men do anything for those tall slender figures, those thin noses, long fingers . . .' He drops his rifle and pulls a knife from his belt while his other fist grips Mum's hand, leaving one of her fingers pointing out. 'We need to remove these siren parts. Perhaps then you will listen.'

'OK, all right, OK. I will do it. It is no big thing. Just leave her, leave her alone,' and Dad tightens his grip on the machete and raises it above his head.

Mum's voice is shaking more than ever now, but it has a power in it greater than any blade or gun out there. 'Do not do it, do not do it, my love, or else you will be as evil as them all. I do not care what they do to me, but do not let them turn you into—'

The man slaps Mum's face to stop her words. 'Get on

with it!' He is shouting so loud that it echoes in the valley and some of the children in the crowd begin to cry. Why do their mothers not take them home? The crowd is getting bigger.

The Interahamwe man loses his patience and cuts off my mum's finger.

The man has cut off my mummy's finger.

The man cut off my mum's finger.

Everything from now on I will tell you like a story. A story of things in the past. *Once upon a time . . . Il était une fois . . .* Because I am not sure that it could be real life. Like stories of princesses, angels, Sebwgugu and his wife and monsters from the forest. Daddy usually started those stories with, *Many years ago . . .* or something like that. And so I knew that they couldn't happen now, however frightening the monsters seemed. But I loved to hear those stories. I loved to sink into them completely. Perhaps because they always had a happy ending. All the suffering and sadness made sense in the end. All the monsters are killed and good people live happily ever after. And so I will tell my story, just like Daddy and Mummy told me stories and perhaps they will turn out the same way, OK?

OK. Here we go then.

Once upon a time . . .

Once upon a time an evil dragon with scales of green, gold and red bit off a beautiful queen's finger. It was all so quick. His teeth must have been so sharp. Queen Chantal let out a scream that was so loud, but so short – it turned straight away into a low muttering – I think she was praying. The dragon did not let go of her hand and a second later both their arms were covered in Queen Chantal's blood. That was when the brave King Jean-Baptiste brought the machete down from above his head. But it did not land on the beaten man at his feet, as the dragon and his goblin helpers had intended. It landed on the head of the nearest goblin. The bright gold and green of the goblin's headscarf turned a dark purple as he collapsed like a doll. King Jean-Baptiste fell over with him because he kept a firm grip on the machete, and the blade was stuck in the goblin's head. The king was struggling to get to his feet when a shot rang out. The whole crowd of onlookers ducked as one. Many of them ran away, and the king released his grip on the machete and hugged his stomach where the bullet had hit.

'No!' the dragon bellowed to his goblins. 'Do not finish him yet. He must see his cockroach wife dealt with first,' and he pulled at the queen's dress with his filthy claws.

I think he expected it to rip straight away, but it did not. The queen herself made that dress. It had green and red oval shapes all over it and inside each oval was a smaller black oval, so that the green shapes looked like avocados sliced in half with the stone still inside. It was a beautiful and bright material. And it was sewn by Queen Chantal, so it was strong. Strong enough not to rip at the hand of some evil beast. But the force pulled the queen's feet out from under her and she fell onto the road, still muttering her prayer. Two more goblins knelt by the king holding his head so that he had to look at his queen and the dragon, who was now lying on top of her, jerking his body as if he was going to vomit at any second.

'Is it the nose that does it for you, Jean-Baptiste?' he said as he got up and knelt by the queen's head.

The king did not answer, he was kicking out at the gravelly road in front of him, as if a wild animal was trying to bite his feet. His face was shining with sweat and he screwed his eyes up tight one moment and then opened them wider than you would have thought possible the next.

The dragon bit off Queen Chantal's nose and spat it at the king.

Could he not see it was a wide nose – a Hutu nose?

When the youngest of them looked towards the house I realized that the squeak had come from me.

'Come, come, come,' I could hardly understand what Pio was saying, his mouth was so full of tears, but I did not need to. He pulled me, just as Mum had done a few minutes before, through the house and out into our back yard. In seconds we were sprinting down the hillside path so fast that I felt as heavy as a man. My bare heels beat the earth like a drummer, absorbing any sharp stones as if my skin was leather.

They should know what is going on out there. They need to know. They need to know how hard they will have to run, how well they will have to hide.

Mum's words were rushing through my head on the wind that roared in my ears as we flew past the banana plantation. Pio skidded to a stop and caught me in his arms as I tried to slow down too. He looked into the banana grove and I could tell he was thinking it would be a good place to hide. Then a scream ended in the explosion of a gunshot, like a firework above our heads. And we were off again.

The sun had set completely by now, so we heard the waters of the Nyabarongo before we saw it. The sound of the river made us slow down. It made my mind slow down too for a moment. Just as it had always done down here – until Jeanette would break the spell and pull me into the water, and we'd splash and shout, laugh and dive.

'In there . . . Clem,' Pio spoke quickly in between huge gulps of air.

He was pointing to the tall papyrus. When I turned back to him to complain about how bad it smelt in the marshes he had pulled from his pockets a yellow plastic bag and the envelope that I had seen Joseph give to Dad at the soccer match. He put the envelope into the bag and tied the plastic handles around his neck.

'What is that?'

'I am not sure, but Dad said it was some very important papers. That I must guard them at all costs. That they could save our lives.'

'When did he give them to *you*?' I can't believe that at a time like this I would be jealous of Pio, but for a moment I was.

'When you and Mum were preparing the food. He told me that if we were all separated we should carry on going south. When we find the United Nations soldiers we must give them these papers and they will save us. Now come!'

I flinched and my skin crawled with every step we took as fingers of papyrus clawed at us, offended that we were entering their world. In daylight I might have been tickled by the leaves against my skin. But on this dark night, I felt scratched.

'How will we know?'

'What?'

'How will we know which soldiers are the United Nations soldiers?'

'They wear blue berets. Come on!'

After a few steps the earth turned to clay and the papyrus seemed to rise around me. Big cool hands of mud massaged their way up my legs. For a second my hot tired limbs enjoyed it, then when I carried on sinking I squeaked like a rat and thrashed my arms about to find Pio.

'Shh, shh!' Pio grabbed my hand before I could slap his head for a second time. 'It's OK, just relax. You will not go under, not unless you want to.'

I did what he said and we just . . . hung there for a moment, hand in hand, up to our waists in the smelly mud. I looked up at the sky dripping with a million jewels as ever, but now it had big papyrus-shaped holes cut in it. And there were no more screams, no more gunshots, just a soft whispering. I kept looking up, as we half floated, and I thought that this must be what it feels like to fly – without the smell, of course.

'All right, Clem?' Pio whispered.

I could hardly see his face, but he sounded so grown up, so in control, so brave . . . Like Dad.

'They might be all right, Pio.'

'Yes. No, they are not all right, Clem. You saw what they did to . . .' His voice broke and he gulped at the air again.

'But they might be alive. Like Augustine and Marie and John. No one saw them dead.'

The only reply from Pio was the rustling of the plastic bag as he turned his head around, listening.

'Pi—'

'We can hide here until tomorrow night, then we will start heading south. The border to Burundi is not that far. Dad said we would see the UN soldiers there.'

'How far?'

Only the plastic bag spoke again.

'How far will we have to walk, Pio?'

'Imagine walking to school. Multiply it by eight. That is roughly how far . . . Shh!'

The whispering was not the papyrus in the breeze. Not just. It was real whispering, people whispering. Pio started to edge forward, so I did too, not letting go of his hand.

That floating, flying feeling had made my heart light for a moment. I knew this only now it started to thump up and down between my throat and my stomach again – the Interahamwe were in the mud too.

We moved further forward into the swamp, but the whispering got closer,

'*Kandiuko guhamya ni uku, ni uko Imana yaduhaye ubugingo bahoraho, kandi ubwo bugingo bubonerwa mu Mwana wayo. Ufite uwo Mwana ni we ufite ubwo bugingo; naho udafite Umwana w'Imana nta bugingo afite. Ibyo ndabibandikiye, mwebwe abizeye izina ry'Umwana w'Imana, kugira ngo mumenye ko mufite ubugingo buhoraho.*'

It was verses from the Bible. I recognized it from church.

'The witness is this, that God has given us eternal life, and this life is in His Son. He who has the Son has the life; he who does not have the Son of God does not have life. These things I have written to you who believe in the name of the Son of God, in order that you may know that you have eternal life.'

Those were not the words of the Interahamwe. Those beasts do not know Imana, they cannot understand the eternal. I pushed through the papyrus stems in front of us and my hand stopped on a smooth warm ball. I snatched back my hand and the bald head poking up from the mud turned round and spoke,

'Peace be with you.'

'S . . . sorry,' I said, as if I'd just bumped into a man at the market!

I squeezed Pio's hand tighter. His plastic bag scarf was rustling more than ever as he realized, like me, that we were surrounded by people. The marshes were noisy with the sound of hundreds of people trying to be quiet.

*   *   *

I felt a million things that night in the mud. I felt relieved, first of all, that we were not alone . . . not completely alone anyway. There were so many people surrounding us that the warmth of all those bodies seemed to heat the clay around me. And I knew that they were all there for the same reason. We were all there for the same reason. And so a bolt of electricity shot through me, just like it had on my first day at school when I stood up with all the Hutus – when I realized I was the same as most of the class. I felt powerful because there were so many others like me. Except this time they were probably all Tutsis. I started to shiver then. Because it was then that I remembered the reason why we were all there. Fear – the complete opposite of power. And it was fear because we were the smallest group, fear of . . . the rest of the class. We may be hundreds in here, but they were thousands out there. My lungs wanted to take a deeper breath and I was nearly sick as I sucked up the smell of forgotten chicken eggs rotting in the sun. Or perhaps it was rotten fish. Something rots in these marshes – life that was free in the river I suppose gets washed up here, stranded on the mud and bakes in the sun.

Then I was annoyed at Pio. Annoyed at him for bringing us to this horrible place. We might get stuck here too, easy prey for the men with their machetes. And then I was annoyed at all the people around us. Stupid people! All coming to the same place, all whispering like they were the only ones for miles around. Shh! You will get us found out, you will get us all killed! All up to their necks in mud. It wasn't like I spent the night meeting new people. I didn't say, 'Hello, my name is Clementine, what is yours?' They were like animals, like a herd, wallowing in the swamp. I tightened my grip on Pio's hand. He had not let me go since we got here. I could not be annoyed with him now. He was my family – all of it now. And he was looking after me. Electricity was back again. Not a bolt, but little pulses, flowing from Pio's hand to mine. I think it was from all the muscles in his body trying their hardest to be strong, because he knew he had to be, for me.

'All right, Clem?'

'I feel sleepy.'

'So sleep.' He pulled my head onto his shoulder and the plastic bag crunched into my hair.

I was not very comfortable like this, but I did not want Pio to think he was doing a bad job. I was so tired. My mind was full of pictures that changed every second – faster than every second. A dragon, a queen, a machete, a dress, an avocado, some plantain, my dad, his tears, my mum, her finger, her eyes looking at Dad, the radio, a newspaper, the church, baby John, Coke bottles in Joseph's hand, Adalbert's bald patches, Paul's horrid grin, Mr Kagina's wide head, Fari in the schoolyard, Fari in Interahamwe colours, green, gold, the second hand sweeping round the face of Pio's watch, red, the eyes of the bird with the white hat, Uncle Leonard in the morning, men at the cabaret falling from their stools, slurring their words, eyes . . . half . . . closed . . .

. . . whistles . . . singing . . . gunshot. I looked for Pio's watch in the blinding light, heard the squelch of mud and the rustling of plastic and remembered we were not at home any more. I blinked the world into focus and saw Pio's face – petrified.

'Clem, they are coming.'

I just hung there in the mud, waiting for him to tell me more – tell me what to do.

The whistles were getting louder, nearer. Men were singing, but not the songs of hate we heard on the radio, not the songs of Simon Bikindi. Traditional songs, songs we all had sung before. Perhaps these men were not the Interahamwe and their followers at all. Perhaps this was the RPF they talked about on the radio, the rebels who were coming to save the Tutsi. I looked into Pio's face to tell him this with my eyes when the singing was interrupted by shouts and the sound of blades swishing through the grass. A woman screamed, a baby started crying, then they both went suddenly silent. And I knew that the RPF were not here.

'Wait until they are close, just before they can see us and then we must hold our breath and sink under the mud, completely, until they have passed. OK . . . ? OK, Clementine?'

I nodded. My mouth was too dry to speak anyway.

We looked up to the tops of the papyrus plants, back towards the road, where the whistles and shouts were coming from, and waited. I did not dare to blink in case the moment I did was the moment that they appeared – I suppose this was why my eyes were watering so much. All we could see were rows of green plant heads against a clear blue sky. Twice or three times I saw a machete blade appearing in the blue and my muscles would twitch ready to start working my body into the mud, but it was my imagination, a false alarm.

When we really saw them, it was not a blade we saw first, but a row of grey domes above the grass. Their black faces and black hair were covered in clay from the swamp, which had dried in the sun, turning them grey. They looked like zombies, living dead wading through the mud. We only got a good look as far down as their foreheads. Before their eyes appeared and caught sight of us we were wriggling down like eels.

I took the deepest breath I could manage without being sick and everything went dark as heavy thumbs of mud pressed at my eyelids. The whistles and screams became muffled and I could hear my own blood thumping through my ears. I tried to imagine me and Jeanette in the river – a few minutes' walk from here – diving under the water, fooling around, holding my breath as I tried to pull her under, gasping for air for fun, because I chose to, not because I might be chopped to bits if I did not.

I still had hold of Pio's hand. He never let me go, but I had no idea what he was thinking, what he thought we should do next, where the men were now, if it was safe to push to the surface again.

The breath ran out. I could either take a lungful of foul mud or get to the surface quickly. My body did not ask my mind what it thought, it just started jerking upwards and swallowed greedy chunks of air as soon as my mouth was clear of the bog.

I wiped my eyes and saw the machete come down. I clawed out my ears and heard the blade thud softly into the bald man's back as he tried to run. He was all grey too, like the man who was chopping him. The killer stopped after three blows and called out,

'Paul, look at the snake, slithering through the marsh!'

The bald man had buried himself in the mud again, as if the men had not seen him yet, and silently wriggled as fast as he could away from them. Paul joined his mate, towering over the bald man, and they laughed and pointed for a minute as he carried on moving slowly away. Although he too was now grey, I could tell that this Paul was the same Paul who drank with my dad at the cabaret. He turned his head to his mate and his ghostly cheeks cracked as he pulled one of his terrible grins.

'Allow me, my friend,' he said and took two steps forward – the bald man had only got that far.

Mud flew up into Paul's face to fill in the cracks his latest grin had made as he chopped at the bald man's back with more dull thuds. The bald man did not scream, he did not make a sound. He just stopped squirming after a while and then Paul stopped chopping.

A woman rose up from the bushes just ahead of them and threw herself forward, splashing away from them. Paul and his mate waded after her, laughing together, machetes over their shoulders as if they were strolling home after a good day in the fields. Except they had a new job now. And they were enjoying this one more. It paid better. I thought of Adalbert and Joseph's homebrew – only the best European beer for him now. They caught up with the woman in no time. She could not get any speed up in this mud, even with her long legs. I have often had dreams where I am running away from a monster, a monster in the story Mum told me before I went to sleep. No matter how hard I try, even though the road is firm and even, I cannot go fast enough to get away from it. It is so difficult to describe when you wake up in the morning. I would often try and tell Mum and she would say she knew exactly what I meant, but I wondered if she was just trying to comfort me. If we had both known what it was like to try and run through the marshes, then I know for sure I could have made her understand my dream.

The woman stood no chance.

Paul and the other grey zombie squelched forward, swishing their blades about in front of them as if it was harvest time in the fields. Papyrus heads spun in the air around them, but I could tell from their grunts and shouts that it was not just the plants they were cutting. I found myself wishing the strangest thing: wishing that these Tutsis, the bald man and the woman, would have screamed more, made more . . . fuss about losing their lives. But they did not. They were almost silent. They did not try and defend themselves, they just ran . . . no, *moved* away without looking back, as if they had all the time in the world . . . foolish people! And when they were cut there were no screams. They just carried on trying to move away, like a millipede chopped in half by a schoolboy, the two pieces quietly wriggling off as if this happened to it every day. They were antelopes caught in the jaws of a leopard, no sound but the snarling of the killer beast. No, not antelopes – not my beautiful antelopes, my favourite animal, like the one I saw not so many days ago, in the old life, hopping high over the papyrus, so graceful and athletic, far from harm's way. There's been no sign of them since we came to the marshes. They are far too quick and clever to be found here now, with all these beasts around. Quick and clever.

What was quick and clever about the bald man and the woman? You fools! Why did you let them catch you? And why did you not cry out in pain? I thought that was what people were supposed to do when they were killed. Do not think me sick, but I wanted the air to be full of blood-curdling cries of terror and gurgled moans. I wanted it so that the killers might not think that they were dealing with animals, snakes slithering through the mud, as Paul's friend had said. On wedding days or at Christmas a man would think nothing of killing a chicken in the back yard. If he was well off, he might even pay a boy to do it for him, and even that boy would think nothing of it – his father would've taught him. Dad taught Pio – it is nothing, it is natural, it is normal. So if these Tutsis die without even so much as a squawk, how will the killers ever realize the wrong that they are doing? If they heard the sound of human terror, of pain, then perhaps they would stop and think for a moment. Perhaps they would feel a moment of regret.

The mud bubbled next to me and exploded in a loud gasp as Pio finally came up for air. I suppose I got my wish – it was a sound of terror all right. But now I wished that I could take my wish back, because Pio's gasp made Paul's disappearing head stop. For a moment he was a statue, still and grey as stone. Then the stone head slowly turned back in our direction.

'Oh . . . ho ho!' That grin of his came bobbing over the grass towards us. 'Élie! Come! I think one may have slipped through the net.'

Pio looked in no condition to dive under the mud again. He was disorientated, he did not know exactly what was going on. I could tell I was going to have to look after him for once. I grabbed his chin and pulled it so that he would look at me. As I did I remembered how Jeanette always did that to me, to get my attention when I was off daydreaming. I always thought it was a nice way to come back to real life, my best friend's touch, and I hoped in that moment that Pio would get some comfort from it too. I pressed my finger to my lips and showed him my idea. I laid my head back in the mud so that everything but my nose and eyes

154

was covered and pulled the papyrus down around us to cover our faces. We were the same colour as the mud now and I hoped it would look like a patch of marsh the men had already trampled so they would not look too hard at the flattened grass.

'Where? Where did you hear it?'

'Back here somewhere. I will not be outwitted by a f—'

My ears were filling with mud again and I could not see them. I raised my head ever so slightly and wiggled my jaw about to try and work out the mud.

'. . . ready been here. It may have been a fish, anything living in the mud.'

'Élie, I know what I heard. Are you calling me a liar?'

'No, Paul, but the teams are moving ahead. If we are seen hanging this far back, we might be branded dawdlers, shirkers even. They might think we are avoiding the work.'

A thick grey leg plunged into the mud in front of me. My heart stopped. My eyes looked up through their woven grass cage towards the sky, but there was no sky. It was as if I was in the sky, so very high, looking down over two enormous mountain sides and the valley between them. A straight road cut its way through the valley. And this road was the seam in the crotch of Élie's shorts; the mountain sides the shorts' crumpled linen legs spattered with brown mud. He was standing astride me.

'You heard the Interahamwe yesterday, the threats of punishment for those who bungled a job, for Tutsi sympathizers.'

'I am no cockroach lover!'

'Neither am I, Paul, so let us go before they mistake us for some.' The sky reappeared as Élie pulled a leg from the mud. 'Besides, Samuel has the beer and I am thirsty!'

Élie laughed, Paul did not, but I saw two sets of legs pass by and soon the only thing I could hear close to us was the whispering again – but this time it was only the papyrus for sure.

11

Sundays are shit, I tell you.

I stood outside the shop, staring at the green metal shutters with narrow eyes – it must've looked like I was trying to burn them open with laser vision. For a second there, I think I was. All I need's a pint of milk for my Frosties – I'd even settle for full fat if you'd just open! Where does everyone go, what do they do on a Sunday? Don't they need things like I do? Or do they spend all of their Saturday making sure they've got enough things in for Sunday? What a waste of time! If the shops were open on a Sunday then people could do all sorts of cool things on a Saturday *and* a Sunday instead of worrying about shop opening times. I tell you, it's like Christmas Day every week . . . shit!

I stomped back to the flat and ate Flora on toast as if it was petrol on polystyrene, angry with myself more than anything that I'd yet again, for the three thousandth time, forgotten that the shops don't open on a Sunday. I didn't even bother to put on the TV – Sunday telly is as bad as Sunday shopping. I washed the toast down with a black coffee, still standing in the kitchen where I'd made it, staring out at the green netting clinging to the scaffolding that had been around the opposite block of flats for what seemed like years. But, I tell you, I don't remember ever seeing a workman on the scaffolding. What was that all about? That would do my head in if I lived there . . . I'd feel like a goldfish being eternally fished from a bowl, my world constantly upset by green-net darkness. And to top it all, my bowl never got clean. It was just the same thin-glassed, undignified, shabby place it had always been, with hypodermics scattered on the floor instead of that pretty coloured gravel . . . Still, central London, forty quid, *I* can't complain . . . I wonder how 'Chelle's getting on up in Leicester . . . Ash, I think you should go back to bed now. My zombie morning brain was just getting my legs to start the difficult trudge back to my bedroom when there was a knock at the door – the best wake-up call. I was suddenly alert, putting my mug down silently on the work surface and creeping like Bugs Bunny with extra long strides to the kitchen door, wincing every time I lifted a slipper and it made a little farting sound as it unstuck itself from the beige lino . . . I thought I'd cleaned the floor well last night! It could be someone from the council, because the buzzer didn't go – they would have their own key for downstairs. I held my breath and, still holding on to the kitchen doorframe, craned my neck and put my eye to the peephole.

I let my breath go in an 'Ah' that said: 'What a waste of adrenaline that was!' and 'I've got no trousers on!' all at once. It was Clementine. I ran to the bedroom and found the trousers I'd worn to the shop earlier. As I pulled them on I caught myself grinning. At what? At the comedy routine I was doing trying to get both feet into one trouser leg? Perhaps.

'*Bonjour, mon amie!*'

'*Bonjour,* Ashley,' she whispered.

I let her in quickly.

'*Une tasse du thé?* Ah . . . er . . . *j'ai* . . . I haven't got any milk . . . Sorry.'

'It's OK. No tea, thank you. I've taken my breakfast before, thank you.'

Taken my breakfast! Excellent! She sounded like a toff from a Merchant-Ivory film or something. But with this soft French accent, it was so much more Luc Besson than Merchant-Ivory.

'I tried to get some milk earlier,' I waffled. 'But everything's shut on a Sunday in this country. Why?' I boiled the kettle again for another coffee.

'So that people can go to church.'

I wasn't expecting an answer to my little rant, but it was the perfect one. The kettle clicked as if to say 'Oh yeah!' and I left my cup empty.

'Do you want to go?'

'To church?'

'Yeah.'

'When?' I could tell those heels of hers were going to levitate if I said it . . .

'Now,' I said. '*Maintenant.*'

Hey presto!

I took her to a church near Highbury. It was the only one I felt confident going into 'cause I knew the routine – I'd been to a funeral there. It was a friend of 'Chelle's. She was really upset. I said I'd support her, but I nearly ended up blubbing myself. The church was big, so it was easy to slip in at the back with Clementine without causing a fuss. There were loads of people there. So this is where all the shopkeepers go on a Sunday!

I led Clementine by the hand to one of the emptiest pews halfway from the front. I wanted her to see everything. She was wide-eyed at the size of the place, at the height of the walls apparently dripping with giant golden icicles, at the massive golden statues and a circular stained-glass window filling the back wall, all deep blues and reds. Most of the congregation was black and I felt strangely proud when some of them turned to see my pasty self leading this little black girl to her seat. As we sat, the pew creaked a bit, then it sounded as if it might snap as the large woman in the middle of it leaned forward to have a good look at us. She wore a little round hat on top of her beige wig and her face was so deeply lined it looked as if she'd just been ploughed. She must've put her lipstick on on the Tube and chosen the colour in the dark, but when she mouthed something at me with those lips and held out her hand as if to try and reach Clementine, I felt nothing but acceptance from her and I knew she was trying to tell me what a beautiful child I had . . . with me.

The singing was shit. I was so disappointed. Once when I looked down at her, I swear Clementine did her tiptoes thing just for my benefit. I didn't know any of the hymns and nor did she, but I expected the congregation to be like Aretha's and send bolts of electricity through us anyway. They didn't, they were pathetic. I laughed at myself as we left; I was as bad as Lola or Sonia. I can hear them now: 'Them type, they can all sing in church like the London Community Gospel Choir, oh yeah, all the same that lot.'

When the heat of the street hit us, I realized how cold it had been in the church. I looked at Clementine, still in the same cherry blossom dress as yesterday, but this time with a pair of old blue shoes that would've looked fashionable on a schoolgirl in the 1950s.

'*Ça va?*' I said loudly over the noise of the traffic.

'*Oui, ça va bien, merci,*' she beamed.

The crowds were getting unbearable, mainly because we seemed to be the only people walking away from Highbury. Arsenal were playing this afternoon – this was where all the other people in the world went on a Sunday! – and there was a river of bodies flowing down the street towards the stadium, threatening to burst its banks at any moment. The hairs on the back of my neck went up and I was filled with that sickening feeling I get when a thousand men start singing about their favourite football team, as if they're about to go into a life or death battle in the Highlands in the 1700s. So aggressive for a game! Clementine squeezed my hand and shouted,

'Is it soccer?'

She looked so excited. I had the urge to say no and make up some bullshit about it being a political demonstration or something.

'Yes, it is . . . Do you, like foot— soccer?'

'The singing will be better there,' she shouted.

I couldn't believe that I, Ashley Bolt – last to be picked in any school team, always booking my violin lesson for the same time as Games so I didn't have to play, rather watch the omnibus of *EastEnders* than sit through football on telly – was standing on the terraces of Highbury stadium on a Sunday afternoon, ripping my throat out singing dodgy football songs with thirty thousand Arsenal fans. I was shitting my pants among all this potential lairiness, but Clementine didn't feel it; she was in her element. The electricity was back. I picked her up so she could see properly over the rows of Jimmy Riddle lookalikes in front and I could feel the energy pulsing through her. It was contagious, and before long we were making more of a scene than anyone around us. For some reason they kept playing a snippet of a classical waltz over the PA and, each time it crashed out of the speakers, me and Clem would stick out our linked hands and I'd start spinning her round in our little space,

'*Un, deux, trois, un, deux, trois!*' we squealed as the JVC shirts either side of us shifted about uncomfortably and folded their arms.

But with Clementine in my arms I felt protected. Anyone that looked at us . . . looked at Clem, even the hardest Highlander, soon had to smile before the red tidal wave swept them up again and they hurled words at the players that I hoped Clementine wasn't picking up.

'Hey, Ash-mate . . . Ashley!'

I looked left, I looked right, I looked in front of me.

'Up here, bruv, behind you!' It was Dave from the flat below, from Number 58. 'All right, mate? Didn't know you were an Arsenal fan.'

I felt the eyes of all the Gooners between me and Dave boring into me. 'Yeah, 'course!'

'Can you stop by later, say before seven?' His Dracula-white neck was stretched so far trying to see me that I thought his sharp Adam's apple was going to pop out any second and land on one of the shaved heads between us.

'Yeah, no problem, mate.' He wanted to buy some pills, but he was trying so hard to keep one eye on me and one on the game that it looked as if he had already taken something.

'Wicked, bruv, wick— O-O-O-O-OOOOOHHH, YOU CUNT!'

Not me. Ian Wright – he just hit the post.

We flowed home. First on the tide of people gushing from the stadium and then on the electric current it left behind. The streets were glowing with it; the dirty air was shimmering with it.

'I bet it's always nice and warm in your country,' I said as we turned into Couper Street.

'It rains a lot too. But it's beautiful.'

I still didn't have the balls to ask her if she had seen anything of the massacres there, although I was burning with curiosity. So when we got to the flat, and I'd turned on the telly for her, and they were talking about it on the news, I left it on that channel for a moment, keeping my eyes on her face.

They were playing an interview with a twat from the US government who was being grilled over their lack of aid to Rwanda. Like her life depended on it, this State Department spokesperson avoided using the word 'genocide' to justify her country's lack of significant help. She just kept referring to any horrific event that the interviewer highlighted as 'an *act* of genocide' – as if that made it less deserving of intervention!

'So Ms Shelley,' the interviewer, Alan-something, said drily, 'how many *acts* of genocide does it take to make a genocide?'

Go on Alan, nice one!

Back in the studio, the newscaster continued over pictures of fishermen hauling bodies onto a shoreline somewhere, in things that looked like those cargo net stretchers they transport dolphins in from captivity back to freedom.

'Every few hours, another boat-load of corpses is being pulled up onto the beach. Fisherman put them into bags and throw them unceremoniously onto a trailer.'

Clementine kept her old eyes firmly on the screen, as if it was nothing new to her, as if she'd seen it all before. But she was the furthest from happy I'd seen her all day and I felt like an arsehole 'cause I was making this happen. I smacked the remote on my knee – it seems to be the way to make it work these days – and flicked over to BBC1.

'"Love Is All Around" by Wet Wet Wet, still your Top of the Pops!'

Christ!

I flicked again. Road Runner was looking smugly at Wile E. Coyote. A second later, wide-eyed Wile E. was catapulted through the yellow sky until his head was rammed through an overhanging rock that he then dangled from by his neck, as if it was a huge ruff like they wore in Elizabethan times. Wile E. looked at the camera, his raised eyebrows bored of it all, as he slowly slipped back through the rock and fell to the bottom of the canyon. Quite violent this, when you think about it – I wonder if I should let her watch it, if she has been through awful things in Rwanda . . . The rock, of course, broke off and followed him down, landing on his head. Wile E. walked from his hole looking like a concertina with the rock still on his head. Clem giggled her high-pitched giggle, clearly loving the show.

You neurotic twat, Ash!

'I just have to go downstairs for a bit.' I handed her the remote.

'OK.' She was absorbed in *Road Runner*.

'I won't be long.' I hovered for a second then went into the kitchen and found a bag of Hula Hoops. 'Have these if you're hungry.' I left them next to her on the sofa, more hovering, then into the kitchen to find a bottle of Pepsi. I opened it and started to pour a glass . . . No, it might go flat before she's ready for it . . . She's a big girl . . . she can do it. I put the glass and bottle on the floor next to her. 'In case you get thirsty . . . OK?'

'OK, Ashley,' she smiled. '*A bientôt.*'

I felt like Hugh Grant bumbling about in that trailer for the new film, the one that poxy Wet Wet Wet song comes from.

She'll be fine. It's only for five minutes. I opened the front door, remembered what I was going out for and went back to my room. I took four pills from the enormous bag-load I was keeping for Jimmy, wrapped it back up in my old boxer shorts and stuffed it at the back of my undies drawer – must find a more inventive place one of these days!

I had to knock a few times – you always do at Dave and Roddy's, whether the music's pumping or not. It takes them a while to work out where the banging's coming from.

'It's the door, you muppet!' a voice went eventually.

'Oh,' said the peephole, 'it's Ashley-mate.'

Dave opened the heavy lid to the tomb that was Number 58. He had one eye closed, squinting in the light coming from the stairwell, or from smoke in his eye from the big white carrot in the corner of his mouth – I wasn't sure. It was always dark in Number 58, whatever time of day you visited. When I went in I always had the urge to pull down the hippy tie-dye throws that were pinned across every window, especially on a beautiful summer evening like this, but if I did, it was possible that Roddy and Dave would curse me and shrivel to dust as the light poured in.

'All right, Ash-mate? Nice to see you, bruv, come in.'

I was nicely light-headed by the time I'd followed Dave's white neck, like a beacon through the dark smoky hallway, the short distance to the living room under mine. It was a bit different to mine, though. Roddy and Dave didn't have a TV in the flat, just an old monitor for watching videos on. They didn't approve of TV, thought it cramped the creative flow. I'm not sure what they were creating, but Dave had an acoustic guitar that he sometimes showed me a bunch of folk-sounding chords on.

'It's the new song I'm working on,' he'd say wisely.

'Sweet,' I'd say, instead of pointing out that he'd been working on this same song for four years now.

Roddy, on the other hand, was a performance artist . . . which seemed to mean he stood at the twin turntables set up on beer crates playing vinyl backwards and reciting poetry about Middle Earth for hours on end. He was there now, but this time playing a white label of the Prodigy's new album.

'All right, Roddy?'

'Man,' he said, putting down the headphones and pushing his amazingly straight long hair behind his ears, 'I take it you've checked out *Music for the Jilted Generation*?'

I guessed he was talking about the break-beats he was playing. 'Not really,' I said, and I shook his hand – he had the longest, skinniest fingers. He pointed one of them to the cushions by the coffee table. I sat on them, but they were so thin I might as well've been sitting on the floor.

'Oh, man, you've got to! I think this is the future . . . seriously.' I wasn't sure if he'd noticed my smirk in the weak lamplight that came from a shelf in the corner. That was the only light in the room apart from the two tiny lighthouses that shone out over the black sea of vinyl on each turntable.

'Yeah?' I fished the pills from my pocket and placed them on the glass table-top.

Dave was down at the table cross-legged in a flash, examining the pills like a jeweller. 'Do you want a suck on this, Ash-mate,' he said, holding out the spliff to me, but keeping his eyes on the pills.

'No, thanks, mate. Got to behave tonight, got . . . visitors.'

Roddy was bobbing up and down behind us by the turntables. '"Voodoo People"'s got to be the best track,' he said, in his West Country accent, to the wall.

'"Full Throttle", easily.'

'You sure, Dave?'

'Positive, bruv.'

Now Roddy was confused. He valued Dave's opinion. So he quickly dug out another record from the cardboard box near his feet and put it on the other deck. Roddy couldn't just pick the needle up from 'Voodoo People' and put it down again on 'Full Throttle' to test Dave's theory. He had to keep the music going, had to mix 'Voodoo People' into another track, then, after that one, mix in 'Full Throttle'. His mixing was appalling – besides, he'd chosen a slow-tempo, mellow track, totally at odds with the hectic Prodigy stuff.

'Choon!' said Dave, lifting a finger into the air.

'You know this one, Ash?'

I was starting to feel like a right old fart, like I always do when I come round here. 'Is it . . . ?'

'Massive Attack. *Protection*. New album. Well, I say new, but it's not out for a couple of months yet. We got this from Dave's mate at Kiss FM, eh, Dave?'

'Choon!'

That was close. I was going to say Everything But The Girl. It sounded like that singer anyway . . . whatsername . . . ?

'Tracey Thorn on vocals, Ash.'

'What from Everything But The Girl?'

'Yep.'

Knew it!

'She's much better singing this kind of stuff, though,' Dave informed me.

We all listened in silence for a minute, bobbing our heads slowly to show that we were appreciating it. This masseuse of a voice sang of a girl needing shelter, doing herself harm, and I found myself thinking of Rachel in Number 61, opposite my flat. Thought it was a long time since I'd heard her calling after Daryl. Tracey sang like some omniscient elf queen from one of Roddy's books, singing about how you couldn't change the way this girl in the song feels, but you could put your arms around her. And I wanted to feel Clem's arms around my neck again.

I'm not sure if it was the smoky atmosphere, but I was floating in that song. I was a bit annoyed when Roddy started mixing in 'Full Throttle' so quickly.

'Aaaaah, Dave, I see what you mean!' Roddy started bobbing faster and deeper.

'Trust yer bruv, bruv,' Dave craned his neck round to enjoy Roddy's dancing and again I was hypnotized by his sharp Adam's apple – it looked like he'd swallowed a chunk of Toblerone whole.

'Aaaaah!' For a moment I thought Roddy was going to pass out. His hamstrings seemed to have permanently short-ened, he couldn't straighten his legs after a particularly low bob. 'This is my church,' he gasped, 'God is a DJ!'

That was the best bit of poetry I'd ever heard him come out with and I told him so.

'Really?' he said, still looking like he needed a shit. 'Nah . . . I don't think so, it's not . . . right . . . I can do better.'

'What are these then, Ash?'

'Mitsubishis, Dave.' I loved making Dave wait as long as possible. He was like a drooling dog waiting to be told it can tuck into its Chum.

'Are they good?'

Try and see! – That's what he wanted me to say. 'Only the best from me, Dave, you know that.'

'Clean on the comedown?'

Have a go and find out! – That's what he wanted to hear. 'As a whistle, of course.'

'Double drop or one at a time?'

Up to you, go for it! – In his head. 'They're good quality, so don't go mad, Dave.'

'How much do we owe ya?'

On the house! – In his dreams. 'Call it thirty quid.'

A twenty came floating down from the darkness above. 'Do you mind if I have two right now, Ash? I think I'm in the perfect place.'

'Go for it, Roddy. . . ! And you, Dave – no need to stand on ceremony.'

Dave unfolded a tiny brown ball, which turned out to be the remaining tenner I needed, and necked one of the little white pills like his life depended on it.

'Tea!' said Roddy. 'Have you not offered our guest a tea yet, Dave?'

'Boys,' I said, after giving respect to Roddy's tea and agreeing that 'Full Throttle' was better than 'Voodoo People' – like I knew! 'Any chance we can have a little listen to that Massive Attack song again?'

'You like it?' Roddy was pleased, his carefully trimmed goatee stretched into a yellow smile.

'Yeah.'

Suddenly Roddy's smile sprung back behind his beard, his jaw shot forward and his eyes disappeared behind fluttering eyelashes. The pills were starting to work. I knew that all he'd want to do now would be to keep riding that wave for as long as possible and the best way to do that would be to show some love to a fellow human being.

'I will put that on with pleasure, my friend.'

It took him a while this time to find the right side of the vinyl and to aim the needle. 'I've got an even better idea,' he said with his nose against the record. 'Why don't you borrow it, you can tape it too then and give it back whenever you want.'

'Ah,' I giggled, 'that's so kind,' and I got up from the floor and gave him a hug.

Roddy's whole body quivered against mine as we 'showed the love'. He squeezed me tight and I allowed a laugh to pop out. I'd already felt what he was feeling . . . today, after the match . . . and I did it without the aid of drugs! And with the spooky telepathy Ecstasy seems to give some people, Dave blew these words up from the floor in a puff of smoke.

'Is that your little girl or something? The one I saw you with at the match today?'

'Yeah,' I reckoned it was best not to complicate things for the boys in their state.

Dave grinned, 'It was the most beautiful sight I've ever seen, bruv . . . truly.'

'Yeah?'

'You whizzing her about, dancing. She looked like the happiest little girl in the world right then, you know.'

'Yeah?' My hands were shaking and for a second I thought perhaps Roddy's tea wasn't just PG Tips.

'And you, Ash-mate . . . You looked happier than I thought it possible to be.' There were tears in Dave's eyes. Perhaps it was the smoke again.

'Did I?'

Dave lay back on the carpet, arms across his chest – he only needed the fangs now! Roddy and I stood looking at Dave, all three of us happy for Happiness. Tracey sang again. She sang of standing in front of someone, taking the force of a blow, protecting. And I saw that blow hit my body like her slow-motion voice, but the blow shattered before it struck because of some new-found strength in my coat. Then I saw Clem behind me clutching the back of it.

'I need to get back upstairs, boys. Sorry, it's been great though.'

My words seemed to drive a stake through Dave's heart and he sat bolt upright, 'Ah, Ash-mate . . . !' But the E-soaked head rush he got from sitting up filled him almost instantly with a selfless compassion, so he added, 'Never mind . . . we understand.'

'I think I see an angel, Dave.' Roddy was staring at a patch of mildew high on the wall.

'What . . . ?'

'I'll leave you two to it,' I was stepping over cushions and ashtrays on my way to the door.

'I see an angel! Really, it's the most beautiful thing I've ever seen. God, I must go to her.'

'Roddy!' I opened the front door and, though the sun was setting, it still seemed bright after Number 58. 'Can you hear me, Roddy, it's Dave. Is there a light?'

'At the end of the tunnel, yeah!'

'Don't go towards the light, Roddy. Do you hear me? I know it's wonderful, but it's not your time . . .'

I shut the door and smiled as I bounced up the stairs with a vision of Roddy floating into the mildew patch, only his bony bare feet left sticking out of the wall as Dave held on for dear life to the ends of his flares, coaxing his friend back from the other side.

I stopped at the landing halfway up and looked out the big window. There was a huge leafy tree in the old playground across the road, a dark silhouette of a tree now, against a pink sky, with a red halo as the sun went down behind it. I did love that view; there were advantages to being stuck up in a tower block . . . OK, *an* advantage. Dave's words about me and Clem rang around my head. Yes, it was Dracula Dave that said it, and yes, he was off his head on E and ganj at the time, but *in vino veritas* and all that . . . I'm sure it applies to all drugs. Anyway, I knew it for myself. I couldn't wait to get back to her and her energy, couldn't wait to see if there was something I could do for her, keep that smile on her face, keep the electricity flowing through her . . .

I'm going to have to change the way I tell this, if you don't mind. There *was* a huge leafy tree? There *is* a huge leafy tree. I seemed to have spent most of my time up till then worrying about what might be or what just happened, so that, if I really think about it, my life felt like an old tired story – one that happened to someone else. There *is* a tree and there *is* a little girl upstairs waiting for me to get back. That's all I'm thinking about, right now, and it's a bit of a relief, I tell you.

'Would you like to see a show?'
    'When?'
    'Right now.'
    'Where?'

'My . . . friend Lola is singing at a cabaret in the West End tonight.'

Clem's face clouds over.

'What's wrong?' I plonk myself on the sofa next to her.

'I'm not allowed in cabarets . . . they are just for the men.'

'Not this one, Clem,' I poke her in the ribs. 'This is definitely not just for men. Besides, Lola will get you and me in as special guests!'

Her face brightens again.

'I promised Lola I would go. I'm her teacher too and if I don't see her show soon I will be in big trouble!' I say with a wink.

And I want to . . . show Clem off to someone . . . It might sound weird, but I want more people to see what Dave saw.

It takes a little persuading by Lola to get the doorman to allow me into a drag club in Soho with a little girl. But Lola, being the prima donna she is, virtually refuses to sing tonight if her 'vocal coach' isn't allowed in. The doorman's unclipping the red rope from its little silver stand so it isn't really necessary, but I can't resist saying,

'She *is* my daughter!' with a squeeze of secrecy to Clem's hand. The doorman thinks this is a great gag, so I add, 'Haven't you heard of mixed marriages?' If he was black I probably wouldn't have tried that one.

'Well, all I can say, mate,' he coughs, 'is your wife must have bloody dominant genes.'

I dive down the stairs into the red light, hoping it'll disguise my glowing face.

There are no high stone arches dripping with gold, statues of Mary and Jesus, red and blue stained glass, and pathetic singers in dodgy lipstick and bad wigs in *this* show. There are dazzling lights, sparkling silver curtains, loud disco music that thumps you in the stomach . . . and pathetic singers in dodgy lipstick and bad wigs. But it's a laugh for me, and Clementine can barely stay in her seat. I'm torn between watching the show and watching her. I love the way her hand is too small for the lemonade glass and she has to use both hands to steady it, taking a while to find her lips as she can't tear her eyes away from the vision of Lola looking like an auditionee for *Priscilla, Queen of the Desert*.

After the show we find Lola and the other girls in a cramped dressing room upstairs – and I'm not sure exactly where to put my eyes when I realize some of the other girls really are girls, so I keep them fixed on Lola, which is where she would want them anyway.

'How was I, then?'

Hello Lola, I'm fine. By the way, this is Clementine!

'Really good,' I say, trying not to sound too surprised. 'But there are one or two things we can work on next time.'

'My God,' she huffs, 'is that really what a girl needs to hear just after a show? Let's see,' and she picks up Clem and sits her on the dressing table, arranging her cherry blossom dress around her as if she was a bunch of flowers from a fan. 'What did *you* think of my performance, sweetheart?'

'It was beautiful,' she says immediately. '*Magnifique! Vous êtes une belle chanteuse!*'

'Oh,' Lola slams one hand dramatically on her chest and the other on the table-top in an explosion of face powder. '*Merci, ma chérie!*' and then in Piaf tones she sings, '*Je ne regrette rien . . .*'

Clem copies her swaying and echoes the lyrics as quickly as she can pick them up.

'Oh, this one's an angel, Ashley!'

Some of the other girls couldn't take their eyes off Clem as they peeled off their dresses, just as I was having trouble keeping my eyes off their jugs.

'Where did you find her, Ash? And don't feed me the same bullshit you gave Ed – she's certainly not your love child.'

This was starting to piss me off. 'Why couldn't she be, eh?' I fiddle with one of the lights around Lola's mirror and nearly burn my fingers.

Lola just raises her pierced eyebrow antenna and takes off her silver wig. It's the first time I've ever seen her real hair. It's greased down flat across her head, quite short and brown. As she cleans off her makeup and shimmies out of the lamé, I can imagine her as a him, sitting behind a desk in a bank instead of a dressing table in Soho.

'Do you have a name, darling?'

I go, 'This is Clementine,' before Clem gets a chance, as if I know better than she does what her name is.

'Clementine,' Lola says like a character from *'Allo 'Allo!*, 'beautiful,' and she gives Clem's chin a little squeeze.

I have the urge to recite Lola back at herself: '*I'm not racist, but, you know . . . that type . . . all the bloody same!*' But I don't, of course.

'Well, it's been a pleasure to meet you, Clementine.' Lola reaches behind her for her handbag and pulls out a box of tablets. She necks a couple with a glass of water and sees me examining the packet. 'Seroxat, better than that bloody Prozac shit. It's the way forward.' I pick up Clem and take her down from the table. 'Where did you think I got my confidence from?' She takes out a Marlboro. 'These?'

I suddenly feel selfish for bringing Clem to this sordid place. I say a quick goodbye to Lola then lead her out, back up the red stairs and past Ed who chuckles,

'Goodnight, Daddy!'

I feel sick.

It's way after eleven when we get home and when I realize the time I feel even worse.

'Will you be all right?' I whisper as we reach my front door.

'Yes.'

I look into her old eyes and allow myself to see an adult so I can be the child for a bit. 'Perhaps you should stay here the night – if you go home now this late you might get into trouble. Then again, if you stay out all night they might call the police . . . God, what should I do?'

Clem takes both my hands. 'It's OK, probably they will not even notice I have gone. Thank you for a wonderful day. I am very tired now!'

'*De rien*,' I say, 'you are *so* welcome.'

Her words are better than any rush I've ever had, from chemical or knife, but then my guts drop down to the ground floor, like Dave and Roddy's will be doing about now as they're faced with the trough after the peak. What happens now? What happens tomorrow? Perhaps this present tense living thing's not going to work out after all.

I turn the TV on and get the crisps and houmous out. And the Red Leicester. I don't pay attention to anything on the screen, my mind is playing a fast-forward jumbled-up film of today to the sound of Tracey Thorn singing with Massive Attack . . . Roddy's neatly trimmed beard, the old woman in the church, the stained-glass window, the roof of King's Cross station, the river of people from the stadium, the classical waltz, Clem's eyes, her toothy smile, Dave's Adam's apple, what he said about us, Lola's real hair, her pills and her fags, the girls' tits in the dressing room Red Leicester the hot light bulbs the blade Ed's chesty chuckle Ah

Ah
Ah

'*Muzima!*' The word comes crashing through the ceiling so hard that I half expect plaster and concrete to fall on my head with it. I throw the knife to the floor and grab my arm, but I'm stuck in the sofa looking up to where the screams and smashing and short bursts of running are coming from. There's him . . . Uncle Leonard, booming about . . . and her . . . her wailing and gnashing . . . But there's Clem too. It's her little blue shoes tapping above my head and it's her squealing in pain after every petrol bomb 'woof' from him.

I rush to the bathroom, rinse my bloodied hand and, all the time keeping my eyes on the ceiling, wrap a bandage badly around my new cut. But you can't hear much in the bathroom, so I rush back to the living room. There's a high-pitched scream from my bedroom. I follow it and stand underneath the spot where he's beating her. She screams some words, some in French I think, some in Rwandan or whatever it is they call their language. I feel anger like I've never felt before . . . I feel so powerless.

I look around the room for . . . help from . . . something, I don't know. I dive into the drawer where Jimmy's pills nest in my old boxers. There's all sorts of shit in there. My passport, my Blockbuster card, a blank birthday card, a pencil, a tape measure, my old photo ID card from the job at the charity. It still has its red necklace thing attached, with the charity's name printed in white all along it. I put it round my neck, pull my sleeve down and run out the flat.

The next thing I know I'm pounding at the door of Number 62 and everything goes quiet inside. Of course! They're hardly going to open up, are they? But at least I may have stopped it for now, I suppose. I wait for a minute, glaring at the peephole as if it's Leonard's own eye . . . I'm thinking about going back downstairs when there's a gasp from somewhere near the door and the sound of a hand slapping skin.

'Clem! Open the door!'

There's a rush of feet in the hallway and the catch opens on the door. Another rush of feet as it swings open a little and the sound of someone being bundled into a room, behind another door. I take the chance and push my way into a flat just like mine, just like Dave and Roddy's. But the smell is very different. It's the smell of food I've never tasted, the smell of old cabbage, the smell of this bloke's breath at a party once who tried to kiss me. Where I have an empty fitting that's been waiting for a bulb for years, this hallway is brightly lit by a bulb with no shade. There's an old-looking man with his back against the living-room door staring at me. His short hair is thin with little curls of grey above his ears. He's still got on the dirty red tracksuit top he was in yesterday, but I can see now he's not wearing anything under it – it's unzipped down to the round belly that's spilling over his tight brown cords.

He shouts at me in his own language and his eyes bulge as if his thyroid just got overactive. They match his tracksuit top – red, like he's smoked too much weed. And when he shouts I realize the smell of stale party breath is coming from him.

'*Allez-vous en! Comment osez-vous?*' He tries it in French instead as I hesitate at the front door.

What am I worried about? Look at the size of him! I hold up the ID badge, praying that he can't read it, and I march forward.

'Social Services.' My voice is shaky. Breathe, Ash! What is the first thing you teach?

Leonard looks alarmed by my ID badge and almost steps aside, but he keeps a grip on the door handle. That's probably the fist he used to beat Clem. To open the door I slam my hand on top of his so hard I almost feel the metal cutting through his bones. He gasps and whips his hand away. Behind him, I see a young woman sitting on the floor with her hand over Clem's mouth. I try to act confidently and quickly, but I'm shocked – first by silly things, like the fact that there's no furniture in the room, just two suitcases puking up clothes in the corner, and a radio on the windowsill chatting to itself in an African language. And then by the fact that this woman seems so young, compared to Leonard. She's thin, her hair in long weaves, tied up like thick rope in a knot on top of her head. Her nose is thin too, just like Clem's, and she sniffs through it a lot. And, 'cause her hand is across Clem's mouth, I can see that she has the longest nails, painted in gold and red. They're so long I'm actually afraid she might catch Clem in the eye with one if they struggle. Then I'm shocked by Clem. Her face looks ashen from crying and one eye has a cut above it that seems to shed its own red tears. Her lip's cut too, and I see hand-shaped purple patches on her arm. I breathe in, from the diaphragm, and shout,

'Social Services,' waving the ID badge again.

The woman takes her hand from Clem's mouth and rubs it across her little broken face as if to show me she is actually looking after her.

'This girl is being abused. She is now under the care of

Social Services until further notice,' I announce, picking up Clem and walking from the room.

'Where will she go?' The woman seems to understand some English. Not sure if this is good or bad.

'You will be notified in a letter . . . tomorrow,' I say. If she could hear me now, Lola's bullshit antenna would be jumping off her face.

Leonard is in the kitchen. As I pass, he raises a bottle of something as if he's toasting us, takes a swig and coughs a single sharp 'Ha!' in our direction.

I wish I had a decent bed to put her in. She almost disappears into the dip in the middle, but she curls up there like some animal getting ready for hibernation.

'You're staying with me, OK?'

She rubs her head against the pillow in a nod and one of the cuts draws a red arc on the blue pillowcase.

'Wait there!' I rush to the bathroom and get my bottle of hydrogen peroxide. If there's one thing I know how to deal with, it's cuts.

I clean the cut near her eye and the one on her lip. She makes no fuss, just whispers, 'How long?'

'How long, what?' I stick a small piece of gauze above her eye.

'How long can I stay?'

'As long as you want.' She looks up at the ceiling where it's all quiet now. I look at the once-magnolia walls and the Led Zeppelin poster with two corners ripped off – I must've been desperate for a bit of paper to do that. 'We'll find a new place to live.'

I stroke her head. Her hair feels like the green side of a scouring sponge. My cuff-linked sleeves brush her smooth cheeks – have to make a bit of an effort going up West, don't you?

'They look like locks . . . padlocks,' her eyes point to the silver squares of the cuff links.

I think about the fresh cut under the sleeve that needs treating and my 'journal' of scars. 'I suppose they are locks, in a way.'

Her eyes are sleepy, but she fights to keep them open and it makes them look older than ever. What's the right thing to do now? And then, just before I panic, an image of Sonia nudges its way into my head and the whiff of hydrogen peroxide around us morphs into one of Germolene smelt by a thirteen-year-old me, soothing, telling me what to do.

'Wait there.'

On the shelf in the living room are some books. Two of them are mine – the one on the birth of British Soul music and the one about Modern Art movements. The rest 'Chelle left here when she moved. Some DIY stuff, some trashy novels and some kids' books for her little one. She joked that I might find them useful, that Aisha had grown out of them.

I'm sitting on the floor with my back to the bed, listening to Clem breathe behind me. 'One day in his village, Botamba the serval cat met a beautiful lady cat from Boende. He wanted her for his wife. Her father agreed and set the bride price before he returned to Boende with his daughter to prepare for the wedding there. In his own village, Botamba danced and danced with joy as he waited for the marriage day to draw near, *kao-kao-kao*.' Clem giggles – at the story or my pronunciation, I'm not sure and I don't care. She's happy again. 'He danced for the bride of Boende.

'Botamba went to the home of his friend, Koto the turtle, to tell him the good news. "Koto," he said, "I have some good news. In two days I am to marry a beautiful bride in Boende." Koto rejoiced, "This is great news indeed. We must celebrate!" And they drank and they danced all night long. *Kao-kao-kao* went Botamba. *Tao-tao-tao* went Koto.' Clem huffed a quick warm laugh into the back of my neck and shuffled about. 'The two of them danced for the bride of Boende.

'Two days later, when they had recovered, Botamba and Koto set out towards Boende. But Koto feared the perilous road to Boende was full of bandits and predators. "We should go to the home of our friend Mpucu the pelican first," said Koto. "She can fly high above us on the journey and see danger in good time." Botamba grumbled, "Mpucu lives a day's journey north of here. And Boende is east." Koto replied, "Mpucu would be offended if we didn't invite her to the wedding and she will help keep us safe." When they arrived at Mpucu's village she was indeed happy to be invited. And *kao-kao-kao* went Botamba; *tao-tao-tao* went Koto; and *seko-seko-seko* went Mpucu. The three of them danced for the bride of Boende.

'But before Mpucu would travel to Boende, she insisted they go and ask Nsonga the panther to travel with them. "He will protect us from any harm I spot along the way," she said. "But Nsonga lives a week's walk west!" cried Botamba. "If we go to his house first we will never reach Boende in time!" Mpucu flapped her wings and said, "Nsonga would be greatly offended if he knew his friends did not invite him to a wedding. Besides, he will keep us safe. Between friends there is only goodness. And I would rather travel a week's walk west first than be in danger on the road to Boende."

'So the friends travelled west until they came to Nsonga's village. He was very happy to see them and insisted they celebrate the good news of the wedding together before they travelled. So they drank and drank. And danced and danced. *Kao-kao-kao* went Botamba; *tao-tao-tao* went Koto; *seko-seko-seko* went Mpucu; and *cwa-cwa-cwa* went Nsonga. All four of them danced for the bride of Boende.

'Two days later, when they had recovered, they began the two weeks' walk to Boende. Through forest and desert the friends travelled and saw no sign of danger at all. When they finally reached Boende, they looked for the bride's house. But it was nowhere to be seen. In fact, all the houses had gone. They had been burned down by bandits and predators, who were still close by and began throwing their spears at the four friends. "But where is my bride?" cried Botamba. The predators snarled back, "We took all the brides for ourselves ten days ago when we attacked the village." And they showed their teeth and began to chase the panther, the turtle, the pelican and the serval cat away. Botamba ran, *kao-kao-kao*; Koto scurried, *tao-tao-tao*; Mpucu flapped, *seko-seko-seko*; and Nsonga dashed, *cwa-cwa-cwa*. All four of them fleeing with no bride from Boende . . .'

She's sleeping.

This is the earliest I've been up in years. I've already been to the shop – never knew it opened that early. Bought everything I couldn't get yesterday and some extra things 'cause I don't know what she might want for breakfast. I got Coco Pops in case she's like every other kid I've ever known, I got some eggs and bacon in case she prefers something hot, and I got some French bread and strawberry jam – well, you never know, they speak the same language so they might have the same habits too. And the paper, I bought a newspaper.

I wore a baseball cap pulled down over my eyes in case I ran into Leonard or his woman, although, when I thought about it, it wasn't impossible that I could work for Social Services and live round here too. It was keeping Clem out of sight that was going to be impossible . . . It might be central London and it might be forty quid, but I could see I was going to have to let 'Chelle know I was looking for somewhere else very soon. But that was exciting, I tell you. Nothing was going to faze me this morning. I must've had a great night's sleep . . . Perhaps I should've started sleeping on the sofa a long time ago!

I'm peeking round my bedroom door, trying not to make a noise, but you can barely touch the thing without it farting and squeaking like an incontinent old lady. Her eyes pop open. She sees me and closes them again with a huge white smile. Oh well, so much for silence. I throw open the door and crouch by the bed.

'Would you like some breakfast? I have eggs, bacon, bread, jam, cereals, all sorts – whatever you want.'

'*Racontes-moi une histoire*,' she whispers, all Jane Birkin to Serge Gainsbourg.

'A what? Not sure if I've got any of those.'

'*Non! Racontes-moi une autre* histoire.' She's trying to teach me.

'*Istoire?*' Ah, *histoire*, like history, that's how I remembered it in school . . . it means story. Another story. Like last night. It doesn't take a genius to work it out.

'OK . . . *D'accord*,' I say. 'But first,' and my heart starts speeding up as I tap her on the nose with the newspaper, scared I could really blow things here already, but I have to know, 'you tell *me* a story first. *Racontes*-moi *une histoire, d'accord?*'

She looks confused. I unfold the paper. 'I want you to tell me your story, *ton histoire*.' I point to the headline on page four.

Children flee to Burundi camps

Six hundred Rwandan children are camping in a huge warehouse in the Burundi capital, Bujumbura, after fleeing the southern Rwandan town of Butare.

'We left Butare on Sunday at the very last minute, during the heavy shelling,' Alexis Briquet of the Swiss charity, Terre des Hommes, said. He persuaded French troops in Butare to organize the evacuation and escort the convoy to the Burundi border . . .

'Did you get away from Rwanda like this?'

She nods. 'A bit like this.'

'Clementine,' I say as softly as possible, 'I want to know everything, I *need* to know what you have been through in case I'm not doing the right things for you.' I tug at my sleeves, 'Between friends there is only goodness, yeah?' and just in case she didn't get my quote from last night's story, 'Mpucu? *Seko-seko-seko!*'

She giggles, a short giggle, then sits herself up, smoothing the blue duvet across her legs, frowning at it as if it's a crystal ball and the story was beginning to appear as she rubbed it more.

'*Il était une fois . . .*'

'Clem, darling, this time I need you to say as much as you can in English.'

She looks up at the wall and breathes in like one of my

students beginning a song. I fix her with my most receptive teacher look as she begins,

'Once upon a time . . .'

At first I thought she was making it up. It was too . . . horrible . . . unreal. If I hadn't seen the footage on TV, if I hadn't read the papers, I might've still doubted, even after all the detail. She tells me all about her family, her dad, her mum, her brother Pio, her friends and life back in a village called Kibungo. Her arsehole teacher and neighbours who turn into murderers. She tells me about the pubs that they call cabarets, voices from the radio, football on a Sunday, the church where she loves to sing and her vicar, Bernard. She never moans or cries as she speaks. When she tells me about her dad and mum getting killed she talks of dragons and kings and queens, but the reality is all too clear. She tells me about her night spent in a marsh, up to her neck in mud, about how close she came to being hacked to death there.

'Hang on, darling.' I stand up and walk to the door so she can't see me wipe my eyes and bite my tongue hard. 'Oh no, it doesn't matter, I can do that later,' I say lamely, turning back and sitting down again on the edge of the bed. 'And how long did you stay in the marsh?'

12

We waited, up to our necks in the stinking swamp, until the sun was low in the sky. After the gunshots and the festival of whistles that seemed to mean the end of the day. 'Work', as Paul called it, was over. This was the time, like yesterday, when they would rush to the homes and the land of the people they had killed and take what they wanted and argue about which part of a banana grove they deserved. They knew exactly whose homes to go to and which bit of land the dead owned, because they knew most of the people they had killed. They were neighbours, they had shared urwagwa at the cabaret, sang next to one another in the church choir, cheered on Nyamata at the soccer game on Sundays.

I bet it suited the killers that the Tutsis were always running away, that they always seemed to land their machetes in the backs of their prey. That way they could not see their faces. They did not have to look into the eyes of the people they killed. The Tutsi could remain an animal, a piece of meat. If they had seen the eyes of the bald man, as I did in the starlight of last night, full of fear, or Pio's eyes when he came gasping for air from the mud . . . if they had cut him then those eyes would have stayed with them for ever, accusing them. That's it! That's why it is so easy for them. Even Uncle

Leonard's eyes stayed with me, red and sore after a long night at the cabaret, blaming me for waking him up so early. Even the beautiful bird with the purple wings and the tall white hat, its eyes stayed with me, disapproving of me for scaring it from its tree – and I was not even to blame!

'Pio.'

'Mmm?'

'Let's make a pact.'

'What?'

'If they ever catch us . . .'

'Clem, they will never catch us. I will not let them. We are too smart for them.' He pulled his arm from the bog and put it around my shoulder.

'But listen,' I said.

'Yes?'

'*If* they ever do . . . we must not turn our backs on them, we must look them straight in the eyes as they do it.'

'I would not run, sister, I am Sentwali, Pio Sentwali!'

I pulled my arm from the mud too – it popped out with a farting noise – and I put it round my brother in return. 'We must look them in the eyes so that they will never forget the evil that they are doing.'

When the sun had nearly set and we were sure they had all returned to the village, we pushed our way back to the path. We had not spoken for hours, we had just suspended ourselves there in the mud, listening and holding on to each other's hands. It was strange to feel the hard ground beneath my feet again. I felt so heavy, as if my feet were made of lead. I looked down at them and they looked as if they were made of lead too, caked in that mud that looks grey next to our black skin. I looked up at Pio to see if he was the same. He was looking at his watch.

'What is the time?' I asked, but I could not think why it mattered any more.

He wiped the watch face a few times before he mumbled, 'Four o'clock . . . it says.' He looked over his shoulder at the disappearing sun. We both knew it was later than that.

Pio looked down again at the watch on his wrist and fiddled with the winder on the side until his hand shot up to his face to catch the tears about to fall from the end of his nose. He sucked in two short, sharp breaths and the plastic bag, still tied around his neck, imitated him. I was going to say, 'Never mind, perhaps we can get it fixed when we reach Burundi. The United Nations soldiers will know how,' but I knew somehow that it was not just the watch he was crying for.

So I started laughing instead.

Pio wiped his eyes and looked at me sternly, like he used to when I caught him in the face during a pillow fight.

'Look! Look at us,' I giggled, 'we look like we are made of stone. And you are the strangest statue I have ever seen with a plastic bag around your neck.' And as I took a step forward, pointing at Pio, I froze.

For a moment he stared at the statue of his sister with its mouth in an exaggerated O shape and wide eyes, then he put his hands on his hips, pulled the widest grin he could and froze too. I was proud that my plan had worked, and so relieved that I laughed even harder this time. I ran at the statue of my brother and tried to push it over. It stood firm for a second then allowed itself to crash to the ground, laughing loudly too. I fell down with him, as if by accident, but really I was glad of the rest.

'We should go to the river and wash this shit off.'

'Shall I look after the bag for a while, Pio?' I said it as if

I was doing him a favour – and I *did* want to do something nice for him – but I also wanted to feel in charge too, especially since I had taken control back there in the marsh when Paul and Élie returned. And it seemed to me that whoever had the bag was in charge.

Pio looked at me, weighing things up for a moment, deciding if I was worthy of the plastic bag.

Hurry up! I'll use the bag more responsibly than you. You see, I would have put my watch inside the bag too, if I had such a lovely thing, then perhaps it would not have got ruined.

He untied the handles, 'It is very important, Clem, no joke. Dad said this could save our lives.'

Get on with it! 'Sure, of course.'

He handed me the bag. 'Let's go.'

'Are you hungry?'

I thought he would never ask! My stomach had been grumbling for ages, but I did not think complaining of hunger was a good way to start my new, responsible job as carrier of the bag. 'A bit . . . yes.'

'Wait there.' Pio ran off up the pathway, away from the river and towards the village.

After a few moments on my own in the fading light, I wanted to run after him. I was worried he would go too close to the village and bump into the killers . . . and self-ishly, I know, I was scared of being left alone. Luckily I did not have to make any big decision then – Pio quickly returned with a handful of leaves. He saw my nose wrinkle as if I was breathing in marshland air again.

'They are cassava leaves . . . it is the best I can do for now.'

I munched on the leaves, wondering why Pio could not

190

have dug a little deeper for the roots – that is the bit Mum always cooked so well. The leaves were never my favourite, even when they were cooked in isombe. But then again, I had never tasted the roots raw – perhaps they were even worse than the leaves uncooked?

We soon reached the water's edge and waded in without taking off our clothes – Pio's T-shirt and shorts, my dress, could all do with the wash too. I left the plastic bag on the bank though. Pio saw and did not complain, so I guess he thought it was the best thing to do. He left his watch next to the bag. The water was cool, but not cold yet, still carrying some of the day's heat. I wanted to splash about and play, like I did with Jeanette sometimes before school, but that was in the old life. I looked at Pio, slowly, gently scooping up handfuls of water to rinse himself with, trying not to make too much noise. His muddy hair looked silver in the moonlight and the careful way he was moving – both made him seem like an old man.

The new life had made us old.

At first I thought it was a rock, a shiny wet rock floating downstream. But rocks that size do not float. As it got closer I realized it was cloth, a sack of something perhaps, with air trapped in it, which made a big dome stick out above the surface.

'What is in it?' I said.

Pio had turned to stop the sack. The river carried it into Pio's arms and he fell back, thrashing his arms about as if he was drowning in the shallow water. The water and the sack were not flowing fast enough to have knocked him over.

'What is wrong?'

The sack was already on its way to me and it was just a moment more before I could see that the sack was a shirt and the shirt had a head and arms sticking out of it. The head of the dead man bumped into my stomach and I too fell back trying to get away. I swam, but not before one cold arm dragged itself along my chest. I wanted to be sick. It was as if this body was conspiring with the Interahamwe, with the dragon with the rifle who liked to force himself on women. In a second the body was gone and I found Pio's hand.

'Shh, shh!' I do not know if I said that, if Pio said it, or both of us, but what we meant was, look!

There were more shiny domes of cloth floating downstream. One, two three . . . ten . . . in front of us, in the deep at the centre, far across at the other bank . . . ten, twenty . . . fifty. It was like a great migration of turtles, their shells blue in the moonlight. If I thought about it like that then it was all right, it was wonderful even . . . Oh, please do not think me evil, it was just such a . . . spectacle.

Pio whispered, 'Oh my God.'

We scrambled out of the way, back onto the bank, and sat shivering, staring at the sight we knew we should not be staring at.

The roar of a truck snapped us out of our trance and we hid behind the nearest *umunyeganyege* . . . you'd call it a palm tree, but it's much smaller. Two men jumped from the front and a third reversed the truck up to the water's edge with directions from the other two. They opened the back and began unloading more dead people, throwing them into the Nyabarongo.

'Fuck off!' one of them shouted at the bodies as if they were listening. 'Fuck off back to Ethiopia, fuck off back to where you came from! The river will take you there, for free, you Tutsi misers. You will not even have to pay. That will please you, no?'

'For free . . . ych . . . misers . . . yeh.' The other one could have saved his foolish words. The valley was echoing enough with the first man's hatred.

The third man just sat in the truck, staring ahead at the hillside. If I had not seen him driving, I would have thought he was dead too. Perhaps he did not want to be involved any more, perhaps he was feeling some regret. Perhaps he was remembering that he was baptized a Catholic, like those he killed. Perhaps he would not be able to sleep tonight unless he whispered 'Sorry' to God as he sat on the edge of his bed, quietly enough so that his wife could not hear. It was a start.

When the truck had gone we started walking. Pio said we should walk as much as possible at night because we'd probably have to hide in the daytime. He pointed which way to go. He said it was south, towards the border and the soldiers with the blue berets. I followed . . . but *I* still had the plastic bag.

And then I had his watch too. It still was not working, but I put it in the bag to keep it safe from any more dirt or wetness. When I got to the UN soldiers I would ask one of them to fix it for me.

I carried on walking south. Alone now. Yes, without Pio. Please, that is all I would like to say about it, about how I came to be without him. OK? I was feeling weak. Not in my legs, or my arms . . . but in my soul. This was the first time I had been alone in the new life and I did not like it. I lasted only a few miles. I suppose I might have been all right if I had gone further, far from anything I recognized. A mile more and I would have been further from home than I had been in my life. But I knew that Jeanette's house was nearby, on the far edge of the thickest marshland, where the village of Ntarama meets the village of Muyange, far from any clear water, far from my home. Jeanette always liked coming to my house because we were close to the river, and because we had cows that gave sweet milk, and because she worshipped my mum and her beauty. And because we were like sisters, best friends.

I had been here only a handful of times, but I knew exactly which way to go. The sun was rising behind me as I entered the village, lighting the way and making the longest shadow in front of me on the orange soil. I imagined the shape was me when I grew up, tall and slender, elegant like Mum. Everything that Jeanette wanted to be. But right then she was more like my mum than me. Jeanette was taller than me, lighter-skinned than me. I smiled to myself – she had two Hutu parents, but she was more Tutsi-looking than me!

Their small *terre-toles* was a lot like ours. Corrugated-metal roof and walls the same orange earth as the yard. Jeanette's dad was a farmer, like mine, although I think we were better off because we had cows. But there was something very different this morning about their house. It was the smell I noticed first, the gorgeous smell of cooking meat. I should have realized then and run away as fast as I could. But the smell paralysed me there in the front yard and sent my mind whizzing back to Joseph's cabaret. I could hear the snake-hiss that the brochettes of goat made when he tossed them onto his grill, feel the hard newspaper in the grass with THE HUTU TEN COMMANDMENTS in it, and hear the angry rock music of Simon Bikindi coming from the radio:

'The majority population, it's you, the Hutu, I am talking to.
You know the minority population is the Tutsi.
Exterminate quickly the remaining ones.'

But the only thing that was just in my imagination was the feel of the newspaper in my hand. The smell of meat was really there, coming from Jeanette's house. At this time of day? For breakfast? And how could they afford it anyway? And the music was really there in my ears too, coming from a radio by the window.

There were three or four sheets of corrugated metal leaning against the wall in the yard that had not been there last time I visited, nearly enough to put a whole new roof on their house. If we sold one of our cows we could get at least twenty sheets of corrugated metal for it. That is why people said we were well off for farmers. I have heard men talk enviously at the cabaret about so-and-so's house, not because of how big it was, but because of how many sheets there were on the roof. Jeanette's family had had some luck, that was for sure. I was suddenly excited for her and I ran for the door, forgetting everything about the last few days. I was too foolish to even think about the angry music on the radio – after all, in the old life everyone used to listen to Bikindi. There was nothing else to listen to anyway, and Tutsis would laugh off the words as a silly joke they had got used to hearing.

'Jeanette, Jeanette! It's me!' I stood by the open doorway trying to peer inside – it seemed so dark compared to out here in the quickly rising sun – but then, trying not to be rude, I turned my face away into the yard, though my eyes kept wandering back. 'It is me, Clementine!'

A chair barked like a dog as it scraped along the floor inside the house and a moment later Jeanette's dad was at the doorway. I was so pleased to see a familiar face that I skipped towards him and took him by the hand,

'Alphonse . . .'

He swatted my hand from his as if it was a tsetse fly. I hit myself in the chin with the force of it. The blow brought me back to real life, the new life. I started to shake. I had always been fearful of Alphonse, but only as you would be of any man you must respect. I did not know him or Christine, his wife, as well as Jeanette knew my parents, but that was because she was always at our house. I thought of Pio then. I wished so much that he was still with me. On our way to school – on the last day the three of us were together – he teased her as usual as we talked of Uncle Leonard and Auntie Rose.

'*What is your Auntie Rose like?*' *says Jeanette.*

'*Haven't you ever met her?*' *says Pio.*

'*Never.*'

'*I am surprised, with the amount of time you spend at our house!*'

I would have come to Jeanette's defence, of course, back then. But now I was angry at Jeanette for spending so much time at my house. Perhaps if I had been at hers more, right now her dad would not be treating me as if he did not know me.

'Go away,' he said quietly, but harshly. 'Go away. Your kind is not welcome here.' His eyes darted back and forth along the road while his tongue tried to wrestle a string of goat meat from between his front teeth.

'I just . . .' I just . . . what? I had no idea what to say, or why I was here.

Along the wall, the blue and white cloth that covered the window instead of glass (just like in my bedroom) caught my eye as it was sucked in and out of the house by the growing wind. Jeanette was there, resting her elbows on the ledge and seeing what her dad had done to me. I ran to

196

her and my eyes overflowed with relief, so much so that she wobbled like that cartoon of the funny coyote on your television, when he goes thin and rubbery and slides down the canyon. I rubbed away the tears.

'Jeanette, Jeanette, I am so happy to see you! You will not believe what has happened to us . . .'

She was not moving her hands from under her chin and she did not smile. She was trying to look stern like a teacher. 'You cannot come in. We cannot hide Tutsis here. What are you trying to do, get me and my family killed?'

'I am not a Tutsi!' It was true, according to the law, but I still felt like the disciple Peter when the cock crowed for the third time. 'My dad is a Hutu, you know that.'

I heard the sound of sharp metal being dragged along hard earth and I knew that Alphonse had picked up his machete. I could hear Jeanette's little sisters whining somewhere inside and Christine telling them they must stay there and do as they were told.

'I have to go to work,' Alphonse said in my direction, 'but I cannot go until you have left my property.'

Your property? Work? If only I had had the guts to say just that to him then, and point to all the stolen things in the yard, stolen from the dead he had gone to 'work' on. Instead I took one last look at my best friend, my sister, before she turned into a wobbly cartoon again. I hugged the yellow bag and it huffed out air as if it was impatient to get going.

So I ran.

The rain started as I headed back down the road. It was only light at this time but I felt as though I was being spat at. My head was spinning and I could not really see properly, so I stopped at a crossroads and tried to compose myself.

Come on, Clem, you have the bag, you have a big responsibility. What would Pio say if he saw you like this? I searched for the sun before it became completely covered by cloud, decided which way was south and looked for a road with plenty of bush along it, in case I needed to hide. I could not wait for night now, not when I was this lonely. I worked out that it could only be another two days walking to the border and safety.

The rain fell so hard now that my dress stuck to me. I felt cold and naked, so I started running again. I ran round the bend and straight into the roadblock.

I saw Fari straight away, not just because I knew him from school, but because he was standing on the back of the muddy white pick-up truck, a machete over his shoulder, higher than the rest, like a lookout. He had on the same colourful shirt of the Interahamwe he had worn that day at the soccer match in Nyamata, but the colours were dull now as the rain soaked it. There were, I guess, about seven more young men and boys, some leaning on the truck, others sitting on the roadside, all of them with a rifle or a machete. The moment I saw them I froze in the middle of the road, my feet in a puddle and orange mud trickling down my legs from the splashes I had made as I ran. The men stopped their chatting and drinking. The ones sitting down stood up and I heard heavy clicks from the rifles.

A man in a red beret holding a machete spoke, 'What have we here then?' He had a scar down his cheek so big that I wondered if he had been cut by a machete himself.

Another man shouted from the truck, 'She looks like a pretty little Tutsi to me.'

The other boys started to whoop like monkeys until the

man in the beret asked me, 'Where arc you going in such a hurry in this weather?'

I had no good answer for him so I thought that it was time to face my death. But then I remembered the pact I had made with Pio, my brave brother. I must look them in the eyes, not turn my back and run. I must make them see the evil they were doing.

The man was standing in front of me now, but every time I tried to lift my head to look at him the rain drove into my eyes and I had to bow my head.

'To destroy the big rats you must kill the little rats,' another man shouted.

'What is in the bag, girl?' Then he boomed, 'Quickly, I am losing my patience!'

'They are – ' the cold rain was taking my breath from me as I tried to speak – 'they are very important papers . . . for no one . . . but the soldiers in the blue berets.'

He snatched the bag from me and pushed me towards the other men. I tried to grab it back, but he just threw me to the roadside like another empty beer can.

'Have a seat,' a boy sneered and the others laughed.

I looked to my left, then to my right, to see what was so funny about where I was made to sit. I was sitting on the back of a woman. She was face down in the dirt and coming from her skirt I could see only one leg. I jumped up and swallowed my scream with a mouthful of rain.

'Oh,' said the sneering boy, 'I think she is angry now. Watch out!'

I kept blinking to keep the rain from my eyes, but if I am honest I think it was also because I expected a blow from a machete at any moment. The boy was not much taller than me so I did not have to look up too much. I made no sound, just looked him in the eyes. The other men cheered and laughed, and the engine of the truck roared as if it too was enjoying the scene. I was glad of the rain then because no one could see the tears running down my face. I was so angry. I could have told them I was a Hutu, but even if they believed me, even if Fari had heard in the schoolyard that I was, I did not *want* to be a Hutu any more. I did not want to be the same as these beasts.

The boy snatched his stupid stare from me. He bent down and scratched a circle in the muddy road around me with his machete. As he straightened up I found his eyes again.

'Well . . . you can run if you want.' He was looking un-comfortable, 'I will give you a chance.'

I shook my head slowly, proud of the effect I could see I was having.

He raised his machete and bellowed, 'Run, you filthy cockroach, run!'

He disappeared.

He was replaced by the hand that had shoved him, sent him sprawling into the mud, which the other men found hilarious. The hand had thick short fingers that looked like they were made of sorghum dough, but they were not soft like dough. They were tough and strong and they held me at the back of my neck.

'What do you think you are doing?'

Nobody answered.

'This is a Hutu girl on an errand for me.'

'We asked, she did not say.' The man in the red beret looked like a schoolboy failing his recitations as the teacher leads the whole class to chant at him, '*You are stupid!*'

'You did not say?' my saviour said to the top of my head.

'Well, you all know who I am, do you not? Do you doubt my word? I know the parentage of each and every one of you, you know that. And you might know also that I have work to do, as you do, and you are not helping by wasting time on little girls like this.'

The man in the red beret looked at the contents of my bag and nodded at the others. He handed it back to me. I took it carefully, waiting for the punch line . . . waiting for them all to laugh at me again for falling for another of their sick jokes. I started shaking. The rain was making me cold, but I think it was disbelief that was shaking me, trying to wake me up to reality.

The thick, doughy fingers led me to an old car and pushed me into the passenger seat. Claudius Kagina got into the driver's seat and closed the door that seemed to flick a switch on the noise of the wind and the rain outside. It was turned instantly into the sound of Ngoma drums being beaten on the roof of the car. He started the engine and I realized that it was this I had heard as the sneering boy laughed at me, not the pick-up truck at all.

We drove through the roadblock and on for a minute or two in silence. Perhaps my saviour was not my saviour at all. Perhaps he just wanted to have me for himself, to torture and to kill me in his own way.

'Did they hurt you?' He spoke only softly but I jumped all the same.

'No, sir.'

'Good. Your family?'

I shook my head.

'Oh. You're heading for the border then?'

'My father told us to go to the United Nations men there and give them these papers.' I squeezed the wet bag on my lap and the little puddles lying on it ran onto my dress – not that I could get any wetter.

Mr Kagina turned a dial and the sound of the wind filled the car again. He pushed a black hole at the front so that it pointed towards me and I felt hot air blasting me, melting me into the car seat of which until now I had only sat on the edge.

'It will not take long to drive there from here. You can rest now.'

The car rumbled along on the uneven road, jostling me about in my seat at every dip and hole, but it was not a bad thing. It was like being bounced on the knee of an auntie when I was smaller. It sent me off to sleep.

'Thank you, sir,' I slurred as if I was drunk, and closed my eyes.

'I am using my position to help bring peace back to this country as soon as possible, not to aid more unnecessary murder. Just remember to stand up correctly next time you find yourself in a class roll call. You may not have such a sympathetic teacher next time.'

I awoke when my teacher banged his fist on the car horn, beeping many times at the crowds of people in the road. There were people as far as I could see and the little car could edge only slowly through them. The rain was long gone and the air was full of dust kicked up by thousands of feet. As we came to the top of a small hill I could see the plain below. Hundreds of brown tents with round walls and pointed roofs formed a massive camp on the far side where all these people seemed to be heading. But heading there too was the strangest thing – a procession of giant silver pangolins . . . a kind of African armadillo . . . their shells glinting in the sun. I pointed to them and asked my teacher,

'What are those?'

'Sheets of corrugated metal on the backs of Hutu men. They are carrying all of value they can. They have carried it all the way from their homes . . .'

And the homes of Tutsis they have killed, I thought, remembering Jeanette's dad.

'. . . They will try to exchange it for safe passage across the border, some food, a place to sleep, anything.'

Then I was filled with fear. 'Are all these people Hutus then?'

'Probably,' said Mr Kagina. 'As soon as the Tutsi rebel army began advancing, almost at the same time as the massacres began, many Hutus fled in fear of revenge attacks. First the Tutsis flee and now the Hutus. There will be no one left in our country if this vicious circle is allowed to continue. Do you understand, Clementine?'

I nodded as he turned his wide head towards me for a moment before beating the car horn again.

'Except the Twa perhaps,' he smiled to himself. 'Maybe that will be the best thing for Rwanda.'

When eventually we reached the city of tents, we left the car and Mr Kagina led me through the crowd towards one of the tents with a big red cross stitched onto the outside. On our way I looked at the faces of the people we passed. Some had traditional Hutu features. Some looked more like Tutsis. All of them looked tired and most of them looked scared and sick. I wondered if they looked at me and wondered who I was, what I was, or if they cared one way or the other now? We passed a wooden fence. Every inch of it was covered in photos of children, with a big painted sign at the top:

CONNAISSEZ-VOUS CES ENFANTS?

Grown-ups gathered around the fence, searching through the photos with frowns on their faces. Some women wailed with delight when they recognized the face in a photo, others wailed because they did not. It was such a noisy place, this city of tents. So many people and they all seemed to be talking at once. I wondered if this was what all cities were like, if Kigali was like this, but with houses of wood and earth instead of tough brown fabric. Perhaps that is why we heard, from the reports on the radio, of so many bad things always happening in Kigali – everybody shouting and no one listening to anyone else.

A tall, thin white man met us at the entrance to the tent with the red cross. 'Ah, Monsieur Kagina, you have another one for us?' He smiled at me as he put on little round glasses. I thought maybe it was because he was so far from the ground that he could not see me properly without them.

'Yes, Monsieur Brunerie, but . . .'

'I am rather run off my feet here, Claudius. Would you mind sorting out her registration for me and I will see to it that she is on the next bus out.'

'This one has a bit more documentation than the others.' My teacher gently lifted the yellow plastic bag from my hand. 'I think she might be able to take a different route.'

Monsieur Brunerie pulled the papers from the bag, which by now had nearly fallen apart it was so worn and ragged. He scrunched up what was left of it and threw it in a sack by the tent doorway. Pio's watch fell at his feet and I threw myself to the floor to catch it before any more harm could come to it. I felt like taking the bag back too. I could not believe the tall man threw it away without asking me if it was OK to do so. For a moment I was angry with him. He had no idea how important the bag was, what a responsibility it was to carry it, how long it had protected the papers and the watch . . . the days since we left home seemed like years. But I knew in my heart that the bag was useless now, so I stood up among the men, their legs like four eucalyptus trees surrounding me, cradling Pio's watch like the head of a newborn baby, while above me they talked of documents, exit visas, an address in London, family, contacts . . . they started laughing and I looked up. The white man called out,

'Lieutenant Remy!' then he looked down at me and said, 'Your family seems to have some very good connections,' he smiled. 'An address in Europe alone is gold dust right now. This little lot is very valuable.'

'Joseph,' I said proudly.

'Mmm?' He had his nose in the papers again.

'Joseph got them for us. People say that Joseph can get you anything you need.'

'Which Joseph is this, Clementine?'

'I do not know his other name, sir, but he has a cabaret in our village.'

Mr Kagina looked out over the plain. 'He may be very useful in helping our cause . . . assuming he is still . . .'

In my mind I saw Joseph's thick beard breaking open into his wonderful smile and I suddenly felt frantic, like the women at the fence of photos. 'Sir, will you find Joseph and make sure that he is OK? Will you let me know he is OK?'

'Well, it seems that I *will* be able to let you know . . .' He pointed to the papers Monsieur Brunerie was now showing another man. 'If I have any news I will write to you at your new address in London, Great Britain!'

I was not sure what my teacher meant, but I was distracted by the third pair of legs in front of me now, the ones belonging to the man Monsieur Brunerie had called over. He wore trousers like yours, but they were tucked into his big black boots. He was a soldier, a white soldier, I could see from his hands. But his face and hat were just silhouettes with the sun behind them shining in my eyes. His hat was a beret, he had a gun in his belt. I quickly moved to his side so I could look up without the sun blinding me. I felt a wave flow through me, as the song spirit possesses thousands of people at the soccer match. The beret was blue.

'Are you a United Nations soldier, sir?'

'I am, young lady.' He turned back to the men, 'She is not exactly an ex-pat though, is she?'

'She has all the necessary documentation, family in England . . .'

'Will you be able to fix my watch?' I held it up to him and the low sun caught a clean part of the frame and it seemed to spark hopefully.

He looked at the watch in silence for a moment then gave a little laugh. He looked at my teacher and the other white man, as if for help, but they said nothing. 'Er . . . well, give that to me,' he grabbed the watch, 'and I will see what I can do on our way to the airport. But we will have to move it, because the next convoy leaves very soon.' He held out a hand to me. I looked to Claudius Kagina.

'Where are we going?'

'You go with the soldier now, Clementine. He will take you to the airport in Bujumbura. There you will get on an aeroplane that will take you to London in Great Britain.' He held me by the shoulders and gave me a little shake as he said this. His wide face lit up as if he thought I was the luckiest girl in the world. 'Your Uncle Leonard is waiting for you.'

The soldier took my hand and led me away.

'Nice to meet you, Clementine!' shouted the tall man as he took off his glasses and frowned at something inside the tent.

'I will let you know the news,' shouted my teacher. 'And you must let me know all about your exciting trip on a plane.'

Everything seemed to be happening so fast. The dusty air made everything seem orange in the low sunlight and, with the noise, I felt like I was having a dream. I was not sure if it was a good one or a nightmare. The soldier's hand was rough and I did not know him. He was taking me to an airport where I would get on the first plane I had ever been on. It should be a very exciting thing, flying in the sky, just as I had always dreamed of, but I wanted to share it with someone – with Pio, with Mum and Dad . . . if not them, at least my teacher, my saviour, Claudius Kagina. But he did not walk after us, he stayed by the tent and waved. The next time I looked back he was gone.

And now another teacher has been my saviour . . . you, Ashley!

When it took off I was so scared by the noise and the feeling that a giant hand was trying to push me by my stomach through the seat and out the back of the plane. A nice red-faced man with a white moustache had asked me in English if I wanted to sit in his place by the window. He said it would be more fun. So, as the plane climbed into the sky, I looked out at the land below getting quickly further away, the roads and the buildings getting smaller and smaller. I only knew the mountains were mountains because of the enormous shadows they cast on the land around them. I wondered if we were flying over Rwanda now. I could not tell where Burundi ended and Rwanda began. I half expected there to be a big red line on the ground like there is on the maps at school so I would know where the border was. I thought I might be able to see the marshland and the Nyabarongo, the banana groves on the hill and our house. Perhaps Mum and Dad would be in the yard looking up and waving at me. My heart jumped – what if I did see them, what if they were OK now . . . ? I never saw them killed for sure, we ran too soon. They might be there waiting for me and I am stuck inside this plane, being taken thousands of miles away . . . I tried to focus on the ground so hard that I stopped blinking and my eyes started to water.

'It's OK,' whispered the red-faced man, 'tomorrow we'll be safe in England.'

I stopped looking at the ground. I thought, if I looked too hard, I might not only see the river and the marshes, but also all the bodies floating there too. I asked the man if he knew where Lieutenant Remy was. He said that he would ask one of the crew for me, but no one seemed to know him. When I explained to the man that Lieutenant Remy was in the camp in Burundi, he said that he was sure that he would still be there. There was no reason for him to get on a plane to England. The soldier had left me and taken my watch . . . Pio's watch. He was supposed to save us. The ones with the blue berets were supposed to be good.

I felt like I had been tricked into this flying prison. I tried to undo the belt across my lap, but I did not know how. As I struggled, kicking my feet into the seat in front until the big shoes they had given me on the bus fell off, the red-faced man asked me what was wrong. He reached over and showed me how the belt worked.

'Now you try,' he said.

I did and the belt fell away.

'Now, where did you want to go?'

Where *could* I go?

13

I point to the newspaper that I've been twisting into a tighter and tighter roll. 'You're not the only one who was disappointed by the UN, Clem. There were Tutsis being murdered a few feet from their camps, Tutsis who had run there for help. And the soldiers looked on. "Not in our mandate!"' I grumble to myself.

I'm glad in a way that I hadn't heard all this from Clem before I'd . . . before she'd become the centre of things for me. This way I know there's more to my connection with her. After all, you'd have to be a pretty heartless bastard to be faced with that story and not want to wrap her in your arms and tell her she really was safe now. Anyone would do that, wouldn't they? But we had a connection before all this. And, although I'm dying to bundle her up in my old duvet right now and protect her from the world, tell her I'll always be there for her, I know that she knows – Christ, of all people she knows better than anyone now – that that's impossible.

'Can we have eggs for breakfast? Did you say there were eggs?'

I'm shattered by her story and it takes me a second to work out what she is asking me, that it's not the beginning of another instalment. 'Er . . . yeah, of course you can have eggs, darling. You can have whatever you want.'

I jump up from the bed and my body stops me halfway to the door for a full stretch. I tell you, I feel like I've just woken from an epic dream. During the stretch, the whole of Clem's story whizzes past my eyes in fast forward and, when my body's done and lets me go again, one question still stops me from going to get the eggs on.

'What happened to Pio, Clem? One minute he was there, the next he was gone. Did you forget that bit?' She slides herself from the edge of the bed onto the floor, her eyes fixed on the carpet. 'What happened to him?' Something tells me to shut up, but my curiosity is getting the better of me. It feels like a power cut in a cinema just before the climax of the film. 'Where is he now?'

She runs past me, 'I need to go to the toilet, please.'

''Course you can . . .' She's already in there and I hear the door lock.

I fry the eggs. I chop an onion too; perhaps I'll fry that as well. Clem hasn't asked for onion and I don't particularly want any, but I can blame my gushing eyes on it if she comes in. I look out at the green net and the scaffolding hiding the other block in Frapper Court away from the world. I'm so happy that Clem is here – and so gutted for her that she's here too. I flatten out the newspaper and hold it down at three corners with the coffee, tea and sugar barrels – they used to be my mum's but she gave them to me when I moved out; she bought new ones to match her new kitchen tiles. I read more of the article on Rwanda. So much of it seems to have been written just for me, answering my questions and doubts about Clem's story:

The roots of the inter-tribal conflict in Rwanda run deep. Tutsis are lighter skinned than Hutus and have always been branded with an 'outsider' status. They are seen as non-Bantu people, coming originally from Ethiopia. In fact, the major reason why the Nyabarongo River was glutted with Tutsi bodies was a perverse symbolic attempt to 'send them back where they came from' – in this case, downstream.

My tongue feels swollen in my mouth, swollen with other questions that I still have for her, but I know that I've asked enough of her for now.

We spend the next few days hiding out at the flat, turning up the music and singing Aretha loudly together, especially when the shouting and banging gets too much from upstairs. We make a game out of running from the flat when we need to go out, trying not to be seen. I take her shopping for some new clothes and give the cherry blossom dress a good wash. I put an ad in the paper. For years I'd relied on word of mouth for getting students because I was too tight to pay for an ad, which probably explains why I didn't have many. But I could see I was going to have to make some extra money now – have you seen the price of kids' clothes these days? I tell you, there's enough material in my top to make three her size, and yet they're almost the same price. I thought about going to the Oxfam shop – just for a second – before it occurred to me that if she was still in the refugee camp that's probably where her clothes would be coming from. So I take her straight to Oxford Street.

The street is as crowded and as hectic as ever, and I can't exactly stick my Discman on to block it all out, not if I have Clem with me. But because she's with me I don't need to block it out so much. She's dazzled by the size of the shops and the millions of things to try on, touch, watch and hear. So, for the first time in my life I don't rush through the shops as if the air in them is infected. Of course, I make time to visit the massive HMV store near Bond Street. I pick her up so she can get a good look at the video wall. She twists and turns in my arms like a fish. Everywhere she looks is water and she doesn't know where to dive in first.

The assistant at Topshop must've seen me hovering round the kids' clothes near the changing rooms, looking like a shoplifter. I think even Clem was getting bored of me asking her if she liked the same green T-shirt every thirty seconds.

'Can I help you, sir? Hello, you,' she rubs Clem's shoulder, 'is your daddy buying you some new clothes?'

I feel so hot suddenly that I wish I could rip off my shirt – or just wear a T-shirt or a vest like most of the other blokes here. I feel hot with pride that the girl thinks I'm Clem's dad and I feel hot with embarrassment at the way she's put Clem on the spot. As much as I'd like her to believe it I say,

'I'm not . . .'

'Yep!' Clem says in the most English accent she can manage.

'Lucky you,' beams the assistant, who looks like she wishes she had a sister like Clem. Her face is almost as black as Clem's, but covered in acne – she's probably only six or seven years older. I find my fingers flicking through the coat hangers on the rail, as if they're prayer beads, and I'm praying that Clem keeps her beautiful smooth skin as she gets older. Perhaps if she stayed in Africa she might have more of a chance. Oh my God! She isn't going to stay like this for much longer, is she? Clem will grow up, be a teenager, fancy boys – even girls – in her class at school . . . What about school? How does that work? What do I have to do? What am I getting myself into . . . ?

'Sir?'

'Oh . . . Would you mind going into the changing room with her and helping her out . . . She doesn't need me in there, you know, at her age.'

On the Tube home we listen on my Discman to bits of the new CDs we bought at HMV. We have an earphone each and sometimes, when there's a bit I want her to hear in all its stereo glory, I put both phones into her ears and her eyes bulge as if there's not enough room in her little head for earphones *and* eyes. I bought Massive Attack's *Blue Lines* for myself and a Soul compilation for Clem. She was happy because Aretha was on it. I catch people looking at us from behind their books or before they flick their eyes back to the advertisements above our heads, and I love it. I love the baby squeaks and the uncontrolled, half-formed notes that bubble from Clem's mouth. Her world is all music and she's unaware that she can be heard in the real world. I look at our reflection in the window opposite to try and see what they all see. I look like a hammerhead shark in a shirt. I slouch down so the curve of the glass doesn't get in the way. Clem wanted to wear her Topshop outfit home. She wears little khaki combats and a white T-shirt. I'm wearing khaki combats and a white long-sleeve top.

'Daddy's little girl!' the assistant winked at me as she showed me what Clem had chosen.

I tell you, the amount of hot flushes I'm going through these days I'm starting to believe this male menopause thing they're going on about.

On the escalator going up I stand behind Clem on the

step below, so my head's just above hers, and I say over her shoulder, 'Clementine Habimana.'

She says, 'Ashley Bolt,' keeping her eyes on the moving steps in front of her and, for the first time in my life, making my surname sound other than something greasy and mechanical.

'Your dad's name . . .' I've been feeling obliged since that moment in Topshop to let her know somehow that I remember him, that he is her real dad still, and this was the only way I could think of. 'His name is Jean-Baptiste Nduwa—'

'Nduwayezu.'

'Right! And your name is Habimana. Why are they different? Is Habimana your mum's name? Do children take their mother's name in Rwanda?'

'No. In Rwanda every family member has a different last name, one that tells you how your mum and dad felt about you the moment you were born.'

'Wow,' I say to the poster for *Oliver* at the Palladium sliding past. Habimana, *God exists*, they thought. And in this moment before she jumps and I step off the escalator, I'm jealous of them.

After a few days of calling the shop, Jimmy finally answers and I rush round to introduce Clementine to him and Elaine.

'Yeah, sorry abou' tha', matey, away on business, you know how i' is.' His eyes are on the TV news, as I'd hoped. I want to enjoy his reaction when he turns round and sees Clem next to me. 'Fink I'm gonna 'ave to invest in one of them mobile phones ev'ryone's goin' on abou'. Could be very 'andy.'

Elaine's white trainers squeak in surprise as she stops in

the doorway, grabbing my attention, and I miss Jimmy Riddle's reaction altogether; just as he would've wanted it! 'Who've you got there, Ashley?' she gasps.

'This is Clementine. Clem, this is Elaine and Jimmy.'

She shakes Jimmy's hand; Elaine scoops her up and gives her a kiss.

'You've never mentioned her before.' Elaine's not waiting for a reply, she's too excited. 'Shall we go and play while the men talk boring business, shall we?' Clem nods and I marvel at the way she seems to trust everyone she meets, after everything that's happened to her.

Jimmy's eyes are back on the TV, 'Wha' you gonna do, let 'er play wiv the piercing gun?'

'Oh, shoosh, Misery Guts! We might do a henna tattoo . . . Ever had a henna tattoo, Clementine?' and she whisks her away next door. 'What beautiful skin . . .'

'Oo the fuck is tha'?' Jimmy looks at me unimpressed.

I nod at the TV screen. The presenter tells Jimmy,

'. . . at the height of the crisis earlier this month, Rwandan refugees were crossing the border into the Zairean town of Goma at the rate of ten thousand per hour . . .'

'You're fuckin' jokin'!'

I grin and say nothing, for once feeling more elusive than the Riddle himself. But he doesn't let me keep one-up for too long.

'Is this a new career for you then, matey? Workin' your way up at Oxfam or somink?'

See!

I fill him in on Clem's story, which every few sentences he punctuates with 'Poor bleeder!' or 'Bastards!' I tell him I need a new place for us to live, cheap, and he says he'll keep his ear to the ground.

'If you want to take another lot off me 'ands, matey, get you some extra cash, you can 'ave Hardeep's lot too.'

'What happened to Hardeep?'

'Nuffink ye', but 'e's abou' to lose the use of 'is legs, 'cause every time I pick up a load from 'im it's 'undreds short, an' 'e finks I won' notice.'

'Cool,' I say, not feeling it.

'Look at this beautiful lady!' Elaine's back and Clem has an intricate copper-coloured design weaving round her fingers and twisting up her arm. She holds her hand out in front of her as if she's admiring an engagement ring on her finger.

Jimmy's different with her now. 'Show me!' he says from his panting-dog face. Clem holds on to his chunky knee with one hand while she flaunts the other. 'Yeah, she ain' done a bad job, 'as she, my little wife.'

Clem nods, then shakes her head, not sure which is the right way to answer.

'It'll wash off in a week or so,' Elaine says quietly to me. But not that quietly.

'Can I have one of these too?' She points to a picture on the wall of a bird tattooed on a white girl's shoulder. 'These ones stay for ever, don't they, Elaine?'

'Yeah.'

'No!' I snap, a bit over the top judging by the reaction of everyone else in the room. 'Clem . . . you should wait a bit till you're sure, 'cause they *are* for ever and, if you change your mind, you're stuck with it, no going back.'

'Very true.' Elaine's looking at me and I've got a feeling she's not talking about tattoos and that she's been listening to my conversation with Jimmy.

'It's alrigh', Clemmy, it's just that Ashley 'ere's go' a fing abou' tattooing being a form of self-mutilation, ain'cha?'

'No . . .'

'I've been finking abou' tha', from when we were talkin' abou' i' before, ya know. An I've go' a feory . . .' You mean, Oprah's got a theory! '. . . a way of understandin' 'ow a nutter does tha' to 'imself, cuttin' an' tha'.'

Elaine goes, 'We're all ears!'

So Jimmy carries on, 'It takes intense feelings to ignore pain, right? You put your foot in the sea, it's cold and you dance around like a pussy, until you gradually, 'alf hour later, shiver in up past ya goolies. On the uvver 'and, if you saw a child drownin' in that same bi' of sea, you'd jump in wivou' a second fought, wouldn'cha? Blockin' ou' the cold, even if i' was winter.' He puts his feet up on the counter, he's on a roll. 'Somefink allows us to ignore discomfort and danger when a higher priority arises, like saving a child's life. Now, ya cutter, ya self-mutilator, whatever you call 'em, experiences their own intense feelings, but they're abou' fings inside themselves, not external stuff like the sight of a child drowning. And this frows a similar switch in their brain tha' allows them to ignore the danger they're pu'in' themselves in by usin' a bloody kitchen knife on themselves. For them, the higher priority is the physical pain, to block out the mental pain.'

It's then that I realize I haven't cut myself in a couple of weeks, since I took . . . since Clem came to live with me.

'Separated at birth, my husband and Kilroy,' goes Elaine. 'And I'm not just talking about the tan!'

A few new students have come round. When they come for their first lesson, Clem pretends she's just had a lesson before them. When she passes them at the front door she turns

218

back to me, beaming, and says, 'Thanks, Ashley, that was great, can't wait for next week!' I have to tell her to calm it down a bit – sometimes it's just too gushing, and then I have to live up to it somehow – but it seems to do the trick, you can see the new student breathe a sigh of relief as they sit behind the skinny music stand, eager to find out what's so great about my teaching style. Most of them have been coming back too.

Lola lets Clem sit in on her lessons. She says it's 'cause Clem wants to see me in action, but I think it's 'cause she can't get enough of Clem herself. There's usually a duet from the two of them before the lesson's over . . . I'm sick of bloody Piaf!

When Levi came for his first lesson since Clem moved in, he stood in the doorway flapping his arms against his baggy jeans and looking at me as if I'd just planted a kilo of coke in them and Clem was a copper. He wouldn't start until she left the flat. When he came round next time we made sure Clem was hiding in the bedroom until Levi was in the spare room with me.

'Purple rain . . .'

We've been on this song for weeks now and I dread this bit halfway through the chorus.

'Purple rain, purple REEEEE . . .' He sounds like an adolescent donkey whose voice is breaking.

'OK, Levi, no worries, we'll . . . er . . .' Quick, think! 'You're keeping that larynx nice and relaxed, low in the neck?'

'Aigh,' he's flapping.

'You're taking enough breath before that line?'

'You know I am, innit.' He's doing that little dance, shifting the weight from one foot to the next and I'm expecting an iron bar round the head any second.

The Reverend Al Green smiles at me from the front cover of his *Greatest Hits* CD on top of the stereo.

I know, I know, Al, but how do I tell him?

There's a tiny tap on the door and, before I can say anything, it's gently pushed open. Clementine smiles at Levi and he stops his little dance.

'What is this, mun?'

'I'm very sorry to disturb you, but I had to say what a wonderful voice you have.'

'She taking the piss, mun?'

'I mean . . . you have a wonderful high voice . . . when you sing false—' she chucks a glance at me.

'Falsetto?' I'm scared to help her out here in case Levi thinks I planned this . . . I didn't!

'Yes, falsetto. It is such a unique sound. I prefer Prince when he sings like that, not like he does in this song,' she points at the stereo, 'like Smokey Robinson, Al Green, even the Bee Gees. Us girls find that style of singing the . . .' The next word comes from Clem's mouth, but it isn't her voice – it's the voice of Richard and Judy, the voice of the ad breaks on Channel 4. '. . . the sexiest.' She smiles at Levi in a way that can only be described as . . . sexy – and I'm not sure if I like it – then she's gone.

I puff out my bottom lip in a what-was-that-all-about face, 'Sorry about that, Levi, sometimes she just can't . . .' Levi stares at the closed door. 'Er . . . so . . . where were we . . . ?' He turns sharply, I wait for the blow . . . he sidesteps up to the window and peers down into the street. 'Should we try an exer—'

'Was I good when I sung in falsetto?' His lips are pulled tight, as if by a drawstring, waiting for an answer.

He trusts you, Ash, don't blow it. 'You were bloody flawless, mate,' the words whoosh out with the breath I've been holding.

'Word?'

I think that means 'Really?' so I say, 'Word.'

'And as for what the girls want . . . she knows better than me or you, surely?'

'Innit.'

'Innit,' I say as confidently as possible in the circumstances.

Something's just occurred to Levi though, and he twists his hat around on his solid hair. 'But how old is she, mun?'

I persuade myself in a lightning-speed debate that, given Levi's size, an average ten-year-old girl could pass for at least fourteen to him. I say, 'Sixteen.' Again, I wait for the blow.

'Word?'

He trusts you, Ash, don't blow it. '. . . Word.'

He looks at me in silence for a bit. At least, I think he's looking at me; his eyes have become even smaller than usual. 'Then what are we wasting time with this shit for, mun?'

'Good question, Levi. I've got something here that'll send the ladies wild if you sing it.' I hand him the lyric sheet to 'Tired of Being Alone' and wink at Al as I open his CD case.

Thanks, Reverend! Perhaps there is a God after all.

'Don't thank me,' says the other Al on the inlay card, 'thank Clementine!'

Of course! I'm trying desperately to stifle a giggle as I press 'Play'. Habimana, Habimana!

Anyone would think the ice-cream man had arrived, with his dodgy version of 'Greensleeves' sounding like it was being

221

played on an old turntable bouncing around on top of a box of cornets in the back. Kids emerge like flying ants from every crevice of the estate trying to get to the big white van first. But this big white van is an ambulance playing something more like a hard House tune, and the crowd wasn't gathering for a refreshing Strawberry Split or a 99 Flake, they were looking for drama.

I'm as bad, I suppose. I stand at the window, with Clem standing on a chair so she can see, waiting for the action. When the lift opens on our floor I run to the door . . . Not sure why, it can only be me or Rachel in 61 that they're coming for (there's only two flats per floor), and I'm pretty sure it's not me . . . but I have to look anyway, through the peephole, to make sure. The paramedics disappear into the open door of Number 61 and come out a few minutes later, a stretcher between them and a pile of bones forming little peaks under a bright blanket, a little red mountain range.

Rachel's starved herself after one too many 'you're a fat whore's from the lovely Daryl. He's nowhere to be seen now, but I guess it was him who called the ambulance and left the door open for them. She's never been anything but skinny anyway, and the last time I saw her, on the stairs, I barely recognized her – assumed she was the junkie from the ground floor and that the pool of sick in the corner was another one of her withdrawal moments that she liked to share with the rest of us.

As the paramedics start the treacherous climb downstairs with a stretcher – too big to go in the lift – Rachel's face, the colour of a fire hours after the last flame has died, passes by the door in fish-eye vision. I presume, because it isn't covered, that she's still alive. I feel guilty I didn't know her well enough to be the one who called the ambulance, to even notice she was ill, to hear her bulimia echoing round her toilet bowl a few feet from my front door. So then I feel angry at her too, especially when Clem asks me what's wrong with her. Oh, she eats loads then makes herself throw it all up again – makes her feel better, thinks she'll be the way her boyfriend wants her to be then, so that he won't leave her any more, won't abuse her any more. I'm embarrassed, to be honest, at the idea of explaining an eating disorder to a girl who, if her father didn't work in the fields every day and her mother walk the hour's walk to the river to fetch water, would not be able to eat at all.

'She's very ill,' I tell her as we both look down to the street, watching the stretcher cut a bright red path through the women, kids and blokes with nothing better to do.

'Legislation will be introduced this month,' says Anna Ford on the news, 'to make Sunday trading legal. Businesses will actually be allowed to take advantage of the change in the law from August of this year . . .'

'About time too,' I tell her, and I actually find myself looking forward to that weekend next month when I'll forget to buy milk on Saturday on purpose, just so's instead I can saunter down to the shop on Sunday and get it. I nudge Clem, falling asleep on my arm, 'Don't you think you should be getting to bed, young lady?'

She shakes her head. I flick to ITV. Marti Pellow tells me he loves me and always will. My God, it can't still be number one! I switch it off.

'Well, I want to go to sleep, Clem, and you're on my bed.' I sprawl out on the sofa to make my point, sliding her to the end.

She sticks to my sleeve and keeps her eyes tightly shut, whining, 'I'm comfortable here!'

A quick tickle in the ribs and she jumps up with a cartoon pout hiding a smile.

'*Bonne nuit, fais des beaux rêves!*' I say like a pro linguist.

'Goodnight,' she says, stomping off to her room.

I try calling Jimmy to see if he's heard of any places going for us, otherwise I'm going to have to start looking the normal way, through letting agents and landlords who'll want a month's rent in advance and big fat deposits. No answer. I'll try tomorrow.

I take off my top and hang it over the back of the sofa before I clean my teeth – if I don't get toothpaste down it, it'll be good for another day yet. As I brush, I watch the different-coloured scars in the mirror – the oldest ones white, the newer still pink – stretching and folding around my elbow joint. I spit and put down the brush, still covered in toothpaste, on the edge of the sink. I have to take a second to feel these scars.

I sit on the edge of the bath and stroke each one; so smooth. Ironically smoother than the rest of my skin. They were so angry and rough once. I try and remember what each one was for, or when it was done. There's so many, it's difficult. The big one here, near my shoulder, I remember that. Did it after Mum died. It sorted me out, I tell you – until then I just had it going around and around in my head that it was typical of her, just sloping off without saying a word, never sticking around to take any responsibility, typical, didn't even have the balls to leave him for another bloke, just had to cop out of living altogether, typical Ah

Ah

'What happened to your arms?' Clem's poking the door-frame and looking concerned.

I jump and my heels whack the chipboard on the side of the bath like a bass drum.

Now she looks embarrassed.

My eyes dart around the room looking for something to hide under . . . my top's in the living room on the sofa, and that hand towel would only cover . . . well, my hand.

Now she looks frightened. She's looking at me and she looks frightened. She's never been frightened because of me and I can't let it start now. I'm so angry with myself, so upset for her, that I make a mental note to cut the living shit out of myself later to deal with this – start on my legs if I have to . . . No, no . . .

'No, no, Clem, angel, it's OK . . . nothing to be frightened of, I'm fine,' and I wave my arms about like Al Jolson singing 'Mammy' to show her that they're the same arms she's always known, that they're not going to fall off. I even pat each arm in turn to show it doesn't hurt. I want to give her a hug, pick her up like I did when I took her away from the abuse upstairs, like I did when we danced like loonies on the terraces up the Arsenal, but I'm scared. Scared that she'll be scared of these things scratched like the wall of a prison cell where a convict keeps a tally of the days he's been inside. And even after this, when my top is on and the sleeves pulled down or the cuff links locked in place, she'll know what's underneath and she'll squirm with repulsion every time we touch. She won't choose my arm instead of her bed again.

She steps forward and her dark brown hands hold on to my arm as if it's something as normal as the white railing at the top of the stairs. She strokes a scar, like I just did and says, 'Are these cuts? From a knife?' She doesn't look up.

'Ye-e-es.' Fuck diaphragm control! My words come like my breath, in fits and starts. 'But they're all old . . . just scars now . . . I . . . it doesn't happen any more . . . it won't . . .'

'Are you like one of the people that Jimmy talked about in the shop?'

'The nutters?' I laugh. Spit and tears shoot onto the back of Clem's hand. I wipe it quickly and leave my hand on top of hers.

She pulls it away and my heart nearly drops into the bath. I knew it; she can't stand my touch any more! But then she lifts the hand to my cheek and wipes away the tears there. The relief just sends more running down to replace them.

'I'm so sorry,' I say.

'*Pourquoi?*'

If I was angry and too embarrassed to try and explain Rachel's self-abuse to Clem, what am I now? You've watched your own mother and father hacked to bits with machetes, run for your life, hidden up to your neck in shit for days, seen more death and destruction in your short years than anyone should in their whole lifetime, and I . . . me, whose biggest stress day to day is that the shop's not open downstairs when I need a pint of milk . . . I deal with my stress by hacking at myself with a fucking cheese knife!

'For not being the "saviour" you think I am.'

She investigates the scars with her fingers a bit more, like a surgeon checking her work. My thighs are going numb from perching on the edge of the bath for so long, but I couldn't care less. She's like a master of Reiki: 'You said you do not do it any more. Why do you not do it any more?'

'Remember when you told me about the bald man in the marshes? And you heard him reciting the words from the Bible?

One bit stuck in my head . . . the bit about *God has given us eternal life . . . ?*'

She nods at me, like I do at a student with no confidence in his own ability.

'*. . . and this life is in His Son. He who has the Son has the life,*' I make sure she's looking right into my eyes. I want to make sure she understands completely my clumsy link. 'Well, do you know what I think, Clem? I think he who has the daughter has the life.' She smiles her toothy smile and I shout up to the ceiling, 'You hear me, God? Forget the Son! He who has the *daughter* has the life!' And the arms she flings around my neck then are like armour which could protect me from any bolt of lightning. He wants to shoot at my blaspheming gob!

On numb legs I carry her back to bed and smooth the duvet tightly around her. She looks a bit uncomfortable and when I ask her what the matter is, my paranoia just starting to rear its stupid head again, she tells me that she needs to go to the toilet, that this was the reason she had got up again in the first place, when she found me sitting on the bath. When she's in there with the door closed, I reckon it's a good time to say from out here in the hallway,

'Nobody else in the whole world knows that, you know.'

I think I'd go to pieces again if I said it while she was looking at me, with eyes big enough to fill a grown woman's sockets. She replies by flushing the chain. I have to smile at that response and, as she washes her hands, I think about all the bathrooms and toilets stacked up on top of each other here in this block. I wonder how many secrets and how much shame, how much abuse and self-abuse gets flushed away every day.

I'm smoothing the duvet around her again, as if I'm moulding clay or something, and she whispers, '*Il était une fois . . .*'

These days I find myself racking my brains, as I wash up or sit on the Tube, trying to remember stories I liked when I was a kid or making up new ones, stocking them up for the times when Clem asks for a story – and she's always asking for a story. I guess this is one of those times. I assume she's hinting at me to begin, until she carries on herself:

'Once upon a time . . .'

14

Once upon a time there was a prince called Pio and his little sister Princess Clementine. They were running through the forest away from a roaring white monster that had eaten many people and was spitting the remains into the river. As the roar of the monster faded into the distance, Princess Clementine felt an uncontrollable urge to go to the toilet, so she stopped running and hid behind a tree to do so. As she began to relieve herself, she noticed a beautiful antelope grazing in the clearing. It was the closest she had ever been to her favourite animal and the white spots on its cheeks shone mysteriously in the moonlight like a second pair of eyes. Prince Pio called out from up ahead for his sister to hurry. The Princess squeezed the golden bag and remembered the great responsibility she had to get the treasure it contained into the protection of her father the king's soldiers as soon as possible, so she jumped up and waved the beautiful creature goodbye. As if startled by the princess, it suddenly lifted its head and fled deep into the forest.

As Princess Clementine was about to leave her hiding place, she saw the shadowy figures of goblins, three or four, one with an enormous belly, surround her brother. In an instant they stripped his clothes from him and beat him with their fists. Princess Clementine wanted desperately to help her brother, but stupid fear nailed her feet to the earth and her hand to the tree. She watched helplessly as they called him names.

'Where is your little sister, where's Clementine, you spawn of a cockroach?' The goblins knew them, knew their family. 'Tell us and we will let you go.'

Prince Pio shouted at them, 'I will never tell you where my sister is and you will never find her!'

One of the goblins pulled out a machete and beat the prince around the face and shoulders with the handle until he fell. Prince Pio covered his head with his hands, his face in the black earth.

'Perhaps now you will tell us!' The goblins stood back and kicked rotting wood at him. 'Look at the insect burrowing through the shit!'

Prince Pio scrambled to his feet and looked into the eyes of the goblin who had said this. He said nothing. His naked body quivered with fear, cold or rage – it was difficult to tell in the half-light. He just stared hard into the creature's eyes. It was then that Princess Clementine realized what her brave brother, Pio Sentwali, was doing. Princess Clementine had made a pact with him, just before they had seen the big white monster. The pact was that if ever they were caught by the evil goblins, they should never run from them, never turn their backs on them, but instead make them look into the eyes of the children they were about to kill, so that they would be faced for ever with their own evil. Princess Clementine was all at once surprised that her brother had remembered her idea and proud that he was brave enough to do it.

'Oh,' said the goblin, looking at his friends for support, 'the insect rises. I think he wants to bite me.'

The goblin with the great belly waddled towards Prince Pio. 'Fall to your knees now, boy, and beg the Lord for forgiveness before you die!'

Princess Clementine recognized the fat one when he spoke. He was Pastor Bernard. But the prince did not fall to his knees, he continued to hold the gaze of the other goblin with the machete.

After a terrible silence, Pastor Bernard raised his voice, 'Are you blind, Pio, do you not know who I am?' The monkeys hiding in the trees screeched as if they were pleading with the prince to say something. 'Will you pray?'

Prince Pio's voice stumbled from his beaten lips as if there was a mouthful of cassava in the way, 'Yes, I will pray. I will pray that you all see the evil you are doing.'

The goblin with the machete gripped it with both hands as Pio's eyes remained locked on him.

'I am the preacher here, little rat, not you. And I bless these men for the work that they are doing.' Pastor Bernard looked around him, then sat on the end of a fallen tree nearby. 'That is the trouble with Tutsis and their offspring,' he waved at the prince or a mosquito – it was difficult to tell, 'they have always thought themselves superior, looked down on us Hutus. My God, they stole Rwanda from us, its rightful inhabitants, and ruthlessly ground the Hutu under their heel in a repressive and bloody regime. Did you know, Pio, that in 1896 Kanjogera, the Queen Mother to the Tutsi King Musinga violently asserted power for her son? You remember your history, I hope? Well, she used to lean on two swords to help her get up from her great throne. Two swords planted between the shoulders of two Hutu children.' Bernard put his hands across his belly and rocked a little, 'Friends,' he smiled at his followers, 'I think *I'd* like to get up now . . .'

After a moment or two the pastor's meaning crept through the thick skulls of the other goblins and they grabbed Prince Pio and tried to push him to the floor next to their leader. The prince struggled silently – the only sounds that came from him were the sounds of air being forced from his lungs as his chest hit the ground – and, as with an eel, the men had a job keeping him where they wanted him. Prince Pio managed to hold the gaze of his pastor for a moment. The fat goblin looked up into the trees while the others forced the prince to the ground. The goblin with the machete held his head, while two others held his legs.

'Keep his arms still!' bellowed Pastor Bernard, annoyed as Prince Pio grabbed at his trousers.

Without another word, the goblin at Pio's head chopped off both the boy's arms. The forest froze with the sound of Pio's scream, but it only lasted a second before his face was shoved into the earth. As the birds cautiously started calling each other again, Princess Clementine remembered the pillow fights she used to have with her brother. His muffled cries then sounded like they did now, except they never tore her heart in two when they came from beneath a pillow.

'Give me that!' Bernard said impatiently. It seemed he was upset he had not been allowed the first blow and he grabbed the machete. 'It is only a shame your little sister is not here on my other side to complete my little re-enactment,' and with a quick glance down at Prince Pio's back he plunged the machete between his shoulders and with it pushed himself up from his rotting seat.

When she was sure that the evil creatures had gone away, Princess Clementine crept from her hiding place. She knelt by the body of her brother and opened her mouth wide. The great cry of grief she expected stuck in her throat, too big for the little girl's windpipe, and the only thing she could say was said by her arms stretched wide, palms to the heavens. After a while she scratched at the earth until her fingers bled. The grave she had tried to make was very shallow indeed, but she pulled her brother into it, all three pieces of him, laying the arms by his side as if they were still attached. She took the prince's watch from the left arm, not because she wanted it for herself, but because that way it would feel like he was still travelling with her on their great journey to deliver the treasure in the golden bag to the king's soldiers. To Clementine, her brother's watch was itself treasure, so she put it in the golden bag then quickly covered the body with a blanket of earth and leaves and set off southwards.

Nobody else in the whole world knows that, you know.

15

All I can think of as I'm hammering on the door of Number 62 is the story of Botamba the serval cat and his friends travelling to Boende. What the fuck is a *serval* cat anyway? And what a dick he is, what a procrastinator – arsing about with his mates so much, listening to their lazy, chicken-shit crap, that he misses out on the love of his life. I tell you, me and Clem laughed at their stupidity; Clem would crack up when I did the funny words that went with each character – *cwa-cwa-cwa* goes the panther, and all that. That was the first story I told her. And that night too I told her we would find a new place to live, away from her pisshead uncle. But that was obviously just another story – another bullshit tale that cons the listener into believing in happy endings. It seems me and the poxy serval cat have a lot in common – just saving up a bit more money from the new students I've got, doing a few more little jobs for the Riddle, so we've got enough to pay the deposit and a month in advance on a flat, perhaps somewhere right out near Finchley or Oakwood where we might get more for our money and the schools won't be as rough . . . don't want to rush into anything, get lumbered with the wrong place, the wrong landlord . . . just hang on in case Jimmy comes up with something after all . . .

And all the time Clem has to sit there with the feet that kicked her stomping about over her head and those vicious arguments cutting into our little world like . . . I keep hammering, even though I have to change hands 'cause the left is starting to feel bruised. The stairwell is echoing with the sound as if the percussion section of a marching band is doing a gig on the ninth floor. But I couldn't care less what people think; not that anyone's coming out to see what all the fuss is about – it's just another psycho making a scene. Safer locked behind your thick brown door. If the police or ambulance arrive then you'll stick your heads out, try and catch a glimpse of the show.

Finally, a female voice from inside tries to snatch a few words between two whacks on the door, 'They're not here!'

I stop for a moment. 'Open up!'

Nothing.

So the hammering starts again, like Morse code spelling out, 'I have nothing to lose and I'll do this all night until you open up.' She gets the message and opens the door. I push past and check every room, every cupboard, the wardrobe. Leonard's bird leans in the bedroom doorway, wearing a dirty red tracksuit top. I'm sure it's the one Leonard wore last time I barged in here. It's quite long on her; she wears it like a minidress. For a moment I think she might be wearing nothing else but, as she folds her arms, the top rides up a bit and I can see black shorts . . . nice legs, but her face is ugly from the hate that contorts it.

'I told you, they are not here.'

'Where are they then?' And to make sure I haven't jumped to completely the wrong conclusions when Clem didn't come home today, I spell it out, 'Where has Leonard taken Clementine?'

She pushes the wardrobe door out of my hand and it slams shut. The white plastic-looking thing wobbles and threatens to collapse in a heap. She chucks herself onto the double mattress in the corner of the room and picks up a packet of Camels. Her lighter doesn't work so she throws it at the wall.

'Do you have a light?'

I feel like chucking her through the window, but I suppose I should try and keep her sweet if I want to get any information out of her, 'No. I don't smoke, sorry.'

She kisses her teeth and I reckon I could kick them all out quite easily from where I'm standing, then she hauls herself up from the floor and drags her feet along the hallway to the kitchen. When I reach the doorway she's lit up from the cooker and is leaning against the sink, peering out at me from under her eyebrows. Her name's Philomena or something like that – Clem told me – so I try the more personal approach.

'Philomena . . .'

'Philomene.'

Great start. 'Philomene . . . I'm really worried about Clementine, as I'm sure you are . . .'

She puffs, 'I am really worried about how the hell I am going to cope in this Godforsaken place without any money.'

The kitchen seems much bigger than mine. There's hardly anything in it, that's why. The surfaces are free of a microwave, a toaster, a breadbin. Only the sink is busy, with loads of dirty plates and pots that fan out behind the red tracksuit top like some elaborate avant-garde bustle. There's a cooker, of course; I doubt the previous tenants could've nicked that monster even if they'd wanted to: it weighs a ton. And there's a little fridge in the corner, playing its buzzing chord to fill the silence while I try and work out whether she's just being supremely ignorant or hinting that I need to pay her for any information. Since I can't work it out that quickly, and I want to keep some kind of control over the situation, I say something before my silence gives me away.

'What do you mean?'

Cool.

'I mean I wish I had stayed in Rwanda,' she launches herself from the sink towards me. For one millisecond I have the feeling she's going to wrap herself around me and try to have sex with me on the ripped lino, but she pushes past me and I mentally slap myself for being such a . . . bloke, even at a time like this. I follow her into the lounge, where there is nowhere to lounge. She's staring out the window into a bright white sky. From where I'm standing you can't see the top of the tree like you can from my flat, just the roofs of the factories that line the canal on the far side of the estate.

'Look at this place,' she snorts at it. 'So many people . . . how is it possible to be this lonely around so many people? So ugly . . . even Kigali was better than this. So my country's at war; it has been all my life. So I could not walk certain roads without being taunted and abused; I could walk others and rub shoulders with high-ranking soldiers, the sons of politicians and rich Europeans. Then I met Leonard. I was pretty sure he was no high-ranking anything, but he was Hutu and he knew how much drink it took for life to look full of potential again.'

I say to her slender silhouette, 'Are you Tutsi?' trying not to sound too surprised.

'One hundred per cent, can't you tell?' and she does a little twirl with her fag held high. 'Some people told me he was married and I know he does not look like a movie star, but much safer these days to walk the streets in the company of Hutus. And then he told me he was leaving his wife, because he was in love with me and he was going to England and he wanted me to come. Oooh, England! I thought, Great Britain!' She kisses her teeth again and it really gets my back up – partly 'cause it says so much about her disgust for my country and partly 'cause I can't do it. 'But he was paying and I could not lose. If the streets of London really were paved with gold, then I would stay. If not, then the word was that Rwanda would soon be under the control of the RPF,' she turned to me, 'the Tutsi rebels . . .'

I nod, confident of the facts and the acronyms, thanks to Clem.

'. . . and then I could return, one of the ruling class again – laughing and drinking with my Tutsi friends while the murdering bastards are tortured in the streets at our feet.'

This room's even emptier than I remember it. Now there's only one sorry suitcase in the corner.

'They killed my parents, just like your precious Clementine's . . . But mine were both Tutsis, so they had no chance . . .'

I tell you, I'm actually starting to feel sympathy for this woman. I need her to do something to annoy me again so I can focus on Clem. 'I'm sorry about that, but—'

'Oh, it was a long time ago. I was still a baby . . . the 1959 uprising.'

The silhouette in front of me is Clem in twenty years' time, full of hatred and thoughts of revenge on the Hutu people who murdered her parents, and my heart plunges the nine storeys to the ground floor under the weight of the cyclical nature of it all.

Philomene turns round and slides her back down the radiator till she's sitting on the floor. 'And now he has gone, used up all the money on two tickets back to Rwanda, but not one for me, so I'm stuck here.' She looks around the room. I suppose she's looking for an ashtray, but she stubs the fag out on the carpet.

'He's flying back to Rwanda?'

She nods with her eyelids.

'With Clementine . . . ?'

'The booze used to make life seem sweet in Rwanda. Here it just made everything seem so much worse. He would sit here night after night listening to the radio.' She threw a thumb over her shoulder at the windowsill, where the radio was last time I was here. 'He would tune into stations that played recordings of transmissions from Radio Libre Mille Collines, soaking up their bastard Hutu propaganda. He slept with the radio more often than with me. And when Clementine arrived he would regurgitate that anti-Tutsi crap and scream it at us both. I thought it was because he was grieving the death of his brother, Clementine's father, but it wasn't that at all. It was this stupid Rwandan obsession with honour and reputation. He had certainly destroyed his with his drinking and his adultery. That is why he flew here, to escape the shame. And then the radio tells him that his brother, his oh-so-saintly brother, has destroyed the family name further; any Hutu who would rather die than kill a Tutsi cockroach, even if it is his own wife, is nothing more than a cockroach himself, bringing dishonour on all his Hutu relations . . .'

I tell you, I'm burning to shout at her, but I'm scared she'll clam up and I'm even more scared at where this is all going.

'When are they flying out, Philomene?'

She puts her elbow on her knee and tugs at a weave hanging from the knot on her head. '. . . So the little devil swimming in his bottle of rum tells Leonard that now is his chance to redeem himself in the eyes of his Hutu "brothers" back home.' Her laugh bounces off the naked walls and makes me feel sick. 'He actually thinks that if he turns up over there and shows some Interahamwe monkeys that he can do what Jean-Baptiste could not, that he can cut his mongrel niece in the name of Hutu Power,' she tugs again, the knot unties and her locks fall down like loads of little arms slapping her face, 'then he thinks that will bring honour back to him . . . the fool thinks he will be such a hero he will win himself a seat in government . . .'

I crouch down in front of her, 'When are they flying, Philomene?'

'. . . Ha! What an idiot. There won't be a single Hutu left in power by the time he—'

I'm not sure if it's those bare walls amplifying everything or if I really do slap her that hard. It's the first time in my life I've ever hit a woman. Don't get me wrong, I'm not proud of it, but it did the trick.

'Tonight.' She doesn't look fazed, she looks like she's quite used to being smacked in the face. 'Seven o'clock the flight leaves . . . I think,' and she flaps a hand towards the phone on the floor. There's a scrap of paper wedged underneath it. Most of it's covered in Kinyarwanda or really bad handwriting – either way I can't understand it.

I'm past caring about raising my voice now. 'Which airport?' I wave the paper under her nose as if it's a bottle of smelling salts, trying to wake her from her selfish stupor.

'Heathrow.'

'Which terminal?'

She stabs a finger at the number four written in one corner. Oh.

I scan the rest of the page for numbers. There's KQ101. I guess that's the flight number, 'What airline is this?'

'Kenya Airways. You have to fly to Nairobi first.'

There's a seven, so I guess she was right about the time. The clouds have thinned a bit and the sun is shining right into the window now. I look at my watch and run.

Five o'clock. Out her flat and down the stairs, I slam into the railing that goes across the big window between my floor and Philomene's and grip it, staring at the tree and its thousands of leaves for answers. I could probably get to the airport before six thirty, but by then they would be through Customs and boarding. I could call the police I suppose, get them to stop him . . . I pick at the flaky paint under my hands and grief runs its fingers up the back of my neck in a way I have never felt in my whole life. She's been taken from me, before I was ready, before we'd even got started, before God knows how many years of ups and downs we would've ridden together . . . the downs might've even outweighed the ups, eventually it might've turned sour, like all relationships seem to one way or the other in time . . . but I wanted the chance to decide that for myself.

I shake the bar in front of me. It doesn't bend.

I tell you, this must be what death does to people, steals the ones you love away before you're ready. But that would be easier – at least you'd have no choice, no way on earth of reversing the situation. Christ, is this what Dad felt like when Mum died? I have to admit that her death didn't really touch me. She was no more than a ghost in the background when I was growing up anyway. But I suppose Dad loved her, or had it already got to the sour stage by then? If it hadn't, how could you ever get over that loss? I'm not going to call the police, even if it is the most likely way of stopping Leonard. Because then they'd want to know who the hell I was to Clem . . . 'Oh, I'm just a drug-running waster living illegally in a scummy council flat who thinks he can look after her . . .' She'll be taken into care before you can say . . . Five past five.

I run down to my flat and make three quick calls before pegging it to the Tube. The first call is to Hammersmith.

'Lola.'

'Who's this?'

'Lola, it's Ashley, look—'

'Oh, Ashley, you haven't double booked yourself again, have you? You know how much I need the next lesson to sort out the new songs for the show.'

I'm out of breath and my voice is trembling – I know you're a formidable dragon, Lola, but do I ever get this nervous about rearranging a lesson with you? That's what I want to say, but, desperate as I am, I reckon it's best to remember that Lola's easily offended. I pick up the phone from its pedestal – a pile of CD cases stacked by the living-room wall with Terence Trent D'Arby's debut on top – and get up from my knees to pace around the room, as far as the tangled wires will let me. Terence has a lock of woven hair hanging down over his nose, just like Philomene did, but his face, inclined downward in the manner of a black Virgin Mary, looks porcelain smooth, like Clem's.

'Lola, it's Clementine, it's Clem, I need your help. There's no—'

'Ha, I wondered when this time would come.'

I look down at Terence's closed lips, scrutinizing them, as if Lola's voice is coming from there, trying to work out if that's really derision I hear. 'Excuse me?'

'They grow up fast, don't they, I knew you'd need a woman's input soon enough! As much as I admire the way you look after her and all that—'

'What?'

'. . . some things . . . *women's* problems . . . only a woman can understand.'

The penny drops and I'm bursting to point out that if I needed help with women's problem's I'd go to a woman, not a bloke addicted to antidepressants who dresses like Lily Savage. I don't, but I'm wondering why I thought of calling her at all. My eyes start to water and I quickly look up from the pile of CDs to the ceiling, as if that would make the tears drain back to wherever they came from. Then I remember:

'Lola. There's no time. You need to get on the Tube now. You're the only person I know who lives out that way, near the airport.'

'I wouldn't say Hammersmith is near the airport, besides . . .'

'You're closer than anyone else.'

'And why would I leave my boudoir for a journey on the Tube at rush hour?'

'For Clem,' I spit through clenched teeth, stabbing the receiver into my hip, 'You self-obsessed tranny.' I look at my watch and hang up. I dial another number. Did I say three quick calls? Make that four.

16

Uncle Leonard said it was safe to go back to Rwanda now, but I was not so sure. I was excited to go back though. I just did not think it would be that soon. And I wished Ashley was coming too. I knew he would want to. He was always asking me about my country, asking me to describe the sunrise and the earth, the way we do things, the foods we eat, our land of a thousand hills. And I would tell him, tell him how the sides of the hills had rich bulging curves, and that the only other places you would see curves like that were on women, women who could afford to eat well. I never saw them on Mum, but I saw them on Auntie Rose and the other women (Hutus as well, I suppose) who she sat with in the marketplace in Nyamata. She used to tell me how it was believed that God would travel all over the world every day on His holy business, but every night, without fail, He would return to Rwanda to sleep, and that is why the landscape looked like paradise. Then I would look at Rose's full body, look to the hills, and tell her if that was so, then God must be a woman.

Ashley would take me to the library to get storybooks and he would find books about Africa and ask me things like, did I know that Rwanda was the lightning capital of the world? When I said that I did not know he would grin and his beautiful green eyes would shine. He seemed so proud to know so much about my homeland. He promised that he would take me back to Rwanda one day, when it was safe, but he said we would have to save lots of money to do that. First, he was working hard to get us enough money to move away from the estate. I think it would be funny walking through Kibungo with Ashley. He was worried about walking through London with short sleeves on, because people would stare at the scars on his arms, but everyone would stare at him in Kibungo, even if his arms were covered, because he has straight hair, green eyes and pale white skin. But I would hold his hand as we walked through the village so that everyone would know he was . . . mine. And I would be proud.

Uncle Leonard said that we could call Ashley from the airport, but if we did not leave right away we would miss our only chance of getting back to Rwanda to see Auntie Rose. When he grabbed my wrist by the ice-cream van I was terrified for a moment. It was the first time I had seen him since Ashley saved me. His grip was uncomfortable, but his face was not angry and his eyes were not as red as usual. He smiled like the boy before me in the queue had done when he'd got his ice cream with a stick of chocolate in it. Uncle Leonard pointed to his suitcase on the pavement and said he had all I would need in there. I looked up to the window of our flat – mine and Ashley's – and I could see the top of Serena's head moving to the rhythm of the song Ashley was teaching her. But I could not see Ashley and he could not see me. If he could then I would know from the look on his face if it was right to listen to Uncle Leonard or not.

'If we go now there is a great chance you will see your parents again too.'

'Are they still alive?' I could not believe what I was hearing, but I wanted to with all my heart.

'Clementine, do you still believe in God?'

I nodded and he let go of my wrist, licking the melting ice cream that had run in a little white river over my hand and onto his.

'Then I swear you will be with them in a few days.'

The Tube train felt as if it was going faster than usual, hurrying along especially for us, to get us to the airport in time. Uncle Leonard could not keep his leg still. It bounced up and down so fast that it looked as if it was part of the engine, pumping tirelessly to help us to our destination. He was smarter than usual, in an orange-brown suit that reminded me of the earth in Kibungo. The crease on his bouncing trousers looked so sharp that you might cut your finger on it. He held me by the wrist nearly all the time. It did not hurt, but it made me feel uneasy. I told myself to be happy that my uncle was a new man, clean and calm and smiling. He talked about God a lot on the journey – not to me really, but he muttered to himself in Kinyarwanda. He said he was sinful, I think, and mumbled about rebellion as evidence of sin, commandments and the year 1959.

A little way after the station called Hammersmith the train burst through the surface of the earth and the hot sun filled the train for the last part of the ride. I wondered how the great tunnel we had been in for so long did not collapse under the weight of all those giant glass buildings and old stone castles that Ashley had taken me to. And the river – what could be deeper than water? Yet the train must have gone deeper than this because I never saw fish pass the window or water drip between the doors. Lots of people looked around and out of the windows as if they were trying to work out where we were, as if we had arrived in a new world, but I knew it was many more hours on an aeroplane until things were really different.

The man opposite me wore a suit like my uncle's, but it was black. He had sat as still as a stone since he got on, staring unhappily at something above my head, but now the sun seemed to bring him to life and he reached into the briefcase on his lap and pulled out a big phone that reminded me of the ones the UN soldiers had used to speak to each other in the camp in Burundi. Some of the people in the train thought it was funny as he spoke about his 'schedule' for the rest of the day, others looked disgusted for some reason. I thought about asking him if he wouldn't mind calling Ashley Bolt on 071 687 5657. Ashley had made me memorize the number. He said I should always carry some silver coins with me so that I could use them in the tele-phone boxes to call him if I was ever in trouble. But I wasn't sure if I was in trouble now, and I did not want to upset Uncle Leonard. Besides, he had promised we would call Ashley when we got to the airport. I knew Jimmy and Elaine's number too. Jimmy makes me laugh and Elaine feels like a big sister.

My uncle's grip on my wrist tightened as the train stopped at Heathrow Terminal 4 and everyone still on the train, including us, got off. When we got to the top of the stairs I noticed the tall blonde woman coming towards us – it was hard not to, she seemed so much bigger than anyone else. Perhaps it was because her hair was so bushy and so bright it was almost yellow, and her red shoes so shiny they looked like they had just been painted and were still wet. Uncle Leonard did not see her, though. He was too busy looking at the television screens that had rows of times, numbers and letters on them.

'Oh my God!' She collided with him and the plastic bag she carried fell, the floor chiming with the sound of broken glass.

'Excuse,' said Uncle Leonard and tugged my arm to keep me walking.

'AHHH!' the woman's deep voice echoed round the huge hall. 'You ignorant little man! Are you just going to walk on as if nothing happened? How dare you!'

Some people walking by slowed down and some stopped to see what all the commotion was about. Ashley hated it when people did that. He always said to me that unless I knew I could help to keep walking, not stand and stare. Uncle Leonard stopped when he realized the woman was shouting at him and that she wasn't going to be quiet unless he did something about it. He looked around the hall nervously as he pulled me back to where the lady was hammering her pointed heels into the hard floor by her bag, as if she was preparing to dance around it.

He picked up the bag. 'I am sorry. Sorry, OK?' He tried to give it back to the lady, but she put both hands on her hips below her short red jacket (as bright a red as her shoes).

'Well, that's no good to me now, is it?' She seemed to know without looking in the bag that what was inside was broken beyond repair.

Uncle Leonard shook the bag as he peered into it, as if he was trying to shake some life back into the broken thing, but the sound that came out just confirmed what the lady had said. He tried again to give the bag to her, but this time she used her hands to burrow into the handbag hanging from her shoulder (red like her shoes and jacket) until she found the cigarettes she was looking for. She pulled out the packet, they were Marlboro ones – red – like the ones Lola smoked. She lifted one to her big lips (red like her jacket, her shoes and her bag) and the lips said,

'I can't believe it! That was a gift for my dying mother. She's obsessed with pigs. She's got pig ornaments all over her house from all over the world, but she didn't have a glass piggy like that. She's got every single one of those Nat West piggy banks, remember them . . . ?' Uncle Leonard looked up blankly at the cigarette waving around in front of her face. 'Don't you remember?' The lady's voice was getting louder with every word, 'There was Woody, Maxwell, Lady Hillary . . .'

'Shh, shh . . . I-I mean listen, please.' I had never heard Uncle Leonard sound so timid. 'Where did you buy the . . . pig . . . perhaps I can . . . give you some money to help buy another?'

I looked hard at the lips. Yes, they were Lola's lips and the voice was unmistakable – a parrot squawking in the Kayumba forest on a warm Sunday afternoon. My eyes moved up to her eyes. They were Lola's eyes, and there was the silver stud through one eyebrow. But because her black hair had become a big bush of yellow she seemed like a different person. Lola is really a man, but we call her a 'she' because she prefers that. As I recognized her, I felt a lightning bolt of excitement lift my heels from the ground. But before I could say anything she looked hard at me and tapped the unlit cigarette on her lips as if it was a finger saying 'Be quiet!'

'No, no, that was the last one in the shop,' Lola's voice quivered. 'It's really quite devastating . . .'

249

'Well, I'm sorry then,' my uncle said. He tugged at my arm again and began to walk away.

'Sorry?' The quivering left her voice with this word. Now it was firm and strong and seemed to hold our feet to the floor. 'A gentleman would at least buy a lady a drink to steady her nerves after such a shock.'

I looked back at Lola, but I could see her straining not to look at me. She did not want my uncle to realize we knew each other and this made me a little scared. I looked up into Uncle Leonard's face. He was squinting, as if in a morning fog on the hillside of Kibungo, trying to work out if Lola was serious about him buying her a drink, trying to work out if telling her to get lost would be a mistake.

'I do not have much time,' he said weakly, as if the decision had already been made.

'I know.'

Lola led the way. As we passed the window of a gift shop my attention was captured by a shelf with a long row of identical glass pigs on it. There were a few people inside the shop looking at them and their faces bubbled up inside each round pig belly as I passed. The pigs were standing on their hind legs as if about to run somewhere, but they seemed chained to the shelf by the white tag tied around each of their ankles with £1.99 written in blue pen on it.

The place where Lola wanted to drink was just like the pub near our flat, but it had no front wall, no doors. This made me think of the cabaret where Daddy used to drink and my heart leapt at the thought of seeing him again soon. But after it leapt, it was as if the ground my heart landed on gave way as I wondered again why Lola was here and why she was acting so strangely? I pushed myself back into a green velvety chair until my feet dangled above the swirly patterned carpet. Lola threw herself into a similar chair and Uncle Leonard began to sit too until Lola said,

'Gin and tonic, please. Double. And what about you, little girl? What would you like? A Pepsi?'

'She does not need a drink. We haven't got that much time.'

Lola sniffed in Uncle Leonard's direction and found a lighter in her handbag for the cigarette she had used to silence me. Uncle Leonard hesitated for a second. I think he wasn't sure if he should take me to the bar with him. I shuffled back in my seat and he went to the bar alone, looking back at us every few seconds.

'Lola?' I whispered.

'Hey, Clem, darling. Sorry about all that. Now it's really important that you don't worry. Ashley called me,' she looked embarrassed for a moment. 'Actually, he called me twice. He asked me to . . . to keep you here until he arrives.'

'Ashley's coming here?' I think I raised my voice too much with excitement and Lola huffed smoke across the table as if to smother my words.

'It's a surprise though. Ashley just needs to . . . to see you and talk to your uncle before you . . . go. But you can't let on that you know me AND THE SHOES ARE FROM DOLCIS, QUITE A BARGAIN. I'M SURE THEY'D HAVE SOME IN YOUR LITTLE SIZE TOO . . .' I was wide-eyed at Lola suddenly talking loudly about shoes, when I realized that Uncle Leonard was on his way back to the table with two glasses. He gave one to Lola and sat holding the small brown drink to his chest like a baby.

'Oh, glad you found time to have a drink with me. Whisky man, are you?'

My uncle gave a tiny single nod.

'Cheers, then,' Lola sipped at her drink.

My uncle raised a shaking hand to his mouth and gulped his down in one go.

'So . . . what brings you two here?'

'Travel.'

'Of course,' Lola gave a delicate cough. 'And where are you two travelling to?'

'Africa,' said Uncle Leonard.

'Very nice . . . On holiday?'

'We are going home. To our family, aren't we, Clementine?'

'Yes,' I smiled a genuine smile at Lola.

'That's nice,' Lola took another sip of her drink, but her lips pursed as if she did not like it. 'And . . . er . . . whereabouts in Africa are you going?'

I jumped in before Uncle Leonard could give another short, awkward answer. 'We are going to Rwanda. It is a beautiful country. The earth is red and you don't have to go to the shops to find fruit.' I tossed my head at the shop opposite the pub with shelves of apples and oranges in the front. 'It hangs from the trees by the side of the road and if you are tall enough you can pluck passion fruit and bananas. Or if you are good at climbing you can get the best fruit from the top of the tree which no one else can reach.'

'That sounds lovely, darling,' Lola stubbed out her cigarette. 'But isn't it a bit dangerous there at the moment?' She spoke to my uncle now, 'With the fighting and killing?'

'No . . . that is all over.'

'Oh,' Lola had some more of her drink, uncrossed her legs and crossed them again as if she could not get comfortable, 'so . . .'

'What?' Uncle Leonard's tongue clicked against the roof of his mouth like the time bomb ticking away before it blows up in Wile E. Coyote's face. 'What else do you want to know about me and my country? I am not in the habit of telling my private life to ugly women I do not know in airports.'

'Hold your fuckin' horses . . .'

The drink was working its evil and the bomb went off. My uncle swore in Kinyarwanda and my heart sped up just like it used to before he started hitting me and Philomene. 'But if you want to know, I came to this ridiculous country because I was a disgrace to my family's name in Rwanda. In fact, they could not do enough to help me get away as quickly as possible. But it was not to help me that they did it. It was to get rid of me and the embarrassment I caused them.' He looked over his shoulder and hissed at the barman, showing him his empty glass. The barman looked offended and served someone else who had just approached the bar.

When Uncle Leonard called her ugly, Lola had lurched forward, sinking her nails into the table and baring her teeth like a baboon. Now she sat back again and sighed, 'It seems like we have more in common than I would ever have imagined.' She threw the rest of her drink into her mouth. 'Have you ever tried Seroxat?' she smirked.

My uncle did not seem to understand what she said. He just looked with longing towards the bar.

'Perhaps you should.' Lola carried on, 'It does wonders . . .' She shifted about in her seat. 'But it plays havoc with the bowels.'

My uncle got up and stood by the bar, waiting to be served. One of his knees was quivering in his trousers.

'Oh another G and T for me then please,' Lola called, but she looked anything but thirsty as she cradled her stomach. She looked me in the eyes and said, 'Listen, I'm not sure how much longer I can wait before I have to go to the

Ladies –' she looked away and spoke to the carpet – 'or shit myself all over this delightful upholstery.'

'Lola, are you all right?'

'I'm fine, sweetheart, but you have to listen to me. It's very very important. Ashley called me and he sounded very worried. He explained that I was the only one he could count on to save you,' she said proudly.

'Save me from what?' I looked over at Uncle Leonard impatiently waiting.

'I don't want to upset you, but you need to know . . . in case I have to go . . . you need to know how important it is not to get on the plane with your uncle today.' She screwed up her eyes and it seemed her head was hurting as well as her stomach now. 'Just wait till Ashley arrives and he'll explain everything, OK, darling?'

I looked around me at the display of oranges and apples opposite the pub, at the stairs with *Departures* written on a big yellow sign over it, hoping Ashley would appear and tell me what was right.

'Listen, Clem,' the voice of a man grabbed my attention. It was coming from Lola's big face, but it was not exactly Lola's voice as I knew it. She wasn't showing off like the parrots in the forest any more. 'I've heard the way your uncle and his girlfriend scream at each other, the way they scream at you. I know they beat you.'

I opened my mouth to explain how Uncle Leonard had changed and what he was doing for me, but Lola leaned closer and continued as I watched the makeup cling to the hairs above her lip like pollen to an insect's leg. 'Clementine, I know what it's like to be beaten up by grown-ups for no good reason. And people that do that are bad people, OK? Bad people don't change. If they've hit you before they'll hit you again.'

'But Lola, when I get back to my country I will be with my family again.'

Lola snapped her lips shut and her eyes seemed to say her stomach was hurting more than ever. Suddenly she whispered, 'Who told you that?'

Uncle Leonard was finally being served.

'Clem, Clem, you precious little thing.' She held my face in her hands. They were cold, but I did not mind. She lurched as if someone had stabbed her in the belly. 'I really have to go, but I'll be right back, OK? Do not go anywhere.'

She looked as if she was in agony, but I could not tell if it was in her guts or an agony of indecision in her mind. Whichever it was, I was no longer sure enough about my uncle's intentions to defend him to Lola, and I had such a fear of her leaving, the kind I had not felt since the first time Ashley left me alone in the flat with Uncle Leonard and Philomene above.

'Why do you have to go, Lola?'

She grabbed the arms of her chair, ready to launch herself upwards. 'The first time Ashley called me I was too self-absorbed to even hear what he was calling about. He called back a few minutes later and . . . well, he spelt out the seriousness of the situation. When it comes to you, darling, I'd do anything, you know. But I'm not as strong a person as you. I . . . I needed some pills to give me the strength to even get out the front door. And I think I might've done too many. Look, I'll be back before your uncle . . . probably.'

And she left.

'Ridiculous country, full of ridiculous people.' My uncle gulped down the drink he had just bought before he reached our table. He grabbed his case and me.

'Shouldn't we wait?' I nodded at the drink he'd bought

for Lola and held on to the chair with my free hand, but Uncle Leonard's grip was strong.

'I'm sure the . . . lady is quite capable of drinking without us. Now come, do you want to miss this plane?'

We rushed past the television screens again. Uncle Leonard looked up at them as we passed without stopping until we reached a desk where a black lady sat with another telly screen behind her. This one said KENYA AIRWAYS in big red letters . . . as red as Lola's skirt. The screen also said KQ101 Nairobi. The lady and my uncle passed papers back and forth between them and I looked around the hall. Other people, mostly black people, were checking in at the desks around us. They put their bags on the conveyor belts like Uncle Leonard did with his. Some of them seemed relieved to get rid of theirs, others seemed concerned and let their hands hover over bulging suitcases for a moment as if to reassure them that they would be OK without their owners until they reached Nairobi. I knew Nairobi was not in Rwanda.

'Are we going to Nairobi, Uncle Leonard?'

He pulled me to the queue by the doorway that said Departures above it. 'No, foolish child.' He stopped and looked down at me, smiling again, like he did by the ice-cream van. 'We will get on another plane at Nairobi that will take us to Kigali, then home.'

I took a look behind to see if Lola had followed us, to see if Ashley was with her.

'Boarding passes as well, please, sir.'

Uncle Leonard tugged on my arm and I had to turn round to see where I was going. He shoved me through the metal doorway that has no wall, that knows if I have any metal in my pockets. The doorway beeped and a guard told me to empty my pockets. I gave him the silver coins that Ashley gave to me and he prodded me back through the frame towards Uncle Leonard. He shoved me back again and I was beginning to feel as dizzy as the ball must in a game of tennis. The doorway did not make a sound this time and the guard returned my coins. I held them out to Uncle Leonard like an offering to a god. They felt hot after being in the guard's hand.

'Can we phone Ashley now?'

'In a minute.' He was busy looking at another screen hanging from the ceiling. I saw our flight number and next to it flashed the word BOARDING and GATE 16. 'Come, quick!'

I was beginning to feel tired with all this running, but I could see that Uncle Leonard was anxious not to miss the plane, and so was I if it meant that I would see my family again soon. When we got to the moving floors I was relieved, but Uncle Leonard still insisted on walking on them, even though the floors walk for you. But at least I could enjoy the way that, with little effort, it felt as if you were walking faster than any other human could. The floor felt like it was melting as it bent under Uncle Leonard's pounding feet, but that could not be, because it was feeling much cooler in these long dark tunnels than it was outside. Numbers, gate numbers I guessed, shone golden in the darkness. Each one was the entrance to a secret passageway that led to a new world. They reminded me of the golden numbers on Pio's watch. Except Gate 3. Pio's watch never had a three on it, because of the space for the date. Only on the third of each month would it look as though it had all its numbers. At three o'clock on the seventeenth I might have grabbed Pio's wrist and said, 'What a funny watch that is. It says it's seventeen o'clock!' Then I would run before he could catch me . . .

My heart dipped with the moving floor then, because whatever Uncle Leonard said, I knew that I could never see all my family again. Not Pio. I was the only one of us who knew that for sure – me and Ashley. The number 5 flew by above our heads and 7 and 9 followed quickly like straggling birds in a migration. I turned round to see them getting smaller. Number 11 joined them, and I tripped on the end of the moving floor. Uncle Leonard still had a tight hold on me, though, and he pulled me to my feet so roughly that it felt like the muscle was stretching and snapping in my armpit.

'This is no time for silly games. I will not miss this flight, I will not!'

He was sweating, but I was shivering in this lifeless place. I had not noticed anyone behind us and I could only see one other person up ahead. We ran onto the next moving floor. Number 13 flew by and number 14 on the other side of this wide corridor.

'Excuse me, sir!' someone shouted from behind.

Uncle Leonard ignored this, his eyes fixed on the number 16 ahead.

'You with the little girl!'

This time Uncle Leonard threw a quick glance over his shoulder. My eyes followed his, behind to the voice, but before they could focus on its owner, they were looking ahead again to the end of the moving floor and the man who stood there. In his blue shirt and trousers with many pockets he looked like a UN soldier, but without the beret. Blood from my arms and legs seemed to flood into my belly and I gripped my uncle's hand, tighter than he had ever gripped mine, to stop myself from falling. It was the soldier from the camp in Burundi, the soldier who took my watch, Pio's watch. I thought he had forgotten about me and let me get on that plane to England without fixing the watch, without even giving it back to me still broken.

I felt a moment of heat for the first time since we started down these corridors, embarrassment at my rudeness. Of course, it would have taken him a while to fix it. With all the other jobs he had to do in the camp, he did not have time before I got on the plane. And now he had made the great effort to come all the way to England to deliver it back to me, because he knew how much it meant to me, how much Pio meant to me.

I looked up at Uncle Leonard to explain who this man was in our way. My uncle's eyes were bulging with fear and anger. He threw his head left and right as we reached the end of the moving floor, like an animal trapped by a hunter, desperate for a way out. The moving floor continued to deliver us into the arms of the waiting UN soldier, but as soon as his feet felt the silver ground, Uncle Leonard tried to sidestep him and push him away. In his haste he slammed his case into one of the moving railings and it split open like a mussel, spilling out clothes. A man in a green uniform ran from Gate 16 to help. At least, I thought he was helping until he said,

'Sir, we would like you to come with us, please.'

'My plane, my flight is here, it is going now, I have to catch it!' My uncle tried to push the clothes back into the case. 'And this . . . this *man* is harassing me.'

'The flight is boarded, the gate is closing, sir, you won't be on that flight today. You need to come with us.' The other man – he was also in a green uniform, but he was much bigger – caught up with us from behind, took Uncle Leonard roughly by the arm and led him away.

I looked into the face of the soldier properly for the first time, wondering why Uncle Leonard could think he was harassing us, searching for answers to all this confusion.

And then, if I am honest, I felt . . . but it was just for a second, for the only time ever in my life . . . I felt a heartbeat of disappointment to see Ashley. Because it wasn't the soldier and I still did not have the watch. But in the same moment I saw Ashley's worried face spread out into a soft smile, like a white sheet pulled tight again over a bed after a rough night. And I bounced into his arms.

The man who had come from Gate 16, who had lots of black hair on the thin white arms coming from his green short sleeves, winked at me as I watched him take a clear bag full of paper triangles from his pocket and tuck it into the suitcase with the rest of my uncle's clothes. It was funny because I also noticed then that there was not one item of my clothing in that case, and yet my uncle had said he had all I would need.

'Come on,' the thin hairy man said to Ashley. 'You're safe now,' he said to me.

I was confused and I had had enough of being dragged around by people I did not know . . . or people I did not know *any more*. So I clung harder to Ashley.

'It's OK,' he whispered, 'they're friends of Jimmy's.'

The office had mirrors on the outside that turned into clear windows when you were inside. It was a small room and Uncle Leonard was already sitting on a plastic chair telling the big officer over and over again that he did not know what he was talking about, that he had nothing like that and that he just wanted to take his niece home.

'I don't think Rwanda is exactly a place to take a little girl right now, do you?'

Uncle Leonard looked at the man in silence for a moment before repeating himself, louder, 'I do not know what you are talking about.' The thin man slammed the suitcase on the table by the mirror-windows. 'I have never been involved with such things.' The hairy hands pulled out a few of Leonard's shirts and underpants. 'I just want to get . . .' Uncle Leonard stopped as a pale hand dangled the bag of triangles in front of his face.

The big officer said, 'You were saying . . . ?'

'What is that?'

'That's what we should be asking you, sir . . . Name?' The big officer sat at a desk, his pen poised, waiting for an answer. I pulled myself onto another plastic chair and watched my feet swinging back and forth.

'This is wrong, that is not—'

'Name!'

Uncle Leonard's silence made me look up. The hairy man was pulling his passport and other papers from the inside pocket of his orange jacket and my uncle just sat there and let him do it. He passed it to the big officer and he copied some words from it onto the forms on his desk.

'Blimey, good job you didn't just tell me, I couldn't've spelt that anyway.' He chuckled to himself as he wrote some more, then put down his pen and picked up a long thin knife with a blue plastic handle. 'You realize that you'll be going down for some time for this amount of cocaine.' He picked up a letter and slid the long blade inside it, slicing it open while the thin man pulled one triangle from the bag and unravelled it under Leonard's nose. It had white powder inside. The thin man licked a skinny finger and dabbed at it. He tasted the end of his finger.

'Mmm, only the best from the Riddler, eh?'

The big officer chuckled again and the thin man pushed the bag into his trouser pocket, where it had come from in the first place.

'It is not mine,' Uncle Leonard's words came out in a sigh.

'That's what they all say, sir.'

I climbed onto Ashley, sitting in the chair next to me and whispered in his ear, 'Uncle Leonard said he was taking me back to Rwanda, he said I would see Mum and Dad.'

Ashley did not whisper back. 'I'm afraid your uncle is a liar, Clem, and a very evil man.'

We were all looking at him. His trouser leg with the sharp crease bounced up and down again and his tongue clicked in his mouth. I should have known then, should have got us away sooner.

The big officer said, 'You two can get off if you like, Ash, we'll be here for some time yet sorting this one out.'

As Ashley stood up, still carrying me, Uncle Leonard started swearing under his breath in Kinyarwanda. '*Igicucu*,' he spat, and said something about doing it here and now if he had to. '. . . *Inyenzi* . . .' he spoke of cockroaches as he leapt from his seat and grabbed the letter opener from the desk. He said something about *umupanga*, a machete, as he ran at me with the blade. In that moment I squeezed tighter around Ashley's neck and felt it grow bigger just like my dad's did when he had shouted to Mum, 'IMPRESSED BY HER BEAUTY AND BRAVERY', as we carried water up the hillside and he told us the story of Sebwgugu. I saw the red eyes of the beautiful green birds with tall white hats, blaming me as Jeanette scared them from the branches of the trees. It was my uncle's red eyes that accused me now as he ran at me, but they quickly turned into red scratches in the air as the image blurred and I felt myself being spun around.

Ashley had put himself between me and Leonard's 'machete' and the two officers pounced on my uncle. I looked over Ashley's shoulder and saw him beneath them, helpless like an antelope attacked by a pair of lions, but the white spots on the cheeks of this sitatunga were tears reflecting the harshly lit walls of the little room.

And then all of us were on the floor – Ashley fell and took me with him.

The ambulance man did not look very happy about me travelling in the back with him and Ashley, but Ashley insisted.

As I followed the stretcher that Ashley was on into the ambulance I noticed how many people had stopped to stare at us as taxis or relatives' cars dropped them off. I realized then why Ashley had told me never to stare unless I could help – it was horrible, why would they want to remember the pain on Ashley's face and the blood all over the ambulance man's hand from where he had held thick wads of bandage against the hole in Ashley's back? I wanted to shout at them, 'A moment ago you would've knocked down anyone in your path to get to the check-in desk first, but now you seem to have all the time in the world!'

As I pulled myself up into the ambulance, I heard a high-pitched voice coming from the crowd.

'Sorry, Clem. Sorry. I tried my hardest to get here sooner.' I saw Levi shifting about from one foot to another and pulling his baseball cap down further over his face with every word. 'I tried.'

I was surprised to feel a burst of warmth in my stomach. I liked Levi, not just his beautiful voice, but his face, closed and secret, serious and hard. I liked it like that only because I had seen it on the rare times that it had broken into a smile.

He started smiling at me on his way out of the door after lessons with Ashley – every lesson since I told him I loved his falsetto voice. From then on he finished each lesson huffing and puffing exhausted, but elated – like a gold-medal-winning sprinter. The smile was a precious pearl because it was usually locked away for so long.

I smiled at Levi to tell him I knew he had tried his best.

'Tell you what, I'll follow in the car.' He looked over his shoulder and darted off across the busy road as two policemen edged towards us.

The other ambulance man was a woman – I do not mean like Lola . . . you know what I mean. She was driving and sometimes spoke to someone through a radio about bringing us to the hospital. She said things like 'splenic trauma' then complained about the traffic.

The man was quite fat and wore glasses. When he looked at me he smiled warmly, but the rest of the time he squeezed his lips tightly together and kept jabbing his glasses into his nose with one finger so hard it looked like it would hurt.

'We need to get some fluids into you, Ash, so we're going to put a drip into your arm, OK?' and he started to roll up one of the sleeves of Ashley's blue shirt, a pale blue like moonlight on water.

Ashley did not stop him, but 'No!' burst from my mouth.

The man jabbed at his glasses again and his hand hovered at his face as if he thought he could hide behind it whilst he stared at Ashley's scars without us seeing. 'It's OK,' Ashley groaned, and I was not sure if he was talking to me or the man, 'old war wounds.'

'Is the other arm the same?'

''Fraid so.'

'Oh well,' the man smiled at me again, 'I'm sure we can find room for another little one!'

Ashley laughed too, but I could not see what was funny. I held on to his other hand – it looked even whiter than it usually did against my black one. And it was damp with sweat.

'Don't worry, Clem, it'll be fine.'

'It's my fault.'

'No, it's not,' Ashley winced with pain, 'don't you ever think that, OK . . . ? OK?'

I nodded, but I wasn't sure.

'I should've got us out of that flat sooner. Don't worry; we're never going back there again now. You deserve better anyway.'

The man jabbed at his glasses and whispered, 'Shit,' then he shouted to the woman driving, 'can't we get things moving up there, Becs?'

'I'm doing me best, Liam, bloody traffic, innit.'

Liam asked Ashley to roll onto his side, so he rolled towards me and I helped pull him with my free hand at the back of his neck. I remembered then how I had felt Ashley's neck throbbing as blood pumped through it when he had spun me round and stood between me and Uncle Leonard. Now it was cold and still as if there was nothing but space inside it. I looked where Liam looked – at the back of Ashley's shirt. It did not look like material any more, not like anything solid, but like a piece of a purple river where the water flowed so thickly you could hold it in your hands. The stretcher beneath was red with blood too and it was dripping to the floor. I had never seen so much blood from one person, even after all the cutting, all the murder in Rwanda, I was sure I had never seen . . .

'So much blood,' my thoughts popped from my mouth again.

Liam smiled at me. 'It's OK,' he said, rolling the shirt up, which stuck to Liam's hands then to Ashley's shoulders. 'You've probably got a ruptured spleen, Ashley, that's why there seems to be so much blood, but we've got it under control,' and he packed more bandages onto the wound and twitched his nose because he had no free hand to jab at his glasses.

'What is a spleen?'

Ashley gripped my hand and I sat closer to his face. 'It's just a place in the body that does the recycling. You know when we take all our bottles to the bottle bank over by the canal?'

We used to love the sound the bottles made when they hit the bottom and smashed – if the bank was full it was no good as the bottles did not have very far to fall.

'Well, the spleen is like a bottle bank, but it recycles old blood instead of glass. That's why it looks like there's so much blood, but it's OK, 'cause grown-ups can survive without a spleen anyway, right?'

'Very good, Ashley, ever thought of becoming a para-medic?' Liam coughed and laughed all at once. 'We'd rather you didn't try and survive without your spleen though, these days.'

'See, angel?' I was staring at Ashley's mouth where little short panting sounds, as if from a dog, came between the words. 'See?' He moved his head so that my eyes met his. 'It's just a scratch, just a scratch.'

Liam checked the needle he had put into Ashley's arm and followed the tube coming from it with his eyes all the way to the bag full of water hanging from the ceiling.

'Clem,' Ashley's voice brought my eyes back to his, 'help

me get this out before I break it.' He was trying to lift himself up on the arm without the needle in it so I could reach in the big pocket of his soldier trousers and pull out his Discman that he had been lying on since Liam had asked him to roll over. 'I had it with me all the way down here, but I didn't listen to it once.' I lay it on the bench next to me. 'Part of me thought I should've listened to something; after all there was nothing else I could do but sit and wait till I got here. Nothing else to do but sit and worry about you and what he might've done to you. But I didn't listen to one song. Because I didn't want to escape from *that* worry and *that* dread . . . I wanted to think about all the possible ways this might turn out and how I was going to make it better. I'll never want to escape anything about you.'

'Becs,' Liam sang his words to the driver through clenched teeth as he grabbed towels from the box he was sitting on, 'fucking hurry up!'

Ashley loosened his grip on my hand and his breaths were even quicker and shorter. His eyes started to close – something told me that was not a good thing so I squeezed his hand and said, 'Ashley, *racontes-moi une histoire!*'

His eyes rolled open again, 'Ha . . . thought you'd never ask.'

'You still with us, Ashley?'

'Once upon a time in the town of London, Ashley the serval cat met a beautiful kitten called Clem that he wanted to look after and love for ever. But one day Clem was stolen away by an evil growling dog, so Ashley set off on a long journey to rescue her. Ashley the cat needed some help if he was to stop the dog before he took Clem the kitten away over the ocean for good, so he called on his friends, Lola the pelican, Levi the panther and Jimmy the turtle.'

I giggled as I saw Jimmy in my mind strutting down the

road with a big shell on his back painted like an England soccer shirt.

'Lola was painting her feathers a pretty colour and she wanted to stay home and finish them. Levi was sniffing at a pile of powder just about to gobble it all up and he wanted to stay home and enjoy it alone. Jimmy was resting his heavy shell in front of the TV and did not want to go out either.'

Ashley smacked his lips together slowly and licked them with a dry tongue before he carried on.

'Ashley was so angry at himself for letting the dog kidnap Clem that he wanted to stay home and cut his own fur with a knife. But he didn't. And when he told his lazy friends that he was calling because Clem the kitten was in trouble, they all jumped up to help. So there was Ashley running *kao-kao-kao* . . .'

Ashley's eyes shone white and I realized it was my teeth I could see in them as I grinned, waiting for the other funny sounds.

'. . . Levi streaking ahead, in someone else's BMW I expect, *cwa-cwa-cwa*, Lola flying from her Hammersmith nest *seko-seko-seko* and Jimmy scurrying . . .'

I could not resist joining in with,

'. . . *tao-tao-tao* . . . scurrying to the phone – it's as far as his little turtle legs could manage in time – where he called the lions he knew in Customs. And . . . well, you know the rest . . . Clem the kitten was saved and lived happily ever after . . .'

'Happily ever after with Ashley the serval cat,' I added.

'She'll live happily ever after,' he looked so desperate for a drink, but I was too selfish to look for one for him, I needed him to end the story my way.

'With Ashley!' I shouted.

'Ashley, mate, stay with us, buddy, nearly there, not long now,' Liam flicked an angry finger at the bag of water and fiddled hopelessly with the needle again.

'You made me happy in a way I didn't think possible, angel . . .' Ashley closed his beautiful green eyes. '. . . Happy ever after.'

The big black nurse in the hospital's Accident and Emergency Department hugged me – I do not think she did that to all the people who were waiting for news of their loved ones. At first I thought she just felt drawn to me because I was black like her. But then I saw other black people on beds behind half-drawn curtains and I guessed she must have felt more sorry for me than anyone else there that evening. As she drew me into her bosom, her tenderness was about to make me cry, but then the coldness of her plastic apron crackling between my face and her chest made me pull myself together and tell her I was all right.

'Oi, Clem!' It was Levi.

'Who's this?' the nurse asked me.

'I'm her brother.'

'Well, look after your little sister.' The nurse seemed a bit agitated that someone else had arrived who was closer to me than she was. 'I'll go and find out what's going on.'

Strangely, I was feeling annoyed that Levi had described himself as my brother, but before I could understand what was going on inside me he whispered, 'They would never've let me in if I wasn't family. Fucked up, innit?'

'It is so nice to see you here.'

Levi rubbed his nose with the palm of his hand and we sat next to each other on plastic chairs, like the ones in the room with the mirror-window at the airport. In England there is so much waiting on such uncomfortable chairs.

'How's Ashley, mun?'

'He's going to be fine, I think. He told me we are going to move out of the estate as soon as he is better.'

'Oh.' Levi did not look very pleased with the news about Ashley, but perhaps he did not believe me, just as I was not sure that I believed myself.

So I said, 'How did you get here?'

'In the car.'

'Which car?'

'I . . . borrowed one. Boy, when Ashley called me I didn't think I'd get to the airport in time unless I used a fast car, innit.'

'A BMW?'

'Yeh.'

I smiled, remembering Ashley's story in the ambulance.

'What?' Levi began to shift from one side of his buttocks to the other, like he might do on his feet before trying a difficult part in a song Ashley was teaching him. 'I might as well not've bothered for all the good it did. I didn't get there in time, innit. I had it all sussed. Ash said I was supposed to mention Jimmy's name and they were going to let me through. Then if no one else had had any luck I was gonna take your uncle down. I would've knee-capped him before I'd let him take you back to the jungle, aigh.'

I felt cold and hot all at once. Levi sounding so protective of me – that was so warm, like the beginning of a bath. But when he sounded so violent towards my uncle – that was cold like the end of the bath when you know it is long overdue to get out, but you just cannot muster up the energy to do so. I looked at the side of Levi's face as he stared at the wall ahead, his beautiful dark, secret face. His eyes were narrowed, searching the Serengeti for prey and for danger.

'Levi the panther,' I whispered loud enough so he was sure to hear.

'What you talking about?' he furrowed his brow as he looked at me, but his mouth was about to break into one of those precious smiles, I could tell.

'Clem, I might have to shoot off for a bit, to sort out the car . . .'

Before I could truly sense disappointment at the thought of Levi going, I noticed the way he stopped looking into my eyes and focused over my head towards the end of the corridor. I turned to look too and saw the big black nurse hurrying to close the green curtain whilst a man in a white coat and another nurse pushed a machine through it towards the bed where Ashley lay. Things had started beeping like lots of little car alarms and it was clear that something was wrong. The big black nurse saw us stand up and told us to wait where we were. She said the doctors needed space to work. Then she disappeared inside the curtain too.

I walked carefully along until I was close then I crawled, like I always did when I got near the cabaret. The grass was cold and smooth tonight as I pulled myself close to the green fence. I lowered my head to the ground so I could peer up through the gap at the base. There were many pairs of feet crowding around the table in the middle. Some of the feet belonged to women – I did not know they had begun inviting women to the cabaret. And so much light. I had never seen the cabaret so brightly lit. I pressed my head closer to the ground so I could see up to the faces. The ground hummed with electricity – I suppose it would in the lightning capital of the world, am I right, Ashley?

Ashley?

He was lying on the table, wires going in and out of him.

There was no Alphonse, no Joseph, no Augustine nor even Paul acting like the king, spreading his arms along the sofa. Just doctors and nurses. One of the doctors held the hands of a machine. The machine had coiled wires for arms that led to a screen where straight lines were being drawn across it. The doctor put the hands of the machine onto Ashley's chest and his whole body jolted violently as if the machine was a lightning maker. A nurse placed a mask with a balloon on the end over Ashley's mouth and she squeezed it. Once, twice, three times, four times. The doctor told her to get out of the way as he shocked Ashley's poor body again. The nurse put the mask back on his face and squeezed, once, twice, three times. But she stopped when the doctor shook his head at her.

The sound of my own sobs surprised me. Not just because of the way they echoed back at me so harshly from the shiny floor. The echo mocked me so that I almost stopped with embarrassment after my first outburst. Almost. But I did not stop. I could not stop. No, the sound also surprised me because over the last few months I had not cried, not like this. The first time I ever saw Ashley, on the stairs in Frapper Court, I saw him through tears, but they were silent ones. These ones made my whole body convulse, just like Ashley's did as they tried to pump life back into his chest. I sobbed for Dad, for Mum, for Pio, for Augustine and Marie and little baby John. I sobbed for the bald man in the marshes and the woman that tried to run. I even sobbed for Jeanette. I cried and cried for Ashley, and for myself for believing in happily ever after and in God, when there seemed to be nothing eternal, nothing more than brief moments when it came to the people that I loved.

1996

I wear my cherry blossom dress as often as possible, before I grow too big for it – it was the one that Ashley loved me in best. Jimmy says that's typical of a man.

'. . . tryin' to keep a woman just as she was a' day one, scared she's gonna change into somefink less beautiful than the vision tha' first captured 'im, and scared of how 'e'll react if she does.'

'I was not Ashley's *woman*, Jimmy.'

'Tha's no' the poin'.' He puts his tanned feet up on the spare garden chair – not one of those white plastic ones. These have green ornate metal frames with springs near the base so you can rock, and soft brown cushions with oriental designs. They're luxurious, like everything in Jimmy's house. 'Women, on the uvver 'and, carn wai' to change their men. Wha' attracts them in the first place is the potenchal they see to mould 'im into somefink they *fink* they really desire.' He takes a huge bite from the barbecued burger in a bun so I can hardly understand the next thing he says, 'Be careful wha' you wiff for, Clemmy!'

Elaine calls over from the other end of the enormous patio, 'Well, whilst we're talking stereotypes, ain't you supposed to be standing here, cooking the meat and stinking of smoke?'

275

Jimmy finishes his mouthful and laughs at me with his tongue out that still has bits of bread stuck to it. Ashley was right, he is like a bulldog. But I love him. He's like . . . an uncle to me . . . the uncle I always wanted. Elaine's my big sister, which makes Lola my . . . auntie, I suppose! And Levi . . . well, we'll see . . . see what I can *mould him into*!

'Wha' you so pleased wiv yerself abou'?' Jimmy's caught me smiling to myself.

'Nuffink, Uncle Jimmy!'

I take the tea towel Jimmy wiped his fingers on and throw it over the Discman, to keep the baking sun from melting it. So I still have a family and I still go to church and pray to God, but I remind myself every day that one or all of them might be gone tomorrow. It's funny how I cannot be so rational when it comes to my Discman. I am truly attached to it – because if everyone else fails me, then I can escape through it to any time or any place. I put in the earphones, the corks back into the bottle, and say, 'Where you taking me today, Ashley?' Massive Attack. Hypnotizing wah-wah guitar, hazy keyboards, Tracey's soft voice caressing the inside of my head, and in no time I am floating above the big houses and well-groomed lawns of Jimmy's neighbourhood until the roads are just seams and the brown, gold and green shapes of fields, villages and gardens are just designs on a busy shirt.

A few thousand miles to the east, a few thousand miles to the south and we are above Nyamata, but it all looks the same from up here . . . the busy shirt wrapped around the Earth is just a bit more red than brown here and the shapes do not have edges as straight . . . red, gold and green, the colour of the Interahamwe. But this shirt will be ripped off the back of Rwanda soon. Paul Kagame and his Tutsi-led army are taking over. Taking revenge? I turn up the music before I see the rivers full of Hutu bodies this time. I float further out to where you can see the awesome shape of the continents sculpted out by the blue sea around them, but not the man-made angles of the countries and borders within.

Come on, Ashley, let's keep on going. Come on! Come on!

Warren FitzGerald was born in 1973. Since graduating from Warwick University he has been a professional singer and worked with children and adults with disabilities. He has undertaken several voluntary projects overseas including building a health centre in Kibungo, Rwanda (the setting for *The Go-Away Bird*). He lives in London.

DEVELOPINGWORLDCONNECTIONS

Developing World Connections is an international voluntary organization based in British Columbia, Canada. Formed in 2005 following a grassroots response to the 2004 Boxing Day tsunami in South-East Asia, the registered charity has grown to now serve sixteen communities in twelve countries across Africa, Asia and Latin America.

Developing World Connections doesn't do "aid". An international volunteer experience offers everyone the opportunity to be of service. Our volunteers work on sustainable development projects through our long–term partnerships with host communities. By committing long–term to the communities we serve, we develop strong relationships with the locals and create a lasting legacy.

These relationships provide our volunteers with the opportunity to make a real difference. However, our greatest legacies are the relationships that provide the windows of opportunity for hope and a better world.

For more information please visit the Developing World Connections website: http://developingworldconnections.org

What's next?

Tell us the name of an author you love

| Warren FitzGerald | Go ▶ |

and we'll find your next great book.

www.bookarmy.com